Praise for C. Hyytinen's

MARIA SANCHEZ THRILLER SERIES

"Hyytinen has 'the touch.' ...stupefying and terror-laden...spine-tingling...a page-turner that can't be put down, even to attend to life's little duties. Hyytinen should have an excellent go as an author...first rate!"

–5 stars from Midwest Book Review
for *Pattern of Violence*

"If you like hard-core crime books, *Pattern of Violence* is a must read. I could not put it down."

–Armchair Interviews

"*Pattern of Violence* is a great book. The characters came to life and the plot was "edge of your seat." I recommend this novel to anyone who likes a good thriller... I'm looking forward to reading more works by this author."

–An Amazon.com Review

A Maria Sanchez Thriller
Book Two

Pattern of Vengeance

By
C. Hyytinen

PATTERN OF VENGEANCE

A Maria Sanchez Thriller

Book Two

An Echelon Press Book

First Echelon Press paperback printing / April 2007

All rights Reserved.
Copyright © 2007
C. Hyytinen

Cover and illustration © Nathalie Moore

Echelon Press
9735 Country Meadows Lane 1-D
Laurel, MD 20723
www.echelonpress.com

All rights reserved. No part of this book may be used or reproduced in any manner whatsoever without written permission, except in the case of brief quotations embodied in critical articles and reviews. For information, address Echelon Press.

ISBN 978-1-59080-520-6

PRINTED IN THE UNITED STATES OF AMERICA
10 9 8 7 6 5 4 3 2 1

Prologue

Two men came out of nowhere.

Stan Bauer *almost* made it to the curb with the last bag of garbage. His immense frame staggered forward, half-asleep. Dressed in only sweats, despite the cold, it went against his grain to hurry. His wife was after him to lose weight–called him a heart attack waiting to happen, and his friends laughed at his expense. Larry liked to point out his bad case of Dinky-do–his belly hung longer than his dinky do. That always got a giant laugh.

Garbage pickup was early in the morning, and he had suddenly remembered the large bag of cat shit in the basement, while listening to his wife snore. Carrie had three fuckin' cats that stank to high heaven. It would sit down there fermenting if he left it for another week.

Two men grabbed him from behind–one on each side. Clouds of spent breath and grunts of exertion clouded the frosty air as his abductors kicked and punched him repeatedly, immobilizing him into submission.

With Stan bound and gagged, they struggled, quickly shoving him into the van. Stan knew his gig was up–all part of the job. The downside so to speak. He tuned them out and reached inside himself, putting his training to use as the driver drove, and his new friends continued their abuse.

Finally, the vehicle screeched to a stop.

Pants pulled down to his ankles, Stan barely heard a young male voice instruct him to bend over. He did not comply, focused on his inner turmoil. Panic surged through him despite his training. He prayed for himself, for his loved ones.

"Fuckin' snitch, this is what you get. Sweet dreams, fat motherfucker."

Pop!

Pain assaulted Stan's senses, as the van resumed moving. A deep wrenching agony encompassed him as he thought of his last hunting trip and the trophy buck he and his son shot, up North. *A keeper.* The head proudly hung in the basement.

The two men dumped the dying Stan Bauer next to the garbage he'd set out for pickup in about three hours, then slowly drove off.

Face down in the snow, bound, gagged, and bleeding, Stan prayed to God again. But now prayed to be taken, begging....

Too weak and consumed with pain to squirm further than a few inches in the wrong direction, tears streamed down his face, freezing as they hit the frigid atmosphere.

A slow bleed ensued in his guts as a white-hot knife of misery divided the center of him. Too much time to think, that was their plan. Think...about being a snitch...going against the Family...being a cop...leaving behind those he loved...begging for death. The pain–he imagined where the bullet lodged. Somewhere past his rectum, the intestines perhaps. *Will I freeze to death or have to endure this...for how long?*

Please God, take me...please. Closing his eyes, he watched a final slide show set in slow motion as his life played out in vivid detail behind tortured lids.

Chapter 1

Detective Maria Sanchez walked into Homicide and slapped the morning Star Tribune on her desk, already in a foul mood. She had picked up the newspaper in front of City Hall and quickly skimmed the front-page article, reading some of her own direct quotes from earlier this morning. 'Agent Stan Bauer was a good man. He didn't deserve this.' *Blah blah blah.*

She had started the day at 3:30 a.m., quickly waking up in below zero temperatures at the crime scene. Maria attempted to talk to Stan's distraught wife, Carrie, who unfortunately had slept through everything. She didn't even recall Stan getting out of bed in the middle of the night.

The killing wasn't done on the premises. They'd taken him elsewhere, probably in a pickup or van, by the fresh tracks in the snow, then dumped him back home, like yesterday's trash.

After giving a statement to reporters, Maria had left two detectives working the case to finish up. She'd gleaned enough information to know it was an inside job. It screamed Mafia hit.

Normally Maria and Joe drove in together. But with the call on Stan at 3:00 a.m. and Joe's schedule with the new chief, Sandra LaSalle, he'd drive in later. The chief wasn't exactly Maria's favorite person, but her boss nonetheless. Perhaps in time they would develop a decent working relationship, although currently it appeared unlikely.

Joe Morgan, her one-time homicide partner, now lifetime partner of ten years, no longer worked directly in Homicide. Currently in Special Investigations, he had spent four years prior in Narcotics. He and Maria worked together more often than not, considering their job duties intermingled. Keeping her last name, Sanchez, in hopes of not drawing attention to the two of them, helped somewhat, but it only went so far.

Maria missed Chief Frank McCollough. He had retired five years ago after a stroke, was doing well, and periodically still stopped in to say hi, however, the visits became more infrequent as the years passed. Sandra LaSalle made the third chief since his departure.

The last case she and Joe worked as partners almost a decade ago was Mafia-related. *The River Rat...* Maria closed her eyes and shook her head. It still hurt. Jack Sanchez, her *supposedly* dead husband, had been brainwashed, his addictions fed with massive quantities of drugs. He *became* JR Franco–a killing machine created by Mafia crime boss Roberto Santini, and underboss Nicholas Freyhoff. When the Minneapolis Police Department got too close to the truth, they'd abducted Maria's daughter, Theresa.

Tess was lucky to survive. By pure accident, Maria had stumbled into the killer's lair to use a telephone after her car broke down. Joe had saved her life, as well as Theresa's.

Those were bittersweet times. The blood bath that took place remained indelibly etched into her memory, but the good things that came out of it counteracted the bad.

Santini's men had murdered Tony's mother, Stephanie Franco, before Joe could get them into witness safety. Joe ended up with a couple of bullets and a hospital stay. The five-year-old boy held a place in their hearts and with no one to claim him, they brought him into their home, loving him as their own. He and Theresa had the same father, who had a brief marriage to Stephanie in his early days with the organization, shortly after his staged death.

Tony's mother was Roberto Santini's half-sister, although she didn't know it until the age of eighteen. Heroin had ruined Stephanie's life thanks to Roberto Santini, her main supplier and controller.

The dead bodies surrounding Maria on that fateful night included Santini and Freyhoff, as well as her husband, JR Franco, the River Rat. In addition, they found Rico Smits, a local drug supplier, rolled in a sheet like a tortilla, and stuffed into the linen closet, minus a tongue for talking too much.

Shortly after, Maria and Joe married, unable to deny their intense feelings, suddenly realizing how close they'd come to losing it all. Two months later, they adopted Tony. They had their fair share of problems, considering the trauma he'd been through, but with proper counseling, Tony overcame a lot of his aggression. He grew up a typical teenager–music and computer games occupied most of his time.

Theresa now attended college at the University of Minnesota and Tony was nearly sixteen. Tony's direct relationship to the Mafia through his mother had been difficult at first, but soon became irrelevant as they grew into a family. Tony was a joy and an integral part of their lives. He and Tess were very close–brother and sister could not even describe them–they were best friends as well

Marco Santini had taken over his Uncle Roberto's role. Ten years into it, he had become a force to be reckoned with. If possible, he had fewer scruples and was more psychotic than his uncle–notorious for whacking his own men in quick fits of rage, reportedly showing no remorse whatsoever.

A couple of years ago, the police department discovered Stephen Freyhoff, Nicholas' brother, also involved in the organization, after a bust with a prostitution ring implicated him. He got off with a fine and no jail time, due to a good crooked lawyer. It appeared these two–Marco and Stephen–had picked up where their deceased elders left off.

Stan Bauer had been undercover for nine months, infiltrating the Mafia and a Minneapolis prostitute ring taking advantage of young runaways who ventured into the city. Some were now showing up on the West Coast. One of the three kids they were following was dead. Drug trafficking also played a part in the scheme, involving local gang-bangers.

Stan had been working closely with Santini's soldiers, finally becoming a confidante to one of them, Vincent Micelli. Stan had only been home five days when Hennepin County Waste Management discovered his body. He was well liked and a good cop–careful, years of experience.

Only a few people in the police department knew Stan had come home–Maria, Joe, Chief LaSalle. *Who else?*

Stan had planned to return to L.A. in a few days–right after Christmas–to continue his investigation. He'd never be missed, or so he'd thought.

But someone felt differently and he got whacked. Someone inside the department leaked the information to Marco and his men. They harbored a snitch, and it wasn't the first time, but were at a loss who it could be. The heat would get turned up, now that Stan was dead.

Chapter 2

"We have now come full-circle, no?" Marco Santini spoke on the telephone, ensconced in his lavish downtown L.A. office. He smiled, listening, then added, "A new generation. New ideas...new opportunities. Eliminate the obstacles and you eliminate failure."

He listened to the response and laughed. "Yes, I will keep in touch and thank you. This will not be forgotten. We owe you, and believe me, that is not common practice."

Marco ended the connection, and leaned back in the leather chair, gazing up at the ceiling. Phone conversations were rare between them–they accomplished most of their communication through e-mail due to fear of discovery. *What a fucking coup.* They actually had their own snitch with inside information on the Minneapolis Police Department. Granted, it was a snitch with a personal agenda, however, favors would be reciprocated. The need for retribution also existed for both he and Stephen. Close family members had been murdered by two of the cops still on the police force. *Payback is a bitch.* Marco smiled.

Marco's brain calculated all the opportunities that came to mind. *This is perfect.* He considered a couple of their relatively big revenue-producing operations based in the Twin Cities; drug trafficking and runaways turned prostitutes. The Minneapolis/St. Paul area was proving extremely profitable.

Must be all the Midwestern corn-fed pussy. He recalled the tall, slender freckle-faced fifteen-year-old in the most recent batch of recruits. *Fresh-faced, but tough.* He grinned, thinking of her sneering, pouty red mouth when he introduced himself–totally unimpressed with him or anyone. He liked her immediately, had slept with her the second night she was in Los Angeles, then killed her afterward for her indifference.

Marco stood and stretched, then walked over to the wet-bar to mix a drink.

Swirling the vodka and vermouth, he took a long drink, feeling the burn all the way to his balls. Checking his watch, he

frowned. *Already 6:30. Where is Stephen?*
The two men worked well together–most of the time. When Stephen first contacted him after his Uncle Roberto's death, Marco was suspicious. However, Stephen proved to be an asset and had helped the organization immensely over the years. He held information no one else knew and had saved Marco's ass repeatedly in the early years, with life-saving insight into some of Uncle Roberto's deals.

Stephen Freyhoff was bringing along the two soldiers who had whacked Leo Gianelli–as well as the details.

Marco added a large Spanish olive to his drink, watched it sink to the bottom. He took another long drink, trying desperately to be patient. Patience was not one of his virtues–he had none to speak of.

A soft rap sounded at the office door. "Yes," Marco said.

The door opened and a blond head popped in. "Hey, man."

"Stephen."

"Hey, Marco. I hate that. You know that. Call me Steve. *Stephen.*" He rolled his eyes as he strode into the room. He dwarfed Marco when they hugged, as custom demanded.

Marco offered a drink, which he accepted. "Where are Vinny and Louie?" He handed his friend a glass of whiskey on the rocks. "I thought they were accompanying you."

The larger man finished off his drink in two gulps and helped himself to another. "Yeah, they'll be here in a minute. I wanted to talk to you alone first." He gauged Marco's reaction and as usual couldn't tell the kind of mood he was in.

"What up?" Marco grinned, getting used to the American expression. Stephen used it quite often.

Steve returned the grin. "Have you heard from our source?"

Marco's smile immediately faltered. He didn't like being questioned about anything. He would give out information, as *he* deemed appropriate. He simply nodded. "All is well, not to worry."

Steve curbed his tongue and finished his drink, thinking, *Fucker.* "I'll go get the boys," he offered, setting his empty glass on the bar. "Be right back." He still didn't totally trust his partner even after all this time. He remembered how his dead brother, Nicholas, felt about the Santini family and had told Steve repeatedly how unscrupulous they were. *Nothing has really changed in that regard.*

Marco freshened his drink and lit a cigarette, looking forward to learning the details of Gianelli's execution.

Chapter 3

Maria called the medical examiner's office requesting an early slot for Stan Bauer, and arranged for an attending detective. Maybe she would send Tom. She frowned, thinking about her partner. Nice enough guy, but unfortunately just didn't have his heart in the job, anymore. With two years until retirement, he'd seen enough dead bodies to last several lifetimes. Burnt out, he would probably transfer to a desk job within the next six to twelve months. However, for now he was her partner.

With Christmas only days away, everywhere she looked, Maria sensed the holiday spirit. It seemed tarnished now, the disturbing image of the scene witnessed several hours ago taking precedence in her brain. Stan lying facedown in the snow at the curb, yesterday's trash–frozen, bloody splotches staining pristine white snow. Christmas lights twinkled merrily on the evergreens around his home and a lighted snowman greeted visitors as they approached the front door. *Merry fuckin' Christmas.*

She shook her head and took a drink of the awful, bitter coffee left from the night shift. *Think happy thoughts.* Immediately, her mind switched gears to her daughter. It was finals week at the University of Minnesota, and she'd be home in a few days. Tess would stay for almost a month. Her new classes didn't begin until the eighteenth of January.

Tess lived in the dorms, but returned home often since it was only fifteen minutes away. What a great family they had created. Maria felt blessed.

She picked up the newspaper again and re-read the brief article on Stan. It would probably be front page in tomorrow's edition, and for days to come.

She scanned the paper, drinking coffee. She caught the article about Leonardo Gianelli, on page three. She set down her cup and read the blurb again. The body was found early this morning in California. Foul play suspected. Maria stood up, stretched, walked around her desk, then sat back down. What she wouldn't give for a cigarette right now. Old habits die hard.

She read the blurb again. Leo Gianelli was *old* Mafia... The talk on the streets suggested that Marco Santini was slowly weeding out the old and reestablishing the new. The organization had become more powerful than ever, infiltrating more businesses than in the past.

Her thoughts went to Stan Bauer. Both he and Gianelli had been taken out about the same time.

The door opened and Joe sauntered in, looking disheveled and crabby. Chief LaSalle followed close behind, nipping at his heels, looking pissed and in a hurry. Giving Maria a perfunctory glance, she mumbled a barely audible "Good morning" and went into her office, shutting the door.

"Trouble in paradise?" Maria asked her husband.

"Yeah, you could say that. What a bi–"

"Easy there, big guy. The walls have ears."

Joe looked frustrated. "You won't believe this–she's already found a replacement for Stan."

Maria just looked at him, surprised.

"From New York...where *she's* from." He nodded toward the chief's closed door.

Sandra LaSalle had been born and raised out East. She'd moved to Minnesota a year ago for this job. A petite redhead in her early fifties with quick wit and a very sharp tongue. No one in the department had seen a side of her other than 'bitch', so if a sense of humor or an ounce of compassion existed, it was yet to be seen.

"Boy that was quick. Who is it? Did she give you any details?"

"Yeah, kinda. Female, Russian, young. Tina something. She's flying in tomorrow."

"So how does Chief LaSalle plan to pull this off? It took Stan months to get into the organization and he's a man for God's sake."

"Different angle this time."

"Huh? What do you mean?"

"Get this–I guess Tina is almost thirty, but looks fifteen according to the chief. Anyway, she'll be going undercover as a runaway, hopefully make it to California, find out what's been happening to our kids, and get close to the source of all our problems–Santini."

"Is this legit?"

Joe Morgan shrugged his broad shoulders, shaking his gray, shaggy head. "Yeah, believe it or not. The chief is adamant about this. Not open for discussion, if ya know what I mean. It's very dangerous, but according to her not only can this Russian Tina person handle it–she'll get results. She's got a track record that speaks for itself."

"You say that like you know for sure."

"I do. Here, check this out." He pulled out a sheaf of paper from his briefcase, handing it to Maria.

Maria took the papers, then remembered the newspaper. "Hey, page one–this morning at Stan's house. Direct quotes from yours truly." She paused, thinking. "Then turn to page three when you're done." She handed him the paper and turned her attention back to the information on Etina Altmark, the new Russian undercover agent.

Joe looked at his wife. They still worked well together and because he loved her more than anything in the world, it made even the most disgusting social injustices bearable. Their jobs sucked the life out of many. A perfect example was Maria's current partner, Tom Powders. Drained, to the point of being dangerous to the department. Something had to be done about him, and soon. Joe worried for Maria, since she had to baby-sit the man, as well as shoulder all duties. He'd spoken to Chief LaSalle about the situation briefly, but with everything else happening, they hadn't pursued it further.

Joe read the short article on Stan, then turned to page three. He didn't see what Maria was referring to–nothing jumped out at him. He opened his mouth to say so, then shut it, as he came to the small notice at the bottom of the page. He looked at Maria as she looked up.

Maria could already read her husband's brain-waves–they were on the same page. *Santini strikes again. What's next on the man's agenda?*

The telephone rang, interrupting their thoughts.

"Sanchez." Listening, she looked at Joe and grinned, giving him thumbs up. "Yeah, I'll be attending. Maria Sanchez."

Powders entered Homicide from the other side of the room.

"Oh and Tom Powders. Put him on the list." She rolled her eyes at Joe, and hung up the phone.

"Why?" was all Joe said.

"Because I *can*." She smiled, adding. "Besides, gotta give him a chance."

"You already have."

Maria shrugged her narrow shoulders and watched her partner slowly maneuver the room, stopping at the coffee maker, carefully adding the proper amounts of cream and sugar. He slowly made his way toward them, to his desk, stopping along the way to talk with another detective.

"Mornin' guys," he offered to Maria and Joe, keeping his head down.

"Good morning, Tom." Maria looked sideways at Joe.

"Mornin', Tom," Joe added reluctantly.

Tom began rearranging papers on his desk, periodically glancing in their direction, uncertainty in his tired eyes.

Maria approached his desk. "How are you this morning? Were the roads bad?" She smiled at him.

"No, no. Roads were okay. Tired though...didn't sleep well last night."

Tom said the same thing every morning without fail. The poor guy never slept well. Maria ran her fingers through her short, dark hair. "Well, don't know if you had a chance to read the morning paper."

Powders shook his head. "Nope."

"Stan Bauer was murdered early this morning."

He looked at her, a blank expression on his face.

"Stan Bauer. Undercover...working in L.A. with the Mafia."

"Yeah, I know who he is." Tom looked down at his shoes. "Too bad."

Maria looked at the top of Powder's head, then at Joe.

Joe shook his head, a strange expression on his face

Maria forged ahead. "The autopsy is scheduled for 10:30. You and I are the attending detectives."

Tom lifted his head and briefly looked his partner in the eye. "I'd rather not, if you don't mind."

"Sorry, Powders. I do mind. I need you there. There should be two of us. You can take notes." Maria's tone left no room for argument. "Okay?"

Tom shrugged his shoulders, obviously resigned to the fact that he'd have to attend another autopsy.

Maria walked back to her desk where Joe waited.

"Told ya." He handed her the newspaper.

"Can I keep the info on the Russian a bit longer?"

"Sure." Joe glanced over at Tom. "Ya know, I'll attend the autopsy with you."

She looked over her shoulder at her partner. "No, thanks. He's going."

"Hard ass." He grinned. "Glad you're not my boss."

At that moment, the chief's door opened and she emerged, an attack dog, a fierce look of determination in her eyes. "Just the two people I want to see. Do you have a moment?" She looked from Maria to Joe, turned on her heel, and retreated to her office. The two detectives followed close behind.

"Shut the door and have a seat, please." Chief LaSalle sat with authority behind a large mahogany desk.

Maria and Joe sat, looking at their new boss with uncertainty.

LaSalle cleared her throat. "Stan Bauer." She paused, adding dramatically, "Leonardo Gianelli."

Maria and Joe sat erect, eyes riveted on the chief.

"I want you two to work the case." She looked at each of them. "This is definitely not standard procedure, but considering we're dealing with the Santini family. You both know 'em well." She snorted. "Let's just say, it's the logical solution."

Maria and Joe were dumbfounded. They hadn't been allowed to work a case as partners in ten years. Yes, they still worked together on many things, but usually under the table.

Chief LaSalle looked at Maria. "Has Joe filled you in on Stan's replacement?"

Maria fidgeted, not wanting to blow the good stuff that just happened. *Me and Joe working together as partners.* "Yes. Tina, right?"

"She's a lovely girl. I'm sure you two will get along winningly."

Maria just smiled.

"Well, that's all I have. You two have your work cut out for you. One of our own was murdered in a way that screams for revenge. It's our job to make certain justice is served."

Once outside the Chief's office, Maria and Joe looked at one another and grinned. "Partner," they said in unison. Shaking hands, they wanted to kiss, but knew that would be inappropriate. They made a handsome couple–Maria her tall, lanky, dark good looks, complimented Joe, with his large lumberjack frame and piercing blue eyes.

They were able to emotionally remove themselves from their personal lives and focus on the job at hand, unlike many couples who worked together. Their detective minds took over the moment they stepped foot into City Hall

Maria walked over to her desk and sat down, still smiling. She looked over at Powders and her smile vanished. She should still make him go to the autopsy, but wouldn't. Joe would take his place. This may be just the case to get Tom assigned to that desk job he so desperately needed.

Chapter 4

The body of Stan Bauer lay prepped for forensic pathologists, Dr Kenneth Lang and his assistant, Dr. Renee Meyer.

Maria and Joe stood aside, watching the grisly scene unfold, in the bowels of Hennepin County Medical Center. HCMC was state-of-the-art and had expanded immensely the past decade. In the old days, there wouldn't have been room for four people *and* the corpse.

The sterile room offered little in the form of comfort. The temperature was set to a cool 62 degrees. A sign hung on one wall, stating, '*Hic locus est ubi mors gaudet succurrere vitae*'– Latin for, 'this is the place where death rejoices to teach those who live.'

Dr. Lang flipped on the recorder and clipped the microphone to his shirt, then turned to his assistant. "Shall we begin?" Giving Maria a smile reserved only for her, he motioned her closer, which she did somewhat reluctantly. Joe followed suit.

"May I do the honors?" Dr. Meyer asked, her hand slightly shaking as the scalpel glittered under the bright florescent light.

"Certainly. Be my guest." Dr. Lang graciously motioned toward their patient who lay waiting on the cold steel table.

Maria looked at Stan's corpse, trying to remember how he looked in life. It was difficult observing an autopsy on a co-worker and friend. It played a number on the brain–watching the procedure, the slicing, removal of organs–even in death, the act itself was disturbing.

Dr. Meyer made a Y-shaped incision from the shoulders to mid-chest, down to the pubic region. Skin wrinkled and puckered as the scalpel made its way. There was very little blood, due to lack of blood pressure.

Dr. Lang spoke into his microphone, stating the patient's name, age and other medical statistics. As he talked, he explored the abdominal cavity. Using a pair of surgical scissors, he began freeing up the large intestine.

Maria glanced at Joe. He looked how she felt. She noticed the perspiration beading his forehead and upper lip. His skin tone had become several shades paler.

Dr. Meyer assisted Dr. Lang, cutting along the abdominal wall attached to the intestine.

Freeing up the intestine took time, especially if only one pathologist was doing all the work. The two doctors worked well together.

With the intestines mobilized, Dr. Lang continued the dissection, splitting them like sausage casings, while Dr. Meyer inspected the chest organs, including the heart and lungs.

"Bingo," Dr. Lang announced, removing a bullet from the middle of the large intestine. He held it up to the light. "This is what killed our friend. Traveled quite some distance."

The bullet was mushroomed, looked like a fang-face. Stan didn't have a chance. Even if he'd made it to the hospital, he would've wished for death. Entering through his anus, the bullet's destructive path had destroyed his bowels and any control over bodily functions.

Dr. Lang removed a good six-inch portion of both the large and small intestine, placing them in a preservative solution.

They continued the abdominal dissection, exploring the bile ducts and removing the liver, weighing and recording each organ on a chart. The major organs–heart, lung, liver–were weighed on a grocer's scale. The smaller organs–thyroid, adrenals–on a chemist's triple-beam balance.

Maria found brain dissection the most difficult to watch. When the doctors removed the top of Stan's skull, she turned and walked to a corner of the room, facing the wall.

Two hours later, Stan was put back together again, like Humpty Dumpty minus some vital organs and with a nasty scar.

Maria and Joe walked out of Hennepin County Medical Center close to noon. Neither had an appetite for lunch.

The autopsy report for Stan Bauer would be several days yet. The pathologists would submit saved tissue to the histology lab to be made into microscopic slides. Drs. Lang and Meyer would then examine the slides and subsequent lab results to make their conclusions for the report.

The crime lab would possibly have something for them later this afternoon, but no one expected any major revelations. They already knew who they were dealing with. Because Stan was killed in another location, crucial evidence was at a minimum. Even if they had it, pinning it on the Mafia would be another story entirely.

Maria and Joe conferred with FBI Agent Peter Slade, who worked in Behavioral Science and had worked with the Minneapolis Police Department in the past. They were old friends. Peter had been involved up to his eyeballs in the Santini case ten years ago, and still followed the Family. He was already investigating the murder of Leonardo Gianelli, as well as the Minnesota connection.

Maria had him on speakerphone as they went over information they had gathered so far.

"This takes us back, doesn't it?" Peter asked.

"Sure does," Maria offered.

"Not in a good way, though," Joe added.

"No, not in a good way." Slade agreed. "I've got some men looking into Mr. Gianelli's murder. He was seen with two of Santini's men earlier in the evening, at an Italian restaurant in the downtown area of Los Angeles. His body was dumped under one of the piers, but whacked elsewhere."

"Yeah, same with Stan. We're dealing with guys who do this kind of thing for a living. It's gonna be tough, pinning anything on them."

"Yeah," Slade said. "But we've done it before. I'll keep in touch."

They ended the connection.

Maria looked at Joe. "Seems like old times, doesn't it?"

"Yeah, but I think it's important to remember it isn't. Marco Santini is *not* his uncle. What we knew about Roberto does not necessarily apply to the nephew."

"Yes, I know. The body of Tamara Wood is proof of that."

Tamara Wood, a runaway found strangled in L.A., grew up in Apple Valley, had been an A student until she became involved with drugs. She'd disappeared, only to turn up dead on the West Coast a month later. According to Stan Bauer, she'd last been seen with Santini–reputed to go after young girls. The fact she hadn't OD'd, and was the second runaway found strangled, caused concern. The first body remained unidentified.

Etina Altmark would arrive in the Twin Cities sometime tomorrow. Maria and Joe dug deeper into their soon-to-be co-worker, and despite their reservations, were impressed. She had worked for Interpol as well as the FBI. Her most recent assignment had been with the NYPD on a terrorist mission. The Russian seemed to get results. She was beautiful–blonde and petite, looked about fifteen years old, although she was twenty-eight.

Maria looked forward to meeting her. Joe was still skeptical, but open-minded. Chief LaSalle was ecstatic.

"Hey, babe, look at the time. Let's split. Tess is coming home tonight."

Maria grinned. "Yes, she is. Just let me gather my things." Their daughter was coming home for Christmas break. They relished the time she spent at home. Theresa brought a special light with her wherever she went.

Chapter 5

Marco Santini reclined on the leather couch, working on his third martini and another cigarette, when Stephen returned with the two thugs who had knocked off Leo Gianelli.

"Hey," they greeted upon entering, hands shoved in pockets, nervous despite their calm demeanor.

"Boys, boys, boys," Marco said. He sat up and stubbed out his cigarette. "I've been waiting with great anticipation to hear your personal account of our friend's demise."

"Friend? Is that what you called him?" Vinny laughed, looking at Louie, who grinned as well.

Marco didn't see the humor and glared at the two men, who quickly turned serious.

Vinny spoke first. "Gianelli was a piece of cake. He suspected nothing, until I pulled the trigger." He grinned, but felt his stomach flip-flop at the thought of it.

Marco studied Vincent Micelli, wondering if he did in fact pull the trigger. Or did he have his friend, Quiet Louie do it with the understanding to shut-up. Perhaps there was hope for him yet. Hard to say. He had debated taking him out, due to the closeness he'd developed with the snitch-pig, Stan, but in the end, Vinny pulled through for the Family. Told of his suspicions despite the friendship. *La Cosa Nostra.*

"Yeah," Louie added. "After a fine dinner, we went for a scenic drive." He laughed, showing a gold tooth.

Marco grinned, studying the two men closely. "Good job, gentlemen," he finally said. "In addition, you dumped the body where we discussed. You actually followed directions this time." He pursed his lips, raising one eyebrow, then handed each of them a roll of cash. "No need to count it. It is the amount we discussed, plus an extra grand for a job well done."

Vinny extended his hand, willing it to stop shaking. "Thanks, man."

Marco stood, grabbed Vinny's trembling hand, embraced him in a hug and kissed his cheek, then did the same with Louie. "You will be contacted in the future. Have a good evening."

Steve offered to escort the two soldiers out, needing time to rethink his strategy. It was almost eight in the evening and dark, inside and out. He slowly made his way back to Marco's lighted office, in no hurry for another one-on-one with the man. Marco Santini was a mind-fuck in every sense of the word. *A fucking hothouse flower. Sensitive and high maintenance.* He had to watch every damn word that came out of his mouth, because the little fucker would turn it around on him sure as shit. *Three things in life mattered to the man—money, his dick, and himself, in that order.*

Steve approached the office door, wishing he could just go back to his apartment and get stoned. Summoning strength, and taking a deep breath, he went inside.

"So, things went well, don't ya think?" Steve strolled into the room, grabbed his empty glass off the wet-bar, and poured another drink. Sitting down, he drained half the glass of whiskey.

Marco paced the length of the room, his expensive Italian shoes squeaking slightly, martini in one hand, Marlboro in the other. He stopped briefly and looked at his sidekick—his bitch—holding Steve's gaze, fire in his dark, Spanish eyes, then resumed pacing.

Steve shrugged his broad shoulders, used to this kind of behavior from the Boss. He knew not to ask any more questions. Marco would speak when he was ready, with much drama if the past held true. He lifted the glass of whiskey to his lips and sipped the icy fire, watching the little Italian pace.

Marco put out his cigarette in the ashtray on his desk. Leaning on the edge, he faced Stephen. "I do believe we've made a dreadful mistake."

Steve wore a puzzled expression on his face, but said nothing.

Lighting another cigarette and blowing a stream of smoke into the already polluted air, Marco continued. "Leonardo Gianelli was killed at relatively the same time as Stan Bauer. This was not wise. Think about it, please."

Steve took another pull from his drink, draining the last of the amber liquid. Picking up his pack of smokes from the coffee table, he extracted one. Fumbling with a lighter, he lit it and deeply inhaled, gazing out the window, knowing he was pissing Marco off.

"Well?" Sometimes his American friend and his lackadaisical ways infuriated him. Americans never seemed to take anything seriously. Everything was a 'Let's just wait and see what happens–to hell with the consequences' attitude. Marco was sick to death of it.

Steve stood and stretched, then moseyed on over to the bar to refresh his drink. He looked at Marco, whiskey bottle midair. "Yeah, you're right. We should have spaced the hits apart a bit more, I guess. Huh?"

Marco couldn't help but grin–despite the fury he felt, he genuinely liked Stephen. "Yes, I *guess*," he offered. "We will have cops and Feds breathing down our necks for some time now."

"Nothing new, there."

"Ahh, that is where you are wrong, my friend. Remember, one of their own was killed. Stan Bauer, a well-loved snitch-pig."

Steve grinned. "Snitch-pig, I like that. Well, ya know, it really doesn't matter. We had no choice but to deal with it. There's no way they can trace the van our guys in Minnesota used. We're safe. As for the boys–Alex and JJ–we'll have them lay low. Maybe take a Florida vacation or something."

"Good idea. Get them out of town, just in case. It was the middle of the night, but you never know what nosey neighbor was out walking their dog or some fucking thing."

Even when Marco cussed, he sounded refined. "I'll take care of it tonight. We won't waste any time," Steve offered. "Don't worry."

"Okay. I won't. I will trust you to take care of all the details. Now, what about *our* snitch?"

"What about him? We need him more than ever."

"Yes, but he could become very dangerous for us, no?"

Steve shrugged his shoulders, running his fingers through his long blonde hair. Scratching a two-day beard growth, he thought for a moment. "Nah. Whatcha worried about? We got our snitch right where we want him. Remember, he contacted us. He needs us. He's looking for ways to ingratiate himself, *and*–this may be the most important–he's naïve as hell. You worry too fuckin' much."

Marco stood and walked behind his desk, feeling anger surge through his blood once again at the way this man so often rubbed him the wrong way. "And you do not worry enough, Stephen."

Steve shrugged. "What good does it do, Marco? Don't you know stress is a killer? Take a chill-pill, man. We'll take extra precautions with the heat on. Okay?"

Marco leaned back in his leather chair and looked at his friend. Smiling through a red haze, he offered, "Okay."

Chapter 6

Maria and Joe arrived home in close succession. Before they married, Maria owned a condo in Minneapolis and Joe owned a small house in St. Paul. Upon joining lives, they sold their properties and bought a house together along the Mississippi. When they purchased the property, it was nowhere near upscale. Now, many of the houses in the area were mansion-like. Some even had names.

Seeing Theresa's beat-up car in the driveway, Maria parked on the street so Joe could get the Jeep into the garage. They met up as he got out of the vehicle. "She's home early."

"Told ya." He grinned and put an arm around her slender waist.

Tess was waiting for them in the kitchen. She threw herself first into her mother's arms, then her father's, glad to be home.

"Sweetheart, you're home." Maria kissed her daughter's cheek and smoothed her long dark hair. She had seen her just last week, but it seemed longer.

"I finished with finals early. Everyone was heading out. The place was deserted by the time I left."

Joe hugged her. "Missed ya, kiddo."

Tess returned the bear hug. "Me, too, Dad."

Joe had been her dad since she was ten years old–the only father she'd ever known. Her biological father, Jack Sanchez, left when she was a baby, returning years later under an alias, and abducting her. He would have killed her…didn't even know she was his own daughter.

Theresa looked back with relative ease now. She remembered it had taken her a full year to get over the initial shock of everything that happened on that fateful evening in September. With therapy and close family ties, she emerged stronger. She thought of what Joe always told her–*If it doesn't kill ya, it'll make ya stronger, kiddo.*

She grinned at her dad. "I can stay for a whole month."

Joe laughed. They had a joke about visitors who brought

large suitcases with nowhere to go. "Good. It's your house, too. You can stay as long as you want, honey."

Maria removed dinner preparations from the refrigerator. "Hey, where's Tony? Have you seen your brother?"

Concern appeared in Tess' eyes. "Yeah, briefly. I think he's in his room–playing computer games."

"Well, nothing new there." Joe headed down the hallway toward Tony's bedroom.

"Ya know–" Tess stopped and frowned at her mother.

"What?"

Tess looked at the floor, then back at her mother.

"What, Theresa, tell me. Please?" Maria took her daughter by the elbow, steering her toward the kitchen table.

"Well, I don't know how to say this without it sounding bad, and it's not necessarily bad. I don't know..."

Maria waited patiently.

"He's changed, Mom."

"Changed?" Maria thought about it. "Well, he's growing up, Theresa. He's becoming more..." Maria struggled for a word.

"Distant," Tess offered.

"Thoughtful," Maria corrected. "He's almost sixteen."

"Yeah, I know, and maybe that's all it is. I hope so."

"But, you think it's more." Maria looked closely at her daughter, who looked exactly as she had at twenty.

Tess glanced down at her lap, then raised her eyes to her mother's face. "Maybe."

"Drugs?" Maria couldn't help but revert to the past. *Perhaps things were not quite over. Was her son following the same path of destruction as his father? Or his mother?*

Tess shrugged her shoulders. "I don't know, Mom. He just seems distant and different. We've always been close...best friends." Her voice faltered.

Maria snapped out of her reverie. She saw the concern written on her daughter's face. If it had Tess this upset, perhaps there *was* a problem. "Don't worry, honey. We'll get to the bottom of this. Everything will be okay. I promise."

Tess nodded, leaned over and hugged her mom, glad to be home, but worried nonetheless. Where had Tony gone? He was right here, yet a million miles away.

The kid was deep into shooting aliens on his computer when Joe opened the bedroom door. "Hey, buddy. What's up?"

Tony got shot down as a result of the interruption, totally blowing his concentration and ending the game. "Shit." He glanced at his stepfather. "Sorry, Joe."

It still somewhat hurt that Tony called them by their first names. He had called them Mom and Dad until around the age of twelve. When they brought it up recently, he shrugged it off, saying it's what he was comfortable with. They had to accept it–everyone's different, and the boy had been through a lot.

Tony turned his attention to Joe, expectantly.

"Your sister is home, ya know."

"Yeah, I already talked to her."

"It would be nice if you came out to join the family. Don't ya think?" Joe touched the boy's shoulder.

Tony flinched slightly, but smiled. "Yeah, okay. Just let me save my game and I'll be right out."

"Great." Joe closed the door and returned to the kitchen.

Maria had marinated chicken breast cooking on the stove and the spicy aroma wafted through the entire house. Tess was busy cleaning lettuce.

"*Hmm*, smells good." Joe kissed Maria on the neck and slipped his arms around her waist.

Tess turned toward them, grinning. "Jeez, get a room you two. You'd think you were just married. Here it's been what, almost ten years and you're still acting like teenagers."

Maria laughed. "It's good to have you home, honey."

"It's good to be home." She turned serious. "I really miss you guys, miss living here."

"I know, kiddo. We miss you, too." Joe enveloped Theresa in his other arm, so they stood in a group hug.

The three of them had always been close, well before Tony came into their lives. They seemed to have a special bond. Joe couldn't help but feel Tony sensed it, possibly resented it. They had given him everything they could. In his younger years, it seemed to be enough, but lately it was difficult to determine what made the boy tick.

Tony came into the kitchen and stopped in his tracks.

Theresa stuck out one arm and broke the circle. "C'mon, little brother."

Tony reluctantly made his way toward them, putting up with the attention. *One big happy family.*

The phone rang and Tony was the first to break away. "It's for you, sis." He handed the phone to Tess, making kissing motions. "It's your boyfriend."

Theresa rolled her eyes at her brother and grinned. Now *that* was the kid she knew and loved. She grabbed the phone and went into the other room for privacy.

Maria extended the dinner invitation to Theresa's boyfriend, Mike, who was already on his way over. He and Tess had a healthy relationship–not too close, school still came first–but they loved each other and planned on having a future together. Both Maria and Joe liked him.

Dinner was a success and even Tony warmed up a bit when Maria brought out the chocolate cake for dessert. They spent the evening together, enjoying good conversation and being a family.

Tomorrow, Maria and Joe would meet the Russian woman. Chief LaSalle was meeting her at the airport, since they were already well acquainted. Tina would hold up at a local hotel, until they set the game plan into motion, and moved her onto the streets, which would be relatively quick. They would discuss everything in detail tomorrow morning at City Hall.

Maria and Joe declined help with the dishes, sending the kids off to do their own things, while they discussed the meeting tomorrow and their new co-worker.

Chapter 7

Etina Altmark packed her belongings. She would miss New York, but remained certain she'd return someday. This city was her home now. She'd come a long way in five years. She had left Kstovo, Russia at the age of twenty-three to finish her last year of training in the United States, and never went back. She missed the place, not the people. Located on the right bank of the Volga River, twenty-two kilometers southeast of Nizhny Novgorod, Kstovo would remain a part of her until the day she died, but with no family left, there was no reason to return. It would be too painful facing the ghosts that haunted each and every path there.

Clearing off the sparse belongings from the dresser-top, her eyes caught the reflection in the mirror. She stopped her task, gazing at herself. Etina was so Americanized she didn't even recognize the old Etina. Even her name–she went by Tina, less confusing. Her short blonde hair made her look almost boyish, if not for her porcelain skin and large blue eyes. Her petite five-foot frame and slender build sliced years off her age. At twenty-eight, she could still pass as a teenager. She was good at her job, better than most.

She grinned at herself, inspecting straight white teeth. Closing her mouth, she attempted a glimpse into her soul, moving closer to the mirror. "Who *are* you?" she asked the woman who returned her stare with crystal blue eyes. There seemed to be a hidden answer waiting to be revealed.

She sighed and continued packing, trying not to think too much about what lay in store for her. It always excited her to start a new assignment–nothing in the world pumped her adrenaline more than working undercover and the thrill of the unknown. She accepted only those posing danger, risk. And the results–so far– were always positive. She had developed a reputation, and she liked it.

She wouldn't be in Minnesota very long. Only long enough to acclimate herself with the other runaways on the street. She had to be one of the chosen for the L.A. circuit. *I can do it...I know I can...I can do anything.* Despite her successes and confidence, a small amount of self-doubt always remained, dating back to her difficult childhood she assumed. Her mother had been murdered one evening while Etina lay sleeping in the next room. Her older brother had been staying overnight at a friend's house, and at the age of fourteen on a bright August morning, she'd discovered her mother's brutalized body.

Closing the large almost empty suitcase, she sat on the edge of the bed, taking in all the details of the small efficiency apartment, committing them to memory. This would be the last time she could do this; she liked it here, nestled in the middle of social chaos. She looked at her watch. Her ride would be here in ten minutes to take her to the airport. With the extra security due to 9-11 and terrorism, and the fact she carried a weapon, she needed to arrive early.

Her flight was due in Minneapolis at 7:35 p.m. Minnesota time. She stood and straightened her blouse, smoothing out the wrinkles and tossing her purse over one shoulder, double checking the small .38 revolver tucked into the inner pocket–easily accessible, but concealed.

Grabbing the surprisingly light suitcase, Etina closed the apartment door on this part of her life, prepared for the adventure. Not even coming close to realizing the eminent danger ahead.

The flight was uneventful and Etina slept most of the way. As the plane descended into Minneapolis, she looked out the window at the winter wonderland, thinking of Russia. She smiled to herself. Perhaps good things would happen here. It was always best to maintain a positive attitude.

She felt different this time, though, and she didn't like it. Trepidation that was foreign to her took residence in the center of her stomach as the plane touched down, bouncing up and down, then finally smoothing out, coasting to the appropriate terminal.

Chapter 8

To appease Marco and all his worries, Steve offered to fly out to Minneapolis, personally, to see that the two soldiers who whacked Stan Bauer disappeared. Two, maybe three weeks. He reserved two first-class tickets on a commercial flight to Miami, Florida, and now waited in the MSP airport for Alex and JJ. He glanced at his watch–almost 7:00. The plane would start boarding any minute. *Where the hell are they?*

Santini's private jet waited for him, refueled and ready for the return flight to California. He was anxious to get home, hated this deep-freeze winter shit. *Who in their right mind would live somewhere like this?* He sat down and waited, chewing his cuticles and frowning.

Alex and JJ showed up, looking stoned and happy, five minutes after they called for initial boarding of small children and the elderly.

Steve stood. "Christ, nothing like last minute, huh guys?"

"Sorry, man." Alex apologized. "We're definitely in vacation mode."

"Yeah, way sorry, man," JJ added, grinning like a fool.

They called for the rest of the passengers and Alex and JJ stumbled into line. Steve stood back and watched as the line slowly disappeared down the concourse.

Once the two were safely on board the 737, Steve gazed out the window at the night sky. A few snowflakes fell under the runway lights, but stars twinkled and the moon flitted in and out behind periodic clouds.

Steve stood, hands in pockets, deep in thought. What he wouldn't give right now to pay their insider a personal visit. They were so close, could practically reach out and touch each other, yet it would be too risky to make direct contact. Their snitch corresponded by e-mail ninety-nine percent of the time. Twice, he and Marco had been contacted by telephone, but were assured an untraceable public payphone was used. Their insider was not stupid. Wet behind the ears, yes, but not stupid. That had been proven two days ago. Who knew what problems the snitch-pig, Stan, would have caused if he had lived to learn more about the organization.

Things are okay. This is good. He watched the plane, with Alex and JJ on board, slowly taxi down the runway.

Steve thought of California and the excellent pot that awaited his return. Suddenly in a hurry, he walked quickly through the airport, dodging people with too much luggage and tired children.

Steve almost missed seeing the most beautiful girl in the world. Racing through the airport, his brain focused on getting home, he glimpsed her on the down escalator.

He stopped his rapid retreat, just as she got off and turned a corner, disappearing into the crowd. He looked for her head and couldn't find it. *Gone. Just like that. Wow.*

He continued at a more leisurely pace, trying to remember what she looked like. There was *something* about her.

Etina looked for Chief Sandra LaSalle as soon as she entered the terminal but didn't see her. "Shit," she whispered under her breath. She checked the scrolling digital display to see where to pick up her luggage, and followed some of the other passengers from her flight.

Waiting by the baggage carousel with the other passengers, Etina was tired and in desperate need of a strong cup of coffee.

She literally jumped when a hand touched her shoulder.

"Tina."

"Sandy. You startled me." She blushed, not wanting to appear anything but strong and confident to this woman, who was a good friend and now her boss.

"Sorry." Chief LaSalle smiled. "Welcome to Minnesota."

"Thank you. It reminds me of Russia."

"How is New York? I miss New York at Christmas time."

Etina smiled broadly. "Yes, it is beautiful."

Luggage started spitting out the hole, making its way around the conveyer belt. Etina spotted her bag–she had tied a decorative scarf to make it unique–third in line. Stepping up to retrieve the large suitcase, she lifted it off the carousel with what looked like Herculean effort considering its size, but was in fact light due to lack of belongings.

Sandra laughed, offering to take her carry-on, which Tina gratefully accepted, then led the way to the car. She made Tina take out her jacket before going outside, and laughed again at the thin, spring jacket the young woman pulled from her suitcase.

They drove in silence to the hotel where Tina would stay for a couple of days, each absorbed in private thoughts.

Chapter 9

The Russian undercover agent already sat in Chief LaSalle's office when Maria and Joe arrived at 7:30 the following morning. They were all scheduled for an eight o'clock meeting.

Tomorrow was Christmas Eve.

Christmas.

It didn't *feel* like Christmas this year. Things were just too discordant. Stan came to mind–dead, facedown in the snow, garbage surrounding him, twinkling holiday lights. But, the funny thing was, December 25th came whether you were ready or not.

Joe had to gather some pertinent information and dived into his PC before the meeting.

Maria grabbed a cup of coffee and sat down at her own desk, going over the detectives' caseload, making notes on what to follow-up on. Her so-called partner should be helping with paperwork, but seemed to have his own agenda lately. Powders and his wife had recently separated, but he seemed even more preoccupied than usual. She tried to give him a break, but how much of a break?

Maria watched detectives filter in and out, getting their assignments.

Powders stumbled in about ten minutes to eight. She watched his progress as he followed his usual routine on the way to his desk. He glanced her way briefly as he walked by to get to his desk.

She gave him a couple of minutes to get settled before walking over, gathering half a dozen folders to be filed which he should have done two days ago.

"Good morning, Tom. How are you this morning?"

He had just taken a huge bite out of a powdered sugar donut and white coating speckled his lips. Grabbing a napkin off a stack that had a permanent location at one side of his desk, he wiped his mouth, apologized, coughed harshly, and apologized again.

Maria just smiled, waiting for him to get the donut down.

After several sips of coffee, he seemed to regain some

composure. "Sorry 'bout that. Went down the wrong pipe." He grinned, showing yellow, tobacco stained teeth.

"Man, thought I was gonna have to do the Heimlich." Maria grinned. "Some files were missed. Maybe you got busy or something." She set the folders on the edge of his workspace, sitting down in the chair next to his desk.

Tom nervously pushed the donut and coffee aside and focused on Sanchez. She was the lead detective and he had been a fuck-up the past few months. He knew it; hell was the first to admit it. Too much booze, too little sleep, not to mention being alone 24/7. A real mess. He'd forgotten about the damn files. He was always forgetting things lately. Too worried about damn e-mails.

"Tom, are you okay? You seem...well, more out-of-sorts than usual." Maria showed genuine concern for the man. The bags under his eyes were darker than ever and his hand shook when he reached for his coffee cup.

"Yeah...yeah...I'm okay. Thanks for asking. Just had a little too much to drink last night. Stayed up too late."

Maria could see he was uncomfortable. She stood. "Well, if there's anything I can do, or if you need to take some time off, just let me know, okay?"

"Thanks. I'll get to those files right away."

"No hurry. Take your time." She walked back to her desk wanting to kick herself. *No hurry. Take your time.* Like she needed to tell him that.

She had just sat down when Chief LaSalle buzzed her, stating everyone was there but her. Maria apologized, grabbed a notepad and hurried to the chief's closed door, knocked once, and entered.

Joe sat in one chair and a blonde pixie sat next to the chief. Maria gave Joe a look for not grabbing her before the meeting. Taking the empty chair next to Joe, she smiled at the stranger.

"You were talking to Tom," he whispered, not wanting to pay the price later at home.

Chief LaSalle looked over her bifocals at Maria. "Glad you could join us, Sanchez."

"Sorry. Had to give some files to Powders."

"He's looking pretty rough around the edges these days.

Everything okay?"

Maria didn't want to get into the sorry state of her partner's affairs right now. "Pretty much," she offered noncommittally. She leaned forward and held out her hand. "Maria Sanchez."

Etina smiled winningly, looking twelve years old, and grasped Maria's hand with more strength than expected. "Tina Altmark," she said, with only a slight accent.

"Maria is Joe's wife." The chief held a look of disdain on her pinched face as she spoke.

Tina looked surprised, and then said, "Cool."

Maria grinned, liking her immediately. She noticed Joe smile slightly, too.

"Okay. I hate to break up newfound friendships, but we need to get down to business. Morgan, have you got the stats to show Tina?"

Joe laid the papers on the chief's desk, flipped through several sheets and got to a map of downtown Minneapolis. "Here's where you'll want to hang." He pointed to a highlighted area, looking over at Tina, who was riveted to the map, eyes twinkling with excitement. "It seems to be the spot where most of the girls congregate," he continued. "The runaways chosen for the West Coast are always younger, fresh, not seasoned junkies, like seventy-five percent of what you'll find down there. I've included several pictures of a few recent missing teens. Hopefully you can locate some of them."

Tina reached for the paper-clipped pages. "May I?"

"Certainly. Study the area and the girls. I've included a small biography on each girl as well, to give you a little insight. In addition, there are a couple of characters you need to watch out for. It's all in there." Joe nodded toward the papers.

Chief LaSalle laughed. "You don't need to worry about Tina. She can take care of herself. A half-pint of dynamite."

Tina smiled at the comparison, blushing slightly. "I am a survivor that is all. And I'm smart," she added, tapping the side of her head. "But the more information I have going into this, the better. Thank you," she said, looking at Joe.

"Tina is staying at a private hotel right now. We'll move her to the streets in a few days, maybe around the twenty-seventh. That will give her time to get into her new character's skin—Lizzy

Fairchild."

Tina grinned at Joe and Maria. "Do I look like a Lizzy?"

Maria nodded. "Yes, you could definitely be a Lizzy."

Joe agreed.

Chief LaSalle stood. "Well, I'm glad that's settled. I don't need to tell you, of course, *everything* said or done in this room *stays* in this room. Tina's life depends on it."

"Yes, that goes without saying." Maria was offended. The chief was always so damn patronizing. What did she think? *We would go into the outer office and call a press conference?*

Tina slipped on her jacket, putting up the hood, and a pair of dark glasses. She grinned. "Incognito."

"Joe would you please escort Tina out? There's a cab waiting out front to take her back. I'll give the two of you Tina's contact information later."

"Sure." Joe moved toward the door, and Tina followed close behind. She only stood about half as tall as Joe. It was comical. She could've been his daughter.

"Tina." Chief LaSalle blew her a kiss. "God's speed. And remember, stay put the next few days. You'll get your chance to explore soon enough."

Tina flashed a toothy smile. "Yes, Mother."

Sandra returned the smile, genuine concern in her eyes, an emotion neither Maria nor Joe thought existed in the woman.

Joe and Tina left quickly, taking the stairwell instead of the elevator, to avoid any curious onlookers.

Maria shut the chief's door and returned to her desk in the outer office. She sat, her mind on a million things, when Powders suddenly appeared at her side.

It was his turn to invade her space. He pulled up a chair and sat by her desk. "Hey, who was that?"

Maria busied herself, shuffling papers. "Who?"

"The kid trailing Morgan a minute ago."

"*Hmm?*" Maria looked at Tom Powders. "Oh, I don't know...I guess the son of some perp. Not really sure."

"Oh."

"Why?" Maria continued separating a pile of reports, wondering why her partner would be so interested in the first place.

"Just wondering." He paused, considering more questions.

Maria stopped for a moment and looked at Tom, trying to figure him out. He seemed to be feeling better–perhaps the caffeine had cleared his head. She shrugged. "Wish I knew more."

She turned to dig some folders out of the file cabinet. When she turned around again, no Powders. He wasn't at his desk, but his coat remained, so he was still in the building. *Probably in the bathroom.* Unease settled over her at his questions concerning Tina.

Chapter 10

Steve woke with a nasty headache. On the flight back from Minneapolis, he got shit-faced on martinis, and he hated martinis. They tasted like foot-sweat. Since Marco was the last one to use the jet, only top-shelf vodka and vermouth were stocked, along with olives, pearl onions, and every kind of fuckin' garnishment for a martini available to mankind. It was either drink it or pass the time sober, which wasn't even an option.

He thought of the girl at the airport. He could barely recall what she looked like now. She was beautiful. He remembered that, and something about her had attracted him like a magnet. *She was...what? I don't know.* Steve shook his head to clear it.

He reached for his pack of smokes on the bedside table, fumbled one out, and put it to his lips, lighting it with a shaky hand. He felt like shit. Hung over. He grinned. JJ and Alex were waking up in Miami, Florida. After hanging in Minnesota for almost two weeks that had to be a real treat. Anything above forty degrees had to be a real treat.

His cell sang a tune on his bedside table. He picked it up, looking at the LED. "Shit, Marco. And two missed calls. Shit." He flipped it open. "Yeah."

"What in the fuck? It is about time."

"Sorry." Steve rubbed his face, trying to focus. "Drank too many martinis on the flight back."

Silence, then Marco laughed. "Martinis? You *hate* martinis."

"Well, let's just say they're an acquired taste." Steve grinned.

"How did it go?" Marco's tone turned serious, all laughter gone from his voice.

Steve had to switch gears. Not an easy feat when the incessant pounding in his head was deafening. *How did it go...how did it go...Oh, Alex and JJ!* A light came on in his strained brain. "Fine. Fine. Watched them board the plane. They're waking up in sunny Florida with probably worse headaches than mine."

"Good. Very good. I want us to get together as soon as possible."

"Why, what up?" Steve sat up, swinging his long legs over the edge of the bed, feeling a wave of dizziness wash over him.

"There is a shipment coming in. We have time to discuss. It is not for a couple of weeks. Big."

"Really?" Steve was intrigued. Marco never handled large quantities–too dangerous.

"More later." Marco ended the connection.

Steve looked at the cell phone in his hand. Closing it, he tossed it on the bed, got up and stretched. "Fuckin' Marco." He dropped to the floor and did ten pushups. He felt as if he was going to throw up when he stood back up.

Time to shower and see what the fuck Marco has up his sleeve. "I love it," he said aloud, jogging into the bathroom, suddenly feeling a little better.

Chapter 11

By late afternoon, the crime lab and autopsy reports came back on Stan Bauer. The autopsy report stated what they already knew–the single bullet had lodged in the large intestine, which resulted in a slow bleed and eventual death.

The crime lab had discovered several things. Tire tracks in the fresh snow left good imprints that appeared to be from a Ford van. The footprints surrounding Stan were clear and concise as well. Size ten Nikes, and size twelve boots of some kind. They also found a small wooden bead. Technicians questioned whether it was part of the crime scene or unrelated. The quarter-inch diameter wooden bead lay embedded in the snow about ten and half feet from Stan Bauer's body, trampled on by the individual wearing boots.

Joe set up camp next to Maria, in an open desk. His duties as Special Investigator were still piling up on his other desk, but Chief LaSalle wanted him here, on this case, working with the lead detective–who happened to be Maria.

Maria returned from the restroom, taking the long way back to walk by Powders. He was busy, or so it appeared, typing like a maniac on his PC. Walking by, she glanced at his work and saw he was in Outlook Express. His *personal* e-mail. The department used Lotus Notes, so this wasn't work related. She slowly continued to her own desk.

Joe had scooted the spare desk up against hers. He watched her progress, a sly smile on his lips. "Maybe you missed your calling, should've been a spy, Ms. Sanchez, *hmm*?" he asked.

Maria sat down quietly. "He looked so damn focused. I had to check it out. Never seen him concentrate that hard," she whispered.

She told Joe about the questions Powders had asked concerning Tina, after he'd escorted her out, earlier this morning. Joe chalked it up to dumb curiosity, not seeing any hidden agenda, as Maria perhaps did. "So? What's he doing?"

"Personal e-mail."

"I thought it was blocked–access denied. I can't get into ours on the computers here."

"Sweetheart, there are ways around it. You've just got to have minimal computer savvy."

"Ouch." Joe was the first to admit computers were not his favorite thing. He could accomplish what he needed, but that was as far as it went. He had no desire to dig around just for the fun of it.

Maria grinned. "Sorry, the truth hurts, doesn't it?"

"So, who was he emailing?"

"I don't know. I didn't get *that* close, or look for very long."

"Well, why the hell not?"

Maria just looked at him and he grinned.

He knew she was a bulldog when she wanted to be, but she also had a soft side–too soft sometimes. She'd been burned in the past because of it.

"Did you get Tina's room number from the chief?" Maria asked wanting to change the subject.

"Yeah, I have all her contact info. We'll go over everything later when we're alone."

"It's going to be a pretty lonely Christmas for her I'm afraid," Maria said.

"Part of the job." Joe was always so centered in reality; whereas Maria let her emotions come into play more often than not.

"Yeah, maybe so. But I thought..." Maria looked at her husband and grinned.

"Oh, no. What? What did you *think*?" He looked skeptical, before even hearing what she had to say.

"I thought we could do a pizza with her tonight. Maybe I'll wrap up a couple of things. Tess was saying how she wanted to have a pizza night with Tony. Just the two of them–hang out, eat pizza, watch a movie, hopefully talk. I thought...we could get a couple of pizzas. Drop one off at home for the kids and take one over to the hotel, hang out with Tina for a while. She's got to feel totally alone–strange city, strange people."

"Wow." Joe laughed. "When you *think*, you really think. Sounds like you've got it all figured out."

"I do. In fact I already talked to Tess and Tony."

"Sounds like all that's left is ordering the damn pizza."

"Yep, that's about it. Even called Tina. She knows we're coming. We should be there around 5:30."

"I thought you asked me what her room number was. How did you know her phone number?"

Maria laughed. "I just asked if you had it. I have all her contact info as well. What did you think? Chief LaSalle only trusted *you* with it?"

"No...I thought...nothing." Joe looked a little hurt. That was exactly what he thought. The chief had specifically told him to share it with Maria–told him he needed to call the shots in this investigation. *Probably told Maria the same damn thing. Women, what a trip.* The chief liked pitting them against each other. She'd done it since day one.

Maria looked at him closely. "What's the matter?"

He nodded toward the chief's closed office door. "I think she's up to her old tricks, again. She told me she wanted me to lead this investigation." He watched the expression on Maria's face change. He knew it; the chief had told her the same thing.

"Well, that makes two of us." Maria rolled her eyes and shook her head. "Bitch."

"Yeah, should we say something?"

"No. Not yet, anyway." Maria looked determined. It was a look that Joe knew from experience meant one thing–*don't fuck with me.* Sandra LaSalle's day was coming.

Chapter 12

Marco had a fresh pot of coffee and an assortment of pastries when Steve arrived mid-afternoon. Steve had hoped for beer and Nacho chips, but this would have to do.

Steve succumbed to the perfunctory hug-hug and cheek kiss. He took the proffered seat opposite the Boss at the small table, facing the picture window that overlooked the city. He could barely see downtown Los Angeles through a layer of hazy fog, leftover from the morning, refusing to dissipate amongst the tall buildings.

Marco poured coffee and selected the first pastry–a chocolate éclair. "Eat, my friend. These are true French pasties–I had them flown in directly from a bakery I have frequented in Paris. Enjoy."

Steve selected a raspberry chocolate number. He wanted to get down to business but knew with this man, it was easier to do as he asked than to face his wrath. He was almost like a chick. The pastries were excellent, though. Steve had never tasted anything like it. Only the best for Marco Santini.

After finishing their second cup of coffee, Marco daintily dabbed his mouth with a napkin and leaned back in his chair. "Well, what do you think?"

Steve always had to play this guessing game and he didn't much care for it. "About?"

Marco laughed, knowing he was a mind-fuck and enjoying it immensely. "The pastries."

"Delicious," Steve answered. "Let's talk about what I came here to talk about."

"Patience, my friend."

"You know I'm not good with that." Steve smiled winningly, showing even white teeth in his rugged, tanned face.

"No, you are not." Marco smiled, thinking back. "Okay, enough torture for now, I guess. We have a big shipment coming in."

Steve sat up straight. "When? What?"

"Easy, boy. Down." Marco laughed, watching irritation fleet across his friend's features. "In two weeks. Heroin." A smile remained on his full lips, as he smoothed his dark mustache.

Steve ran his fingers through his long blonde hair, thinking. "How big?"

"Big. Compressed blocks. A box full."

"A box full...how big of a box and the how the hell ya gonna ship it?"

Marco smiled. "It's all been decided, my friend. Books." Steve studied the impeccably dressed man, who had risen and now paced the length of the room. "Books? Wanna explain?"

Marco Santini laughed, relishing the game. He stopped pacing for a moment while he spoke. "Yes, books. Hollowed out textbooks, if you will. The first layer will be legit, and perhaps the bottom. But in the middle we shall ship blocks of compressed Mexican heroin."

Steve grinned. "I like it. Just might work."

"Might?" Marco frowned. "No, it *will* work. However, if it doesn't, we'll make sure we have a scapegoat. It won't be connected to The Family."

Steve nodded. It wouldn't be the first time things were *handled*. Marco Santini had a knack for staying clean, even in the dirtiest of situations. "Sounds like a plan." He lit a cigarette, then refilled his coffee cup with the rich Nicaraguan brew. "How soon again?"

"Two weeks...give or take a day or so. The heroin will be brought across the border into Texas and from there will be packaged into the books and shipped via a private flight to one of the smaller airfields–I'm not certain which one yet." He looked at Stephen, already gauging his reaction. "I know, I know, it is a risk flying."

Steve shook his head. "Road trip is our best bet. You know that. That's how we brought the coke in."

"Time is money, my friend. The cocaine is gone. The streets are almost dry. I want to move before someone else does. And what fun is life without a little risk here and there, *hmm*?"

Steve knew exactly who Marco was referring to–a long-time rival to the Santini family. Anthony Rossi, had been looking for a way to take over as top dog, keeping the supply and demand going in the drug trade. He smiled. "I understand."

"Good. I knew you would. I already have a stooge set up to tag along. He will take the unfortunate fall if necessary."

"Where's it coming into? L.A.?"

"No, no, that would point to us. Minneapolis." He grinned at his friend.

"Minneapolis?" Steve thought about it and smiled. "We can pick it up the same time we bring back a couple more girls."

"*Hmm*, I didn't think of that. Yes, that will work. We did that once before, didn't we?"

"Yes." Steve remembered the redhead and brunette who each carried a makeup case filled with meth. "Indeed we did."

"Okay. Well, that's all I have. I have other appointments to attend to."

Steve took the cue. "Later, Dude." He gave Marco a peace sign. "Have a day, man."

Marco smiled and waved him off, then picked up the telephone and started punching numbers.

Steve grinned all the way down the hall. *The man was definitely a force to be reckoned with. Always had a million things going at once. An inspiration, that's what he was. Selfish, yes, but also an inspiration to hard work, dedication and the almighty buck.* He knew he could learn a thing of two from Marco Santini, and he was definitely eager.

Chapter 13

Dropping off one pizza at home, Joe and Maria drove to Etina's hotel room. The smell of pepperoni and sausage assailed their nostrils the entire way, taking all the willpower they had not to sneak a piece.

Joe pulled into the hotel's private lot and parked the Jeep. At home, Maria had managed to gather a few unassigned gifts. She had a box of chocolates and a scented candle. She added a good luck charm bought at the last minute–spying a gold horseshoe necklace in the window of a boutique store next to the pizza joint. She had popped in while Joe picked up the pizza, and only spent ten dollars. It was a spur of the moment thing, and perhaps Tina didn't even wear jewelry, but Maria thought it was a nice gesture.

"Ready?" Joe asked, eyeing his wife's armload of gifts. He shook his head as he grabbed the pizza and two bottles of champagne.

"Yes. Let's go." Maria grinned, and followed her husband to room six.

Tina opened the door a crack, gun drawn, then opened it wide upon seeing them, smiling.

"Merry Christmas," Maria said. "Don't shoot. I hope you're hungry. Joe ordered a large pizza with everything on it."

Tina tucked the small pistol back into her belt. "Ooh, a garbage pizza–my favorite." She looked like a kid.

Joe grinned. "That makes three of us. Only kind of pizza there is if you ask me."

Joe sat in the only chair and the women sat cross-legged on the bed, devouring the greasy pizza. The hotel had supplied several plastic cups, and they toasted the holidays with champagne.

After twenty minutes of stuffing their faces and keeping talk to a minimum, Maria leaned back. "Wow, I'm really full." She pushed away her plate.

Two pieces remained.

"Okay, I'm game if you are." Tina looked at Joe who laughed.

"I probably ate more than the two of you combined."

"I don't think so...eat." Tina shoved the box toward Joe who groaned and complied.

Maria laughed. "I'll be the one who's sorry. Tonight in bed."

Tina grinned. "Too much information," she said between bites.

Joe refilled everyone's wine and cracked open the second bottle.

"Well, that was delicious," Tina said with a sigh. "I want to thank you both very much. It was very kind of you. This must be what they mean when they say, 'Minnesota Nice'."

"Oh, God. Here we go." Joe looked at Maria. He hated the 'Minnesota Nice' crap. "Suppose you saw the movie Fargo, too."

Tina laughed. "Why, yes. Yes I did. I liked it. Very much."

"At the risk of adding to the whole thing...I...we brought you a few gifts...for Christmas," Maria faltered.

Tina was genuinely touched. These lovely people probably didn't think she'd live to see the New Year...due to her new assignment. "Thank you. How...nice." She smiled broadly.

"Well, we figured you're away from friends and family. That and I knew we'd be friends when I met you." Maria grinned at the other woman. "I don't know what it is."

"You are both 'go-getters'. That's what it is." Joe looked at the two women.

Tina laughed, and said to Maria, "He thinks he's got us figured out."

Maria grinned. "Yeah, right. Good luck with that, buddy."

The women laughed at Joe's expense, but he didn't care. He was enjoying himself.

"Open this one first." Maria handed Tina the box containing the horseshoe charm necklace.

Tina tried to avoid getting too close to people, because with closeness came pain. She tried to dodge it whenever possible, but sometimes life gave one no choice. She found herself genuinely liking Maria, despite what Sandra had told her. She carefully opened the small box, revealing the glittering horseshoe pendant. "Oh, it's beautiful." She held it up to the light, then tried to clasp it around her neck.

"Here let me help you." Maria instructed the other woman to sit still, then closed the tiny clasp.

Tina looked down at her throat, then sprang up and ran to the mirror in the bathroom to get a closer look. "I love it," she said, walking back to where Maria and Joe sat. "Thank you."

Maria thought her eyes looked wet. "You're welcome. I hope it brings you good luck. I don't know about you, but I'm very superstitious."

"Superstitious, yes. Me, too." Tina rubbed the horseshoe.

Maria grinned at her new friend, and handed over the other two gifts.

Tina tore into the chocolates, declaring 'dessert'. She inhaled the candle's scent and promised to use it tonight in her bath. "Thank you, thank you, thank you," she said kissing and hugging first Maria then Joe.

They talked for another hour or so and learned that Etina Altmark had no family to speak of anywhere. She missed Russia but loved it here. She had never been married and had no intention of doing so.

Maria gave her the rundown of who she would ultimately be dealing with–Marco Santini–and the story behind Jack Sanchez and Roberto Santini. "So, there's a history there, and the Santini's seem to get more diabolical with each new generation."

Tina absorbed it all, knowing it could save her life. *Knowledge was power.*

When they left, Maria couldn't help but wonder what it would be like the next time they got together, or if there would even be a next time.

Maria and Joe hadn't been gone five minutes when a soft knock sounded on Tina's hotel door. Once again, she opened the door a crack, gun drawn.

Her visitor held up her hands. "I come bearing gifts." Sandra LaSalle stood with an armful of old clothes for Tina's new assignment and a sarcastic grin on her face.

"Sandy...Mom." She opened the door and hugged the older woman, who really was like a mother.

When Sandy and Tina had worked together in New York,

they became very close. Sandy was going through a nasty divorce when they met and Tina was fresh out of college, no parents, and no friends. She had only been in the United States a short while and still learning the American way, but she showed extreme dedication to getting the job done right. Sandy had seen a version of herself in the younger woman and taken her under wing. They shared dinners and movies and talk at a time when both women needed something. They never let work issues, or strong personalities affect the quality of their friendship.

Sandra looked around the small room, taking in the large empty pizza carton and two empty bottles of champagne. She eyed Tina up and down. "Hungry?"

Tina laughed. "Joe and Maria were here."

"Really..." Sandra looked mildly surprised, then annoyance crossed her face.

"Yes, they just left as a matter of fact." Tina adopted American expressions on a daily basis.

Sandra looked at her friend. Tina was a little shorter than she, so they were eye level. "Did you have fun?"

She met the older woman's gaze. "Yes, we did. Very much so."

"Well, that's good. I'm glad to hear it. Just remember what I told you about Maria Sanchez." Sandra smiled and walked to the other side of the small room. She set the stack of old clothes on the chair. Sandra did not entirely trust Maria Sanchez for some reason, and she had filled Tina in before her arrival. *Gut instinct.* Chief McCollough had been too soft. Things had happened in the department that never should've happened. Sanchez had him wrapped around her little finger. Those days were over. Things would be straightened out by the time her reign was over.

"I suppose I should straighten up a bit." Tina grabbed the empty pizza box and spent bottles of wine, depositing them in the garbage.

Sandra sat on the bed and watched Tina pick up napkins and plastic cups, patiently waiting for the girl–that is how she thought of her–to settle down. *Patience.* Surprisingly, she had learned to have considerably more over the years than she used to possess.

Tina finished by washing her hands in the bathroom sink. Drying them on a hand towel, she returned to where Sandra waited. "Sorry. You know how I hate a mess."

Sandra grinned. "I couldn't have phrased it better myself. That's why you're so good at what you do."

Tina thought about this. "*Hmm*, I never thought of it that way. Maybe you're right." She smiled. "Now, you have my undivided attention." She sat on the bed, hugging her friend briefly before tucking her legs underneath, focused.

Sandra stood and took the few steps to grab the pile of things she'd brought, and sat back down. "These are for you. They're clean. I know they look shabby, but we want you to look like you've been on the streets for a while. You're certainly skinny enough. Jeez, Tina–do you eat?"

"Like a pig."

"Figures...the envy of every woman." The older woman frowned, then smiled. "That's okay, sweetheart. I still love ya."

Tina sorted through the clothes–two pairs of jeans and three tops, a relatively warm jacket with a hood, an old hat, and holey gloves. She would wear her own worn-out sneakers. An old tattered backpack was included as well.

"Oh, I almost forgot. You have to be Lizzy Fairchild all the way down to your underwear." She pulled a plastic bag out of her large purse and tossed it to the girl, grinning. "Hand-me-downs."

Tina opened it and pulled out a ratty bra, three pairs of nearly worn-out underwear and two pairs of socks with no holes but a little threadbare. "So this Lizzy Fairchild–where does she come from? What are her parents like? Why did she run away? Any ideas on how I should become her?" It was paramount to any undercover case. The agent had to develop his or her fictitious character well, in order to be believable. Once there is doubt, discovery and possible death shortly followed.

"I think the usual...you could take a bit from each girl on the history Morgan gave you. Or make up your own. Your basics– middle class family. Parents too busy working to pay attention to their kid. Perhaps throw in an alcohol problem with one or both parents. Just misunderstood. Simply misunderstood."

"The plight of any normal teenager."

"Exactly." The chief had her try on the clothes to make sure they weren't too big. They fit and Etina Altmark looked good in anything, whatever the quality. The girl would look ravishing in a burlap sack. "I hate to run, but I'll come see you tomorrow and each day you stay here."

Tina knew once on the streets, she'd be on her own. Wearing a wire or anything at this early stage of the game was not an option. Once she worked her way into the Santini family, they would find a way to bring him down. That was too far down the road to consider though. She hugged her friend and boss. "I will see you tomorrow."

Sandra returned the hug. "Tomorrow," she promised, shutting the door. She had mixed emotions, but tried to be strong in front of Tina.

Once in the car, she felt a single tear slide down her face. "I hope I haven't signed the girl's fate," she said aloud. She turned the key, watching her breath frost the window.

Maria couldn't get Tina off her mind. She hated this part of the job. Danger was always a factor in police work, but undercover became an entirely different ball game. She wouldn't dream of doing undercover work at this stage in her life.

She thought back to her brief attempt at it years ago. She remembered thinking she had pulled one over on Roberto Santini, posing as the daughter of a rich tycoon, looking for ways to invest money. Roberto was onto her from the beginning. It had become ugly, quickly. She shivered, thinking about it.

Joe entered the bedroom. "Hey."

"Hey." Maria sat on the edge of the bed.

"You okay?"

Maria nodded. "Think so."

Joe sat next to her, put an arm around her shoulders. "What's wrong, baby?"

"Ah...nothing really. Just thinking." Maria looked at her husband.

"About?"

"Tina. How dangerous it is. Thinking back to Roberto and our little office visit."

Joe rolled his eyes, remembering. "Maria Sands."

Maria smiled, recalling her ruse.

"You could've been killed. I was pissed, and lying in a fuckin' hospital bed in Ventura, California, so there was nothing I

could do about it."
"I was fine. I had protection."
"Yeah, I know. Not enough, considering what we know. I will say it again–you were lucky to walk out of Santini Reality alive, darlin'."
"Well, think of Tina. On the streets, for God's sake. It's cold out there, and we both know that's not the worst part. I don't know. I like her. Just worried. Don't want to see her dead, that's all." Maria kissed her husband and stood to undress for bed.

Tomorrow was Christmas Eve. Sunday was Christmas. Tina would hit the streets some time on Monday. Maria climbed between the sheets, snuggling up to her husband.

Joe wrapped his strong arms around her, holding her. They made love, then fell asleep in each other's arms.

Tina sat alone in her hotel room, going over strategies, then fell into shallow dream-filled sleep.

Chapter 14

Maria woke early. They always celebrated Christmas on Christmas Eve, having a big dinner, then opening gifts. She felt tired and preoccupied, but was prepared to go through the motions.

She and Tess planned to bake a couple of pies and get a lot of the pre-meal prep work done this morning. That was *if* Maria could wake her. Theresa was taking a heavy load in college. She wanted to be a doctor or psychologist, and still wasn't sure if she could handle the intense schedule, but so far had managed. The first year she had some adjustment problems in addition to the difficult coursework. This year she finally seemed to be getting it together–exhausted, but still receiving good grades. *Maybe I'll just let her sleep.*

Maria poured a cup of coffee and sat down at the kitchen table. She loved early morning. It was *her* time. Something about being alone in the darkened world while everyone slept, knowing daybreak and the busy day would start all too soon. She relished these quiet moments.

Startled by the telephone, she checked the caller ID. Unknown Caller. She picked it up, anyway. "Hello."

"Maria, it's Chief LaSalle."

"Chief. What's up?"

"Is Joe up?"

Maria bristled, but kept her cool. "No, still sleeping."

Silence from the other end.

"Shall I wake him?"

The chief cleared her throat. "No, just tell him, Melanie Davis…"

Maria knew the name. A runaway who shouldn't have been. Melanie came from a wealthy family and had a relatively good relationship with her parents. They were half-expecting the girl to return home any day now. "Dead?"

"Yes, very. Her body was found on Hennepin Avenue about an hour and a half ago. Drug overdose."

"Drug overdose?" Maria ran her fingers through her short dark hair, sitting down hard on a kitchen chair.
"Cocaine."
"Shit. They find any on her?"
"No, she was naked. Found in an entryway of a storefront. Parents already ID'd the body."
"Who's working the case?"
"Well, let's see. Technically, it's not really a homicide if the overdose was self induced, which by the initial run-through from the M.E., appears to be the case. However, as I look at the other information–*hmm*–runaway, linked to drugs and the Mafia. You tell me who should be working the case." Chief LaSalle laughed.

Maria felt heat flush her face as anger rose to the surface. The woman had a way of pushing her buttons.

"Olson and Hadley–Narcotics–are on it right now. They'll turn over to you and Joe. Does that answer your question?"

Maria felt her anger fade a bit. "I'll wake Joe."

"Don't rush. The girl's dead, crime scene has been processed. Forensic Techs and BCA will be done shortly if not already. It's Christmas. I'm going home."

"We'll be there in an hour." Maria disconnected and went to wake her husband.

Joe was softly snoring when she entered the quiet bedroom. She shook him gently by the shoulder.

He rolled over, shrugging her off.

"Wake up, Joe. Just got off the phone with Chief LaSalle."

"Wh-what?" He turned his head, looking at his wife, sleep trying desperately to retreat as his senses slowly came to life.

Maria sat on the edge of the bed. "Melanie Davis was found this morning. Dead. Drug overdose. Cocaine."

Joe let it sink in. "Damn. I was hoping she'd make it back."

"I know. Me, too. I told the chief we'd be in the office in about an hour. Olson and Hadley from Narcotics are on it for now–long story." Maria rolled her eyes. "Chief said there was no hurry, but–"

Joe made a mental note to ask his wife about that conversation later. She appeared pissed. "Okay." He looked at her closely. "You okay?"

Maria nodded.

Joe let it go, knowing Maria. She was upset about something, but that seemed to be the norm with their new boss, unfortunately. "Yeah, let's wake Tess; let her know we gotta run. She can hold down the fort for a while."

"It's Christmas Eve, Joe."

"I know. Death sucks."

"You jump in the shower first. I'll go wake her up."

Tess woke with relatively little complaint. She was used to growing up with police emergencies, and simply dragged her blanket to the living room couch and fell back asleep. She mumbled a sleepy good-bye when they left, with a promise to feed Tony and start the Christmas pies.

By the time they reached City Hall, a light snow had begun to fall, dusting cars in the parking lot in a white fluffy blanket. It was beautiful, pristine, contradicting what they were here for–death of innocence. Another young life destroyed.

Maria wasn't surprised to see the chief when they walked into Homicide. She had just started a fresh pot of coffee.

"Well, well, well, if it isn't the Dynamic Duo. Now we can all rest easy." She smiled but it didn't reach her eyes, which held contempt or something similar.

Joe grinned easily enough, but Maria simply looked at her. The title had been given to them long ago when they were first partners, because their success rate was high and they worked well together.

"I've got all the info on the latest OD. We need to talk. You two get settled a bit, grab a cup of coffee, and meet me in my office, please." She left them standing in the middle of the room and quickly departed to her sanctuary, shutting the door loudly.

"Dynamic Duo…why does it piss me off when I hear *her* say it?"

"I don't know, darlin', you used to like it. We both did."

"The woman hates me for some reason."

Joe looked at his wife. He would like to argue the point, but unfortunately, she was right. For some reason Chief LaSalle did not like Maria. Hate was too strong of a word, but intense dislike appeared distinctly possible.

"See, you won't even disagree." Maria appeared crestfallen.

Joe couldn't help but laugh. "Like it would do any good."

"It might," Maria offered feebly.

"Well, for the record, I do think hate is a bit strong, but–"

"Thanks for your support." Maria walked to her desk, and tossed her purse into the center of the mess, throwing her coat over the chair.

Grabbing a couple cups of coffee, Maria followed Joe to the chief's office. They knocked twice, and opened the door. Sandra LaSalle was on the phone, but motioned them in.

"Yes, tonight. We'll be in contact later. I can't talk now." She ended her call and looked up at them. "Sit down, please." She shoved a mountain of paperwork in their direction. "Courtesy of Narcotics–what we have so far on the Davis girl. I'm not sure when they'll get to the autopsy, since it's Christmas. It's an open and shut OD, so they may just keep the kid on ice for a while."

Joe winced.

The chief noticed and grinned. "Sorry. Sometimes I can come off as a cold-hearted bitch, can't I?" She looked at the two of them for confirmation.

Neither Joe nor Maria said a word, although Maria noticed Joe's mouth quiver and was worried for selfish reasons. If she suspected even a small smile, she would totally lose it–burst out laughing. That would not be cool. *Not cool at all.*

"No comment, huh?" Chief LaSalle laughed. "Smarter than you look I guess."

Maria narrowed her eyes at the woman, wondering what the hell made her tick.

Joe picked up the paperwork, sensing a need to get Maria out before she said something that couldn't be unsaid. "Okay, we got the paperwork, anything else we should know?"

"Yes."

They both looked at her expectantly.

"Damn, wish I could have a fuckin' smoke." She opened her top desk drawer, pulled out a foil pack of nicotine gum, punctured two compartments with a long red fingernail, then popped both pieces into her mouth. "Tina's going early." She returned their gaze evenly.

"Because of Melanie Davis?" Maria leaned forward in her chair.

The chief nodded.

"How early?" Joe asked, concern in his piercing blue eyes.

"Tonight," the chief said simply, chewing her gum voraciously, attempting to glean each and every buzz of available nicotine.

"Christmas Eve..." Maria gazed out the window. The snow was still falling, had picked up a bit.

"It doesn't fuckin' matter, Sanchez. Don't be so damn sentimental. Tina, or should I say Lizzy, is ready. More than ready. Don't underestimate her. This is a piece of cake compared to some of the other shit she's done."

Maria watched the chief, sensing an emotion that wasn't usually there–concern maybe, and anger. Always anger. "Okay."

Joe looked at the two women. *What the fuck.* He was at a loss.

"We'll keep an eye on her." LaSalle stood, forcing her visitors to stand, too. "I'm going home. I believe it's Christmas Eve." She looked directly at Maria although it strained her neck to do so.

Maria looked down at the chief, who only came up to her breasts, and wondered why exactly the woman hated her guts. "Merry Christmas, Chief."

Chief LaSalle kept a straight face and walked past them through the office, then out the door to whatever excitement awaited this special night.

Chapter 15

Marco loved this time of evening. The sun was setting and children were nestled all snug in their beds on this so-called *magical* night. Christmas meant nothing to him, just another day. Perhaps it would take on meaning if he had someone special to spend his time with.

He stood on the balcony of his penthouse suite, martini in one hand, cigarette in the other, gazing out over the darkening world. What he wanted more than anything in the world–a devoted wife and family–he felt he could never have. It never worked. He had tried. Numerous times. Two failed marriages–almost three if the last one hadn't cheated on him–child-support continually drained his resources. His own children barely knew him. This was proof, but still he dreamt of the unattainable–the perfect woman–not realizing the rejection and mind games he doled out to those he loved, corroded each and every relationship. Nevertheless, women loved him, despite his toxic personality.

I am a good man. A passionate, loving man. Marco told himself this repeatedly. He knew exactly how to satisfy a woman. Completely, time and time again. He smiled. He loved to perform cunnilingus. It was one of his favorite acts. He touched himself, getting aroused at the mere thought. The fact he was well endowed and could go for hours, helped to endear every woman he had relations with even more. There was never a lull in conversation either. With immense knowledge in many areas, he felt an expert in human behavior. Overall, he was perfect. The main issue seemed to be a lack of understanding on *their* part.

Marco checked his watch. He had to leave shortly to meet Stephen and the go-between at his favorite Italian restaurant. They would finalize the plans for the heroin shipment coming through. They had bumped it up, decided to go after Christmas but before the New Year. The supplier promised this batch was pure, better than usual. They could get top dollar. It wouldn't take long to triple their profits.

Marco drained his martini and took a last filter-hit off the cigarette, flicking it over the balcony. Perusing the night sky, he took a deep breath, filling his lungs, and closed his eyes. He said his version of prayer, which was more satanic than Godly, wishing for things to go his way and that those who dared cross him burn in the fiery pits of Hell.

Steve Freyhoff arrived at the restaurant early, wanting to tip back a few before the Boss and go-between grunt arrived.

He needed to gather his thoughts. They upped the date for the H shipment, but he just discovered another small problem. Probably nothing in the entire scheme of things, but when all the little coincidental crap was added together, sometimes it turned into one *big* problem.

He debated if he should tell Marco about the dead girl in Minneapolis–the last batch of cocaine had done a number on her. One of their contacts on the streets called him last night. Melanie Davis was a rich kid, which always gathered more attention than a nobody. Their contact, Tiny Tim, was a smalltime pimp and drug-dealer, but he usually came through, despite his loser mentality. He received a kickback for keeping an eye on things. So far, it had been working out. Tiny and his buddy, Nick had a pretty sweet deal. All the girls and drugs they could ask for. Steve grinned to himself, wishing his life were a tad simpler sometimes.

He sat down at the bar, and ordered a whiskey on the rocks. Draining half the glass, he played out the evening in his head, wanting to get everything finalized and set in motion.

He glanced at his watch. They were due to arrive in about half an hour. He waved the bartender over for a refill, needing all the courage he could muster.

Chapter 16

It was almost seven o'clock by the time Maria and Joe arrived back home. *Another fucked-up Christmas.* The job was always an interference, especially with both of them in the same line of work.

They opened the door to a beautiful sight. The table was set with their best dinnerware and crystal. The smell of turkey breast and sage stuffing hung in the air. Two pies sat on the counter and Tess was placing everything on the table while Tony furiously mashed potatoes.

Maria laughed. "Wow. You two should go into business for yourselves. I'm impressed."

"Me, too." Joe removed his coat and offered to take Maria's, then hung them in the hall closet, returning to the kitchen to help.

They all sat down as Tess lit the candles in the centerpiece. Holding hands, they said the same prayer offered every year, simple and thankful. The dinner was delicious with nothing forgotten–not even sweet potatoes and cranberries.

The kids were getting along well. Maria noticed Tony more in tune to the family. He hung on every word his older sister said. Tess in turn, made sure she included him in conversation, making frequent eye contact. She was like a ray of sunshine in the house.

Maria and Joe were way too busy with work. She could suddenly see that now, as she watched her family eat, talk, and laugh. Perhaps some kind of change was in order, so one or both of them were home more often.

Tess stopped talking and looked at her mother. "Right, Mom?"

Maria looked up from her plate. "I'm sorry, sweetheart. What?"

Tess laughed. "Jeez, where were you? A million miles away."

Maria smiled. "No, not really. Thinking how great it is having the four of us together like this. Like old times." She smiled at Tony, and when she caught his eye, blew him a kiss.

He grinned and pretended to catch it in midair.

Finishing dinner, they indulged in pie for dessert, then retired to the living room to open gifts. They never went overboard, trying to instill what Christmas was truly about, instead of just presents. Theresa gave everyone University of Minnesota stuff. Tony got an MP3 player and was in heaven, anxious to try it out as soon as possible.

Maria and Joe sat together on the couch, watching the kids and recalling their first Christmas together. Tony had never experienced snow, and they bought him a bright red sled, called The Screamer. The look on the boy's face was priceless and then on Christmas morning they tried it out, going to a well-known sliding hill. Good memories throughout the years, and things were still good. Different but good.

That night, lying in bed, Maria turned to Joe. "What are you thinking about?"

Joe faced his wife, wrapping his arms around her. "How lucky I am to have someone as beautiful as you in my arms right now."

"No, try again." Maria kissed him on the forehead.

He frowned and looked at her.

Maria read his thoughts, which she'd become very good at over time. "Me, too. It's cold tonight."

"She'll be fine."

"Yes, fine."

Chapter 17

Lizzy Fairchild was alone and cold, but determined. She didn't see any other runaways, yet. *They must be holed up somewhere, staying warm on Christmas Eve.* She looked at her four-dollar watch. Only nine o'clock. *Maybe there's a movie theater around.* She had ten dollars and hated to blow half of it on a movie, but maybe she could talk the ticket person into a discount. She had a knack for getting deals.

She grinned, picking up the pace. Moving kept her warm. She walked along the cold empty streets, hoping for a friendly face, going over all the information she had memorized.

No movie theater, but she found an open all-night diner. Through the window, she saw a group of girls sitting in a far corner booth. She touched the horseshoe necklace. *Good luck.*

Taking a deep breath, and becoming Lizzy *completely*, she opened the door. A bell sounded, making the woman who was waitress, cook and owner, look up, half-asleep. She smiled briefly and put down her magazine.

Sliding into a stool at the counter, Lizzy removed her tattered gloves and shoved them into her coat pockets.

"What can I get ya, honey?" The waitress placed a glass of water in front of the girl.

Lizzy thought for a minute. She really wanted coffee, but should order hot chocolate to play the part. But she needed the caffeine. "Large Coke."

The woman looked at the skinny kid. *Another runaway*, she thought. "Anything to eat?"

"Um, how much for an order of fries?" She met the older woman's eyes and smiled uncertainly.

The woman looked at the kid. "All you can eat for one dollar."

Lizzy nodded. "Great. That's what I'll have."

"Sounds like a plan. I'm Janet, by the way." The waitress smiled, showing tobacco stained teeth, and friendly brown eyes. She filled a large glass with ice and soda, returning it to the girl, then wandered back into the kitchen to make a fresh batch of fries.

Lizzy sipped her pop and looked around the diner, her eyes coming to rest on the three girls. One girl looked her way and smiled. Another seemed to growl, and the third huddled up in a corner of the booth, asleep. Lizzy smiled back at the friendly one and returned her gaze to her glass, waiting for the French fries.

Five minutes later, the waitress brought a heaping plate of steaming fries and a bottle of ketchup.

"Wow." Lizzy grinned broadly. "That's a lot of fries."

Janet grinned. "Looks like you could use it." She looked the girl up and down. "Skinny." Refilling her Coke to the top, she trotted back into the kitchen, leaving the girl alone with her food.

Lizzy ate half the fries. Glancing at the girls in the booth, she mustered up the courage and grabbed her half-eaten fries and pop, jacket, and backpack, then made her way toward them.

The friendly girl smiled and said 'Hi.' The mean one said nothing, but glared, and the sleeping girl didn't move. The latter appeared wasted on something. It looked more like unconsciousness than sleep.

"Can I join you? I come with food." She smiled nervously.

"I've had enough." Lizzy placed her hand on her stomach.

"Sure, sit." The friendly girl slid over and patted the booth next to her.

The mean one sneered, tossed her dreadlocks, and scooted further down in the booth. The stoned girl slept, taking up more than half the booth.

"I'm Lizzy." She sat down, placing her plate of fries in the center of the table.

"Beth." She held out a hand. "Are you an Elizabeth, too?"

The question took her off-guard for a moment. *Was Lizzy a spin-off of Elizabeth?* These first days were crucial in developing her character and not making stupid mistakes. "Yes, yes it is."

"Wow, me too. That's Tiara." She pointed to the angry black girl with dreadlocks. "And that's Kathy, or just Kath is what she goes by." She grinned showing scummy teeth.

"Nice to meet everyone." She recognized Tiara from one of the photos Joe had included with the runaway bios.

"Where ya from?" Beth pulled the plate of French fries closer and began devouring three, four at a time.

"Um, around here." She looked at the other girl. "You?"
"Same," Beth said between bites. "And Tiara–"
"Nobody's damn business." Tiara Jackson glared at Beth, then the newcomer, challenging both with her dark, angry eyes.
Beth closed her mouth, and grabbed another handful of fries to occupy it, a half-apologetic, half-scared look on her face.
"So why ya runnin'?" Tiara asked.
Lizzy fidgeted in her seat and looked down at the table. "Lots of reasons, main one is my parents." She shrugged her shoulders. "School sucked. Everything sucked, ya know what I mean?"
Tiara grinned, showing perfect white teeth against chocolate brown skin. "Man, don't I know it. The sad thing is, it sucks everywhere." She looked around the small diner, then back at Lizzy.
"If it wasn't so freakin' cold." Beth chimed in. "Maybe we'll get to go to L.A."
"L.A.?" Lizzy looked at the slightly chubby, mousy-brown-haired girl with trusting eyes, and smiled.
"Yeah, there're a couple guys we know. They mentioned California to Tiara and–" She stopped, catching the look Tiara directed at her. "Well, they just mentioned it." She finished, picking up her empty glass of pop, making loud sucking noises to get every remaining drop.
Lizzy let it go. She would know more soon enough. Tiara watched her every move with suspicion. *Why? Maybe that was just her nature...suspicious.* Lizzy returned her gaze then looked away when the other girl wanted a stare down. Tiara Jackson was beautiful. She would make a lot of money in Los Angeles for the Santini Family. Lizzy had definitely connected with the right girls. Hopefully she'd get to meet the guys who offered Tiara a free trip to La-La Land.

Chapter 18

Steve was halfway blitzed. With no food in his stomach, he began *sipping* the fourth whiskey, waiting for the Boss.

When Marco arrived, he found his friend in the bar. "Stephen. There you are."

"Marco, my man." Steve stood and stumbled slightly, then sat back down hard on the barstool.

"You are intoxicated, my friend."

Steve grinned. "Yesss, I am getting there, my friend."

Marco frowned. "We have important business to discuss. I would appreciate you taking matters seriously. This is unacceptable." He looked at Stephen with disgust.

"Oh Christ, take a fucking chill-pill, man. I'm fine. I'm serious. What the fuck? You know I do my best planning and negotiating fucked up. It's when I'm *not* wasted that I usually have problems."

"I am ordering coffee for you." Marco pranced to the bar, impeccably dressed and demanding attention, which he received immediately.

Five minutes later Stephen and Marco sat in the dining room, sipping strong coffee and speaking in quiet tones while waiting for the third person in their party to arrive.

David Finch entered the posh Italian restaurant with trepidation. He'd heard tales of Marco Santini and what a ruthless bastard he could be. He wasn't too worried. He could run with the best of them and he definitely had size and muscle on his side, but anyone as powerful as Santini always made him nervous.

Steve was on his second cup of coffee when he saw the young man standing by the front of the restaurant. "That him?" he asked Marco.

Marco turned, taking in the burly young man with reddish brown hair. "Yes, I believe so. He fits the description." Marco stood and looked directly at the man, nodding when their eyes met.

That's him–the Boss. Deep breath. Finch made his way

toward the expensively dressed Italian man and his blonde counterpart, who looked like a surfer dude.

Marco smiled charmingly as the man approached the table, and then extended his hand. "Mr. Finch I presume?"

Finch grabbed the man's hand. "Yes, sir."

"Marco Santini. And this is Stephen Freyhoff." Marco gestured toward his table companion.

Steve pushed his chair back and rose with some reluctance, extending his hand. "Nice to meet ya."

"Have a seat, please." Marco sat, as did the other two. "Wine?" he offered.

Finch nodded. "Sure."

Marco raised his hand to summon a waiter, and one appeared instantly. "We'll begin with the wine now, please."

"Certainly, sir." The waiter hurried away, returning in less than a minute, always prepared to please the Boss.

Marco filled everyone's glass. "A toast. To new alliances." Clinking glasses, he smiled at Finch, who nervously returned the smile.

As always, the wine was delicious and after some perfunctory small talk, they were ready to get down to business.

Steve became impatient to end this little get-together and get back to his apartment and the woman who waited in his bed. With an ounce of really good dope and a rock of cocaine, by the time he returned, she'd be so fuckin' zonked, he wouldn't get any sex. "So, what do we got in the works so far? Let's go over the finer points, shall we?"

David Finch leaned forward. "Sure." He lowered his voice. "It's coming into Texas from Mexico. There it will be placed in the hollowed out textbooks then flown via a small private plane to our destination point in Minneapolis, where the pickup will take place by your people. The rest, of course, is up to you." He drained his glass of wine, then reached into his pocket and pulled out the flight itinerary.

Steve took it, and glanced at the information, noting approximate arrival time and location. He handed it to Marco. Thoughts of the dead girl floated into his mind. The cocaine that came in a couple of weeks ago was dangerous stuff. He wondered just how pure it was; wasted on just two lines. *They had paid top dollar but it was worth it–good shit, almost too good.* In fact, the last rock remained at his apartment. He looked at Finch. "So how good?"

The go-between looked at him. "Real good. Definitely high quality. Ninety plus percent pure. Guaranteed."

"Guaranteed?" Marco looked up from the flight itinerary.

Bells went off in Finch's brain. "Yes, to a point."

"Ah-ha. I get it." Marco grinned. "Who, per se, shall guarantee it for me?"

Finch looked at his empty glass, suddenly thirsty and in need of fresh air. "I'll get you a name by end of the day tomorrow."

"No later, please. The deal goes down the day after–the twenty-seventh." Marco gazed at the man over his half-full wine glass, dark eyes pinning him down.

"Yes, yes. I know. No later, I promise." David Finch glanced at his watch. "Gotta run. I'll contact you tomorrow." He stood, suddenly in a hurry to leave. He should have never offered them a name. Now he'd put himself in a jam…would have to deliver, though. *No question there.*

Steve watched the man's rapidly retreating back. "Way to go, Marco."

Marco wiped his full lips with a napkin. "What?"

Steve grinned. "What? You have *the gift*, man."

A slight smile played at the corner of Marco's mouth.

"Guarantee, my ass." He looked at the Boss with new respect.

"Shall we order now? I'm suddenly starving." Marco picked up the menu and studied it intently.

Fuck, Steve thought. *So much for getting back to my apartment and Denise, who was probably done with the coke by now and had moved on to other things.* He considered bowing out, then immediately dismissed the idea, knowing he would pay the price later. Steve glanced at Marco, then picked up the menu, focusing on pasta and a long night.

Lizzy and the girls woke up to a pancake breakfast. Janet took mercy on them since it was Christmas, and had let them crash in the diner in the booths. It was the cleanest and warmest place the other three runaways had spent the night in a long time.

Janet let them sleep in and then woke them up with the smell of blueberry pancakes and a mountain of bacon. She heated four different kinds of syrup and offered a variety of juices, too.

Seeing the looks of brief joy on their normally lost faces was the best Christmas present Janet could ask for. The holidays were still rough since losing her husband of forty years, only two years ago. This was fun in a sad sort of way. She felt sorry for these lost kids. It wasn't a very nice world out there.

The four girls polished off three tall stacks of pancakes. Janet offered them the use of the bathroom and gave them each a clean towel. It was as good as a gift. They each took their time, even the new one, Lizzy. She was different, though. Something about her... Janet couldn't quite put her finger on it. She liked her, but *something* differentiated her from the other girls.

She shrugged it off, finally kicking the girls out into the bright Christmas sunshine.

Chapter 19

Christmas day was quiet. They were all content to do their own thing. Since the kids were small, they woke up to Christmas stockings stuffed to the brim and one gift for each of them under the tree from Santa. The tradition continued as Maria and Joe sat on the couch, watching Tess and Tony.

Tess had become a beautiful young woman. Her long dark hair and large expressive brown eyes along with a sparkling personality captivated everyone she met.

Tony was almost as tall as Joe. He'd grown almost four inches this past summer. He and Theresa looked alike since they had the same father. Tony's mother had been dark complected, too, and Joe always said he had her eyes–beautiful, sad eyes.

They all laid around until mid-morning, then the guys made the traditional pancake breakfast.

Maria telephoned her brother, Carlos, in Chicago. He, his wife, and their five-year old son were the happiest family she knew. She'd thought her brother would never remarry after his first disastrous marriage. But Ellen was the woman meant for him, and their adopted son was the light of their lives. Carlos promised a visit to Minnesota soon, and Maria promised to hold him to it.

Maria and Joe had the Monday after Christmas off, because the holiday fell on a Sunday. The mall and all the stores were madhouses with returns and sales typical on the day after.

Maria hated to be out in this mess at all, but Theresa had a million errands to run. Maria offered to be her chauffer for a couple of reasons–first, to talk and be together, and second, the city was crazy to drive in on a normal day. Adding the day-after-Christmas shopping frenzy and Theresa's driving record, the result became an accident waiting to happen. She didn't mention the latter to her daughter.

Mall of America wasn't too bad, but they arrived relatively early. Tess had a couple of stops to make, which weren't too painful, and they were out within the hour.

Maria offered to buy her daughter lunch at one of the many restaurants they frequented on Eat Street, an eclectic array of eateries, which ran nearly fifteen blocks along Nicollet Avenue. She let Tess pick and wasn't disappointed. The Indian cuisine was an experience to behold, with excellent food–spicy and delicious.

Afterwards they drove by City Hall. Since they were in the neighborhood, Maria thought she'd stop in Homicide and pick up a file pertaining to the case, she had left.

"You planned this all along didn't you, Mom?" Tess looked at her mother, with raised eyebrows.

Maria laughed. "Maybe, do you mind?"

"Nah, brings back memories," she offered, as they parked the Jeep Cherokee.

"Yeah, it does. It's been a while since you came to work with Mommy, hasn't it?" Maria grinned at her daughter who now stood two inches taller than her.

Tess leaned over and hugged her mom. "Yes, and I miss it. I miss my Mommy."

"C'mon, honey." They got out of the Jeep and trudged through the sloppy parking lot. It had snowed just enough to be slippery, but not enough to get the snowplows out on the streets.

Unlocking the office door, they assumed they were alone in Homicide.

Tess let out a startled cry when Tom Powders came around the corner. Tom fell back a step, clutching his chest and turning pale.

Maria was surprised as well. "Tom! Jeez, what are you doing here on a holiday weekend? How did you get in?"

He looked down at the ground, guiltily. "Oh, um....Got a key from the janitorial service. They're working today...doing carpets. I um...just wanted to um...file some stuff I forgot before I left." He fumbled for words, then headed straight to his desk. The fact was his Internet connection wasn't working from home and he had to check his e-mail for an important reply he was expecting.

When Maria walked back to her own desk, she noticed his PC powered on and his personal e-mail on the monitor. *File some stuff, my ass. I must look really fuckin' stupid.*

"Whose desk is this? Practically right on top of you." Tess sat at the desk scooted next to her mother's.

Maria grinned. "It's Joe's. He's moved in because we're working this new case together."

"My God. I can't believe you didn't tell me. I thought you guys were acting different–secretive, happy. That is so cool. How many years has it been?"

"Close to ten, I think." Maria looked at her daughter.

"Must be an important case, huh?"

"Yep." Maria busied herself looking for the file on Melanie Davis.

"Is that all you're gonna say? C'mon, Mom–at least give me the basics...no names. Jeez, you and Dad working as partners and you won't fill me in. What is it? Some deep, dark secret?"

"No, honey. It involves runaways and the Maf–" Maria stopped herself–too late.

"The Mafia?" Theresa looked at her mother, suddenly very interested.

Maria gathered the file she had come for. "Shall we go?"

"You're not working on Santini again are you? I heard the nephew is a bigger bastard than his uncle." Theresa Sanchez tossed her dark hair over one shoulder and gazed directly at her mother, expecting a challenge, knowing she'd get one.

Maria shook her head and grinned. "Where do you get your information, child?"

"Well, actually, a couple of places."

"*Hmm*, I can only think of one." Maria frowned.

"Well, there's the obvious. I've gleaned bits and pieces off you and Dad for the past decade, and then there's Linda." She looked at her mother and glanced away, wondering how much information she should divulge. She never promised Linda anything, but still felt funny about telling a cop this kind of stuff even though the cop was her own mother. *Weird.*

"Yes, I'm listening. Linda?"

"Yeah, a woman who works in the library at the university. Linda has a sister who lives in L.A., who's best friend dated Marco Santini a couple of years ago."

"Oh, really? A friend's sister's friend?"

Theresa thought about it for a minute, then nodded, realizing

how goofy it sounded. "I know, I know. A friend of a friend of a sister, whatever, but I guess the guy's a major creep."
"Well, that's a given. Okay, I'll bite. Why? What did he do?"
"Well...now this is second hand of course, but Linda doesn't spread gossip. She's not like that."
"Of course." Maria loved her daughter more than anything, but the kid drove her nuts with the beating-around-the-bush crap.
"Go on," she encouraged, appearing patient.
"Well, concerning the sister's best friend–the woman who dated Marco Santini? I guess he literally swept her off her feet She was married, two kids, met him I don't know where, but he wouldn't take *no* for an answer. They had a palpable chemistry and she tried to fight it, but he convinced her it was the right thing, that she was the woman of his dreams, meant to be and all that garbage. Promised her it would be the most beautiful relationship and she'd never regret it."

Maria grinned, watching her daughter gain momentum as she told the story. Surprised at the cynical tone she heard, but not necessarily sorry to hear it. Tess was getting a close and personal view of the world living on her own. It wasn't always nice.

"Anyway, he messed with her head so bad, she ended up committing suicide."

"Theresa, my God, that's awful." Maria shook her head. "So, she's dead?"

Tess nodded. "Yep, dead as a doornail. And all because of Marco. I guess he's a real nut job. He set her up, played her for a fool, used her for his own advantage, and disposed of her in the only neat way that didn't implicate him–suicide. Gives whole new meaning to the term *Lady-killer*, doesn't it?"

"Yeah, it certainly does. Sad for the woman's family."

"I know. Linda said they've been having a rough time. The kids are really messed up. I guess the older boy found his mother's body in the bath-tub."

Maria shook her head. "Man, it just keeps getting worse, doesn't it?"

"Terrible, but true."

"It's what we call hearsay in the business, sweetheart."

Tess rolled her eyes. "I know, Mom. But it *is* true. Linda

didn't make it up. She's not like that. She's an older lady who has had quite a difficult life, with no need to make up tall-tales. Just thought it might be of interest to you, that's all." She knew her mother would be skeptical. It was the *cop* bred into her.

"Okay." Maria did appreciate this bit of insight, whether true or not. "Thanks, I will take everything you said into consideration."

Tom Powders seemed to be packing up. Maria watched him out of the corner of her eye, ready to leave as well, but wanting to wait until her ex-partner departed. *What the hell was the guy up to?*

"Are we gonna get out of here anytime soon, Mom? I still gotta stop at the drug store."

Powders slipped into his jacket and headed out, not saying good-bye.

"Good-bye, Tom. See you tomorrow," Maria called to his retreating back.

Tom responded with a brief wave and quickly left.

"Okay kid, let's go," Maria said to her daughter, as she picked up the folder to take home.

They left, locking the door to Homicide, trudging through the snowy parking lot to their frigid vehicle.

Chapter 20

The girls stayed in a storeroom at the back of a gas-convenience store, on Christmas evening. They spent the next day looking for somewhere to keep warm and make a buck or two. They set up at a mall entrance and preyed on shoppers who entered, having it down to a science within an hour. Lizzy played a good part–since she was so skinny, people felt sorry for her.

She missed Maria and her daughter by only twenty minutes.

They had a better place to stay tonight, according to the girls, but Lizzy remained skeptical. Kathy, the doper had come back to life, and it wasn't pretty. They had stolen a bunch of munchies for breakfast and she'd been nursing a stomachache all afternoon. Beth swiped some antacids but they weren't helping.

Kath sat on the corner of the street, head between her knees.

Tiara walked around, hands on her hips. "See, girlfriend, that's what you git for doing that *bad* shit. Takes days to get outta your system." She spoke from experience.

Beth offered her friend more antacids, but had her hand slapped away. She appeared on the verge of tears from the rejection. Emotions were definitely running high for everyone today.

"Well, maybe we can cruise by Tiny and Nick's place a little earlier than planned." Tiara stood, hands still on her hips, but a look of compassion on her face for both Beth and Kathy. "Maybe." She shrugged her shoulders.

Kath looked up, misery wracking her abused body. "Think I gotta poop," she offered reluctantly, trying to rise. She finally made it with a helping hand.

They slowly made their way to the nearest bathroom, which happened to be a McDonalds, on the next block.

Lizzy bought a large pop for them to share, as they waited for Kath to do her business. She figured being the new kid in town she needed to ingratiate herself. "So where does this Tiny person live?"

Tiara glared at Lizzy, wondering what the girl's real story

was. *Pretty little white girlie.* "Seventh Street."

Lizzy had no idea where Seventh Street was. She racked her brain, searching for the maps Joe had given her for memorization. She mentally pictured downtown Minneapolis, but wasn't sure what street they were on now.

"I hope she's alright in there," Beth said worriedly. "Maybe I'll go check on her." Her motherly concern was touching–to Lizzy, anyway.

"For Christ's sake, can't the girl even take a shit in peace?" Tiara put her feet on the booth across from her.

Beth looked hurt.

"She just wants to help," Lizzy said, challenging Tiara.

Tiara stared at her. "Who the fuck asked you?"

Lizzy met her stare.

"I said, who the fuck asked you?"

"Knock it off you guys," Beth said in a shaky voice.

"Sorry," Lizzy mumbled, looking down at her hands folded on the table. She inspected her dirty fingernails. She glanced up at Tiara, surprised to see the girl smiling.

"You're okay. I was just givin' you shit." Tiara still grinned.

Lizzy tentatively smiled back.

The bathroom door opened and Kath emerged, looking pale, but at least walking more upright than when they first came in. She sat next to Lizzy. "Ugh."

Tiara laughed. "You gonna make it, girlfriend?"

"Not sure. Think so."

"No more of that shit you been shovin' up your nose. I won't take you with, if you're gonna do it again." Tiara's gaze never wavered.

"Yeah, right. What ya gonna do? Leave me here?" Kath asked, reaching for the community pop, taking several small sips. She challenged the black girl with her eyes.

"That's exactly what I'm gonna do–leave your sorry white ass right fuckin' here." Tiara glared at Kathy, with a look that said, try me.

Kath sat up straighter, a frown creasing her forehead. "Alright already. I get it, okay? I'll play it cool." *Just won't do too much like last time.*

Tiara looked at her friend, and didn't trust her. The girl had a definite addiction problem. Kathy was running from an abusive stepfather. Her mother had died two years ago and her stepfather resented everything about her. He had started beating her, then he raped her. She had left in the middle of the night. Drugs helped the girl forget, and Tiara understood, but didn't want to see her end up like Mel. Melanie had the same addictive personality, in addition to being the typical poor little rich girl, and now she was dead.

A group of black boys entered the restaurant. The five boys slowly made their way to the counter. One of them spotted the girls and nudged his friend, who whistled.

"Shit," Tiara said under her breath. "Let's go."

They slid out of the booth, and Lizzy dumped the empty pop in the garbage.

The boys approached. One tall lean kid walked up to Tiara. "Hey, T baby. How's it goin', girl?"

"Fine, Jerome. How are you?"

"Better now." He grabbed his crotch and his friends laughed.

Tiara Jackson smiled outwardly, but inside was ready to punch him in the nose. Her eyes shot daggers at him, showing the true hate she felt. He must've sensed it, because he took a step back. She pushed past him.

The other girls followed, quickly exiting McDonalds into the crisp winter air.

Tiara took a deep breath and held it a moment, before blowing out a cloud of frosty steam. "Man..."

"You okay?" Lizzy touched Tiara's arm.

Tiara looked at her. "No, not really."

Lizzy could see tears standing in the tough girl's eyes. She was upset about something.

"I blew Jerome for ten bucks a coupla weeks ago. Hunger will do that to ya. We all had to eat, and had twenty-two fuckin' cents between us. That's all. No biggy." She grinned, blinking the unshed tears from large brown eyes. "Literally, no biggy."

Beth and Kathy laughed, remembering how Tiara had commented on the little weenie, after blowing the kid in a back alley. They had hamburgers that night.

Lizzy smiled, getting the joke. "They're assholes."

"Who?" Tiara asked, knowing the answer. She wanted to

hear what the new girl had to say.

Lizzy thought for a moment. "Boys, not just *those* boys. All boys."

The girls all nodded in agreement.

"Yeah, they only want one thing," Kathy offered, already thinking that's how she'd get more coke tonight. *Hey, supply and demand.*

"Pussy." Tiara grabbed her crotch much like Jerome did in the restaurant, making them laugh.

"They don't want mine," Beth said, looking sad. Even with the lack of food, she was thirty pounds overweight.

"Oh, yes they do," Tiara said. "What's the matter with you, girl? Don't you know? Sometimes *any* will do. Besides..." She looked at her friend. "You ain't so bad–skinnier than when I met ya."

Lizzy smiled. If that was Tiara's way of paying a compliment, it left a little to be desired.

"You think so?" Beth asked hopefully.

Tiara nodded, and looked at Kathy who immediately agreed. "Okay. Now that we have that settled, let's go to Tiny's. I'm freezin' my cute little black ass off, and it's already starting to get dark." Tiara took off walking at a fast pace, the three girls following close behind.

Chapter 21

Steve had already talked to Tiny Tim, his contact in Minneapolis. There was a definite market there for the H. They could unload half of it, then bring the rest back to L.A. Dollar signs danced in his brain.

He and Marco were meeting this evening to discuss the final plan, before it was implemented tomorrow. Marco had heard back on his so-called *guarantee* from the go-between. He'd even spoken with the source in Mexico, who personally promised the quality of the heroin.

Steve spent the day cleaning his apartment, which was unusual for him. Normally he lived in a mess until the maid came in, once a week, to do a thorough cleaning. Oddly enough, he felt the need to get things organized. He needed to focus and felt he could only do it in a tidy environment, which hadn't been his apartment. Now it was.

"I could get used to this," he said aloud, looking around his surroundings. He had a thought and laughed aloud. Marco was neat as a pin. Perhaps he had developed more of the man's traits than he realized.

He glanced at the clock. The day was getting away from him. He still had to grab a shower before going to the office to meet Marco. After a last gulp of cold coffee, he dropped to the floor and did a quick twenty-five pushups, then headed for the bathroom, whistling a tune as he went.

Marco had just fucked one of the service personnel. It was his special offering to a less fortunate one. He had arrived at Santini Realty after lunch, the offices empty due to the holiday, which made it perfect for the maintenance service to do their year-end cleaning.

He was unlocking his door, when a young, gorgeous Latino woman, with broken English, asked if she could clean his office. Marco never allowed the cleaning service into his private office. He and Stephen were the only ones who possessed keys.

There were too many *things* to find–guns, drugs, information.

He opened the door, replaced the key in his pocket, then turned his attention to the beautiful girl and smiled. "Hello."

"Hello, you like me clean office?" she asked again.

His gaze quickly traveled, resting first on the swell of her breasts, then her hips, returning to her dark flashing eyes. A subtle smile played on her lips as she watched him drink her in.

"Yes," Marco said. "Please, come in." He held the door open for her, then quietly closed and locked it.

Luisa busied herself dusting the blinds that covered the large picture window, while the handsome man sat at his desk, watching every move.

She cleaned the wet-bar, spraying it down with a solution and wiping it clean. She made her way around the room, wiping down everything in sight, finally coming to his desk. "You like me clean desk?" Luisa smiled, playfulness lighting her eyes as she waited for a response.

Marco sat, his chin resting on steepled fingers. He smiled broadly, scooting his chair back so the girl could get to the desk. He was a very organized man. Never liked a mess, would not tolerate it.

Luisa smiled tentatively. She raised the spray cleaner, but before she could spray the surface, she felt a gentle hand on her upper arm. Turning, she met the eyes of the rich, handsome Italian man. Setting the cleaner down, she didn't notice it tumble to the floor.

Marco kissed her, exploring her mouth with his tongue. He unbuttoned her denim shirt in record time, tasting her neck and breasts.

She responded to him and unbuckled his pants, while he slipped her shirt off and unhooked her bra. He traced a finger down the center of her soft stomach sending shivers through her, then unbuttoned her jeans, pushing them down to her ankles.

Marco inhaled deeply–her white ruffled panties smelled of rose water–he found himself lost in her beauty. His tongue explored and she moaned, more than willing.

He knew he'd made her happier than she'd been in a long time as she *popped* in his mouth, her back arched. He took her repeatedly, on the desk, in his chair, experimenting with what felt good to both of them.

As quickly as Marco accosted her, he had enough. Satisfied, he commanded her to dress quickly. She complied, worried she'd done something to offend the important man.

Luisa thanked him when he handed her a hundred dollar bill. A strange look on her face, she suddenly felt like a whore, and didn't quite believe what had just happened. Guilt and shame quickened her pace.

He grinned wickedly, watching her leave. "Please shut the door, sweetheart."

She turned briefly and smiled shyly, still shaking from the passionate encounter with this strange, exciting man. She would definitely never forget him–Marco Santini of Santini Realty. Reality hit her in the face once she emerged into the hallway. One of the other cleaners had been sent to find her. She was in trouble for not vacuuming the front hallway. Luisa followed the other woman into the main reception area, trying to keep her knees from shaking.

Mixing a martini and lighting a cigarette, Marco returned to his desk, and leaned back in the comfortable leather chair. He put his feet up, satisfied, patiently waiting for time to pass. Soon Stephen would arrive. *Stephen.* Could he really trust the man? *How much?*

You can never really trust anyone...but yourself. He remembered the words from his own father, who died at a young age. Marco was only twelve years old when the man had a heart attack. He remembered his father as angry and possibly not the brightest man, as well as a womanizer in the highest degree. Marco strived to be different and *thought* he was.

The sun was sinking and his favorite time of day descended around him. He looked out at the city of Los Angeles. *My city. This is my city of angels. And I am its axis of evil.*

Chapter 22

When Maria and Tess arrived home, they found the guys in the living room half-asleep, a football game blaring in the background.

"Jeez, where ya been?" Joe asked, stretching and getting up with some difficulty from the couch. He took in all the bags. "I thought you were *returning* stuff."

"You know the kid," Maria said, rolling her eyes.

"Hey. I spent no money–well hardly, and the reason we took so long was Mom had to stop at work, and then that goofy guy was there." Tess rolled her eyes, much like her mother, in exasperation.

"You stopped at Homicide?" Joe looked at his wife, and noticed the file tucked under her arm. He turned his head sideways and read the tab–Melanie Davis. "Okay. Who's the goofy guy, um…let me guess. Tom Powders?"

"Yep. Guess he got the janitorial service to open the door for him." Maria set the folder and bags down on a kitchen chair. "Or so he said."

"What the f–" He caught himself. "What the heck was he doing there on a day off?"

"Oh, this is good, said he forgot to put away some files. Insinuating I'd chew him out again. So, it appears it's his dedication to the job that brought him to City Hall on an extended holiday weekend. Of course, his PC was on…"

"No doubt in his personal e-mail," Joe added.

Maria nodded affirmation. "Weird."

"That's putting it mildly. Even I find his behavior disturbing." Tess added her bags to her mother's pile.

"What do ya mean?" Joe was curious.

"He acts like he's got something to hide, like he's sneaking around."

"You've been talking to your mother." Joe looked from mother to daughter.

"No, we haven't talked about Tom Powders, we talked about

Marco Santini," Maria offered. "Theresa is just an insightful girl."

Joe sat down at the kitchen table. "Honey, we're not supposed to discuss the case."

Tess sat down, too. "Mom didn't tell me anything. I had info on Marco. A friend of a friend kind of a thing."

Joe looked confused.

"I'll tell you later," Maria promised, as Tony walked into the kitchen. "Hungry, sport?"

"Yeah...could eat," Tony said. He opened the refrigerator and examined the contents.

"Leftovers okay?" Maria stood behind him.

"I guess. Lemme know when it's ready, 'kay?" He went back into the living room to zone out.

Maria looked at Joe and said quietly, "How's he been today?"

"Quiet," Joe offered. "We both slept quite a bit, he goofed around on his computer for a while."

"I'll go hang with him," Tess offered. She got up and joined her brother in the living room.

Before long, they could hear laughter.

Joe helped Maria put a quick supper together. The next few days would be crazy with the new case–long hours required. They were lucky to have Tess home from college. With Tony on Christmas vacation, they hated to leave him alone all day even though the kid was almost sixteen years old. He seemed to be more in need of adult supervision than ever before.

Chapter 23

"Okay, this is it." Tiara led the way up the narrow metal stairs to an apartment located above the fast-food Chinese restaurant on Seventh Street. With no moon to light the way, it was difficult to see where they were going.

"Are you sure this is it?" Beth sounded worried.

"This is it," Tiara said. "The last time you were here it was daylight. Looks different at night, that's all."

Once they reached the door, they could hear the deep bass beat of music.

Tiara knocked loudly to be heard over the tunes.

No one came to the door.

She knocked again, louder and longer.

This time, the music was turned down a notch and the door opened a crack. A young face peeked out. Tiny Tim stood behind the young girl at the door, to check out the visitors.

"T...and the gang." He stuck his head out the door and took in everyone, noticing Lizzy. "And a new face."

Tiara grinned. She kind of liked it when he called her T. "Hey, Tiny. How's it hangin'?"

Now it was his turn to grin. "Well, how do you think it's hangin', girlfriend? Long and hard for you, sweetheart. Come on in, bring your friends. The more the merrier."

"Is Nick around?" Tiara asked, stepping into the warm apartment. Dope smoke hung thick in the air, and the girl who'd answered the door, sat on the couch with another youngster, stoned and half-naked. Neither looked older than twelve or thirteen.

"Yeah, he'll be back in a while. Had to make a liquor run." Tiny Tim ushered them all inside, looking the new girl up and down. She was a keeper. *Cute little thing about my size.*

The girls stood together, relishing the inviting warmth.

"Make yourselves at home. Sit." Tiny grinned. "Nick will be back with booze and munchies in about five. I was just about to fire up a twister of some *really* good weed I came across."

Kathy and Beth sat on the floor. Tiara took an old kitchen chair and Lizzy sat on the couch next to the two girls.

Tiny Tim lit some incense then the joint, passing it to Lizzy, watching with interest.

Lizzy put it to her lips and sucked, getting way too much and coughing, then passed it back to Tiny. She was not about to give it to the kids next to her on the couch.

Tiny Tim passed the joint to the two girls, grinning at Lizzy. She glared at him, still coughing.

Neither girl appeared interested, but Tiny insisted. "You can't stay here unless you at least *try* it. C'mon, Dani, you first." He handed it to the girl who had answered the door.

Danielle took the joint and took a small puff, blowing it out immediately.

"No, inhale. Like this." He breathed in deeply.

The girl tried again and started coughing.

"There ya go. You know ya got a hit when ya cough like a bastard. Pass it to Shawna."

Dani passed it to her friend, who followed suit, coughing and gagging.

Tiny laughed. "Good girl." He passed it to Kathy. "Now I know I don't have to encourage you."

Kathy took a deep toke and passed it down the line.

When it came to Lizzy again, she tried to pass it up but wasn't allowed. She hated to be one of the sheep following the herd, but had to fit in at any cost.

Tiny's roommate, Nick, arrived with a 12-pack of Coke and a bottle of rum. In another bag, he carried potato chips, pretzels, and popcorn. "Hey." He took in the crowd, his eyes coming to rest on T's beautiful face.

He poured the munchies in a couple big plastic bowls and set the rum and Coke on the table. "Let's party."

Tiny laughed. "Hey, man, sounds like a plan. We started without ya." He giggled. "Smoked that joint…" He grinned up at his friend, eyes glassy.

Nick looked alarmed. "The one laced with dust?"

Tiny nodded, a huge grin plastered on his sweaty face. "Man, it's getting warm in here. Think I'll take off some clothes. Are you girls warm?"

"Easy, big guy," Nick said, not giving a shit if the comment pissed off his roomy. He could see this getting out of control. *Little fucker. Angel dust for Christ's sake. Who knows how it will hit the young ones. And who was the little blonde hanging with T?* He looked at Lizzy, who met his gaze and looked away. She was a cutie. He caught T's look and got busy mixing drinks.

"So, how is everyone feeling?" Nick passed out the drinks. He looked around the room. Dani had her head back on the couch, staring at the ceiling. Her friend looked to be asleep. Someone had thrown a blanket over them. The little blonde, Lizzy, glared at him, fear or something like it in her eyes. Tiara looked absolutely fine. He scooted another kitchen chair next to T and sat down.

Tiny had his shirt unbuttoned; sweat glistened on his face and made his hair appear wet. He looked more wasted than anyone so far, but this shit crept up on you.

"Drink up," Nick said, holding up his glass. "Toast. To us."

Those still awake echoed, "To us," and drank.

Lizzy pretended to drink, but didn't. She would dump it out behind the couch if necessary. She didn't like this feeling. Her mind was not under control. She felt herself slipping farther and farther away as the angel dust took effect in her system.

Chapter 24

By the time Steve arrived at Santini Realty, darkness had fallen. The place was deserted–Marco appeared to be the only one in the building, although there were probably others.

Steve softly knocked on the office door, and Marco quietly ushered his friend inside. He was in a pensive mood, and resumed his position on the leather couch, working on his fourth martini.

Steve helped himself to a drink and joined the Boss. "Well, tomorrow's the big day, huh?"

Marco looked at him over his martini glass, not saying a word, his fierce gaze never wavering. Plucking out the large Spanish olive, he popped it into his mouth, licking his lips, watching Stephen squirm.

"What the fuck's wrong now?" Steve couldn't help but get pissed. He was supposed to be a goddamn mind reader and he wasn't good at it, not at all.

"You're late, first of all."

Steve rolled his eyes and downed his drink in two swallows, then stood up to pour another. This conversation was gonna require some major fortification. *Fuckin' hothouse flower.* He smiled to himself, thinking how apt the description fit Marco Santini.

"What is so amusing?" Marco joined his friend at the bar.

Steve looked down at the man. Marco came up to Steve's chest. He was short, but muscular. He worked out several times a day–a bit excessive about it. Still, Steve could crush him like a bug in hand-to-hand combat. "Nothing, why?"

Marco freshened his drink. "Because my friend, you were smiling."

"*Hmm*, I don't know. Guess I'm just happy." Steve returned to the couch with his drink, not in the mood for a fight. Marco was *always* in the mood for a fight. He frequently stated how he hated to fight, didn't want to fight, would not tolerate it, was a peaceable human being, and could not stand arguing. However, in reality the man thrived on it. It was an integral part of his personality.

Marco joined him, trying to remain calm, finding it difficult. Americans angered him with their lazy ways. Always looking for the easy way out. It was sickening.

"So is the H coming in tomorrow or not?" Steve sipped his whiskey, trying to pace himself and trying to be patient with the mind games.

Marco looked at him and imperceptibly nodded.

"Yes? Is that what that means? Yes, the heroin is coming in tomorrow as planned?" Steve looked frustrated.

Marco laughed. "Patience is a virtue, dear man, and you have none of it, do you? Yes, the heroin is coming tomorrow as planned. Okay?" He sipped his martini, the smile never leaving his dark sparkling Spanish eyes.

"Still coming into Eden Prairie?"

"Yes. Everything has been arranged. It is already packed into the hollowed out textbooks. I spoke to the drop man in Texas. Tomorrow by this time, it should be hitting the streets of Minneapolis, and shortly thereafter, L.A. Now, I have a question for you." Marco raised an eyebrow and paused to light a cigarette.

Steve waited, patiently.

"Can your contacts in Minneapolis be trusted to successfully deliver this much dope? Please do not answer right away, take a moment." Marco took a long drag off his cigarette and blew smoke dramatically into the air, then stubbed it out and turned his full attention to Stephen.

Steve had thought about this earlier. His first instinct was yes, however, the more he hashed it over in his mind, the more uncomfortable he became. Tiny Tim and Nick had proven themselves trustworthy in the past. They handled the cocaine when it came in a couple of weeks ago. Met the drug-runner, handled the money, drugs. No problems. Of course, there was the dead girl that Marco didn't know about.

"Well?" Marco asked, waiting.

"Honestly?"

"Of course." Marco tensed a bit, studying him.

"I don't know. Maybe I'll make a trip, especially considering the additional risk we're taking. Flight risk." Steve still didn't like the idea. After 9-11, the fuckin' airports were a disaster, but this was a private plane and a less-traveled, smaller airport. Hopefully, they could land without going through all the regular bullshit. It would take finesse though. Tiny Tim and Nick Dupree did not have it. He decided he would pick it up and deliver it to them personally. Half of it, anyway.

Marco thought about it and nodded. "Perhaps that would be a good idea. We have more at stake than usual. We don't want any *fuck-ups* as you would say."

Steve looked at his boss. "Yeah, no fuck-ups." He thought of Tiny Tim and all the runaways that filtered through his apartment. "That way, I can bring some back with me."

"Some what?" Marco grinned. "Pussy or H?"

Steve returned the grin. "Both."

"Pack your bags, my friend." Marco continued studying Stephen, wondering once again just how much he could trust him. He remembered the wise words, *trust no one*, on a daily basis.

"Man, seems like I was just there." Steve had a sudden flash of the beautiful girl he'd glimpsed in the Minneapolis/St. Paul airport.

"You were." Marco laughed. "Bring a warm jacket."

Steve remembered how cold it was. It would definitely be a quick trip.

"Thanks." Steve stood, anxious to return to his clean apartment, and out from under Marco's microscope.

Chapter 25

Maria had a fitful night's sleep. She dreamt of being cast out in the cold, on the streets of Minneapolis. Homeless, freezing, hungry. She awoke at five-thirty, completely uncovered and shaking from the cold. Joe snored softly, wrapped in a cocoon of warm blankets.

She got out of bed reluctantly, but determined to shake the stupid dream that still hung onto her psyche, haunting her.

They had a busy day ahead, so she made the coffee extra strong. She'd let Joe sleep another hour. That would give her quiet time to think about the day's upcoming events.

Maria sat at the kitchen table waiting for coffee, head in hands. The dream was bizarre, very real. She knew her Russian co-worker definitely played a role in the dream sequence.

Lizzy, who had been in contact with Chief LaSalle whenever she could, reported she was with a key group of girls, and staying with a well-known small-time pimp and drug dealer, Tiny Tim, and his cohort Nick Dupree. Maria knew them well. They'd been busted before on marijuana charges and loitering. Rumor said they'd gained momentum over the months with pimping the runaways, as well as dealing drugs, and they had developed tenuous ties to the mob.

This was perfect. It certainly hadn't taken the Russian very long to make headway. Chief LaSalle was definitely right about this one. Etina Altmark was good.

Maria checked on the coffee. Close enough. She placed a cup under the drip and poured coffee into another cup, quickly replacing the pot.

She sipped the strong brew and looked out at the dark night, wondering what catastrophes the day held. The moon reflected a luminous glow on the snow, creating a mysterious path out past the grove of trees, down the hill, and onto the Mississippi River beyond. It shone invitingly, possibly offering some kind of revelation.

* * *

Everyone was sound asleep. Lizzy wondered if she should risk making a phone call. This was big. They could have a *major* bust on their hands. A large shipment of heroin was coming in on a private flight tomorrow, sometime in the afternoon. She heard Flying Cloud–Eden Prairie. She assumed it was an airport. That's all she knew. She overheard Tiny Tim telling his roommate, in the hall, before they retired for the evening.

The angel dust they had shared in the joint earlier had finally worn off enough to where she could trust her wobbly legs. She still felt strange in the head–worried about what the crap did to her brain. *What was it? Pig tranquilizer?* She remembered reading that somewhere. *Shit. All in the name of duty.*

The two young girls were asleep on the couch. Everyone else was scattered throughout–Tiara in Nick's bedroom, and no sign of Kathy or Beth. Maybe they were in Tiny's room.

The telephone was in the kitchen. Lizzy tiptoed, cringing every time a floorboard creaked. Picking up the phone, she went into the far corner, away from the bedrooms. In case someone came out, they wouldn't see her right away.

She carefully dialed the number, knowing it would be answered immediately.

Sandra LaSalle picked up on the first ring, despite the late hour. "Yes."

The Russian relayed what little information she had, quickly and succinctly, ending the connection as soon as she finished. She didn't trust herself to hold an intelligent conversation right now and she didn't want to worry the chief.

Replacing the telephone where she'd found it, Lizzy tiptoed back into the living room and resumed her position on the floor, keeping watch over the youngsters on the couch.

Sleep didn't come. She lay awake watching the sky slowly lighten outside, wondering what the day would bring.

Homicide was a zoo. Maria and Joe arrived early, and the chief pulled them into her office immediately. All flights at Flying Cloud Airport in Eden Prairie would be monitored beginning mid-morning.

"Plan on being here well into the evening. Make any necessary calls to home, whatever. It's going to be a long day. I'll buy supper." Chief LaSalle placed her desk phone in front of Maria. LaSalle continued talking to Joe while Maria called home to report their late arrival tonight.

Tony answered and said they'd have leftovers or Tess would get a pizza–not to worry. Maria tried to listen to the chief tell Joe the details of the heroin shipment and talk to her son at the same time.

"Who's talking?" Tony asked, listening to the grating background voice.

"Um, I'm in the chief's office, honey. It's crazy here today."

"Yeah. Okay. Hey, I gotta go. I'm expecting a call from Derek, okay?"

Derek lived down the block and seemed like an alright kid. "Okay. Sorry about tonight." She hung up and slid the phone back toward the chief.

"Did you hear my conversation with Joe?"

Maria looked at the woman who was her boss, and thought, so did my kid, but said, "I heard the part about heroin coming in on a private flight this afternoon."

"Well, that's about the extent of it. It sounds like a for sure thing, though. Thanks to Tina." The chief softened at these last words.

"How is she?" Maria wanted to know.

"Hard to say. It's not like we had any kind of real conversation. Short and sweet."

"She seemed okay, though. Right?"

The chief raised her eyebrows. "Sure, she seemed okay. Why?"

"Oh, I don't know. I had a weird dream last night." Maria blushed, looking from the chief to Joe. "Dreamt I was homeless–cold, hungry. You stole the covers," she said the latter to Joe.

Sandra LaSalle looked at her as if she had two heads. Joe grinned, his eyes showing sympathy.

"Just made me think, that's all," she said in defense. Her momentary caring for another human being, obviously wasn't allowed in this department, under the watchful eye of the new chief.

Stephen didn't really look forward to going back to

Minneapolis so soon, but had now committed himself to the idea. He was surprised when Marco telephoned, as they were prepared for takeoff. He almost didn't answer, not wanting to have a one-on-one with the crazy little Italian right now. But he did.

He listened, feeling anger course through him. "What? Are you sure? How could *he* know?"

Steve ended the connection. "Shit." He threw the phone in the seat next to him. *Change of plans. Somehow, the fuckin' cops got wind of the shipment. Not good. How in the hell did they find out?*

It was pure luck they even got a heads-up. This could have been a major disaster. Their personal snitch came through for the Santini family once again. Marco would now be indebted, he'd said as much. *Interesting.*

They would still fly into Minnesota. Only now, the drop-off had changed. In addition to renting a goddamn car, he now had to drive a couple hours to get to the goods. "Mistake from the start..." he said aloud.

Steve had a bad feeling. When a job starts out with problems this big, it wasn't a good sign. Normally, he wasn't superstitious, but all the bells and whistles were going off in his head. He wished he could just get off the fuckin' plane, go back to his apartment, and smoke a doob.

The jet prepared for take-off and he buckled himself in, looking out the small window at sunny brown California.

"Here we go," he told himself, as the small jet taxied down the runway, Minnesota-bound.

Maria interrupted Tom Powders while he was engrossed in his personal e-mail. She took perverse pleasure in startling the man so much he literally jumped. He quickly minimized the window, and turned his attention to her.

He grinned, showing yellow teeth. "What can I do for ya?"

Maria debated asking him about his e-mails. She just wanted some damn answers, but held her tongue. *In good time. Patience.* "You're scheduled to attend the Davis girl's autopsy." She watched the smile disappear from his face.

"Well, I have things to do here—"

"*Things* can wait. You're the only available body. Someone

has to go. Melanie Davis is part of the big picture. You're going." She spun on her heel, not willing to hear any more argument, and headed back to her desk. *Pansy-ass*, she thought, taking her seat. Tom hated Sanchez. She was a bitch. *A bossy bitch. One of these days, the bitch will get what's coming to her.*

Chapter 26

Lizzy and the girls decided to lay low today, since they had a roof over their heads and food to eat. Everyone was still recuperating from last night's party.

Tiny Tim waited for the word on the smack coming in. The last he heard, the shipment was coming into Flying Cloud Airport in Eden Prairie. He checked his watch, wondering what time Steve would show up. He said he would call first. Steve planned to make the pick-up himself, which was unusual.

Nick and Tiara came out of the bedroom, laughing. He was pale and thin, with long dark greasy hair and gothic features, while Tiara was chocolate brown and very athletic looking. They made a strange, but engrossing couple.

"And why are you two so bloody happy?" Tiny asked, as they joined the rest of them in the living room.

"Don't know," Tiara said, shrugging her shoulders.

"Well, I do." Nick Dupree grabbed T as he collapsed into a chair, bringing her down on top of him.

Tiara screamed, laughing. She really liked this guy. He was cool. She'd do just about *anything* for him, and he knew it.

Nick was her ticket outta here. That's all she wanted in life right now. She had to split before her father caught up with her. Only a matter of time. And when he did? That would be it. He'd kill her, she knew it. He was just crazy enough and if he was drinking… She let that thought linger a bit. He was one scary old man–so scary her mother had fled, leaving Tiara all alone with him.

"Who's hungry?" Tiny Tim inquired.

No one said anything.

"Oh, come on now! I thought I'd make sloppy Joes." He grinned, one hand on his hip. "Wanna help, girlfriend?" He looked at Lizzy.

"Me?" She touched her chest, surprised. He held his hand out for her to take. She really had no choice, so grabbed his hand and groaned, reluctantly getting off the couch.

"Rough night, love?" Tiny led her into the kitchen, smiling the entire way.

"Yeah, little hung that's all." She used the term she heard Kath use yesterday.

"Feel up to helping me I hope."

Lizzy smiled uncertainly. "Sure." This guy freaked her out. She didn't like the way he looked at her.

She hoped she wouldn't have to sleep with him, but knew it could happen sooner or later. If she wanted to infiltrate deep into the Santini family, she'd have to work for it, and unfortunately, some of that work would be extremely distasteful.

Tiny Tim grabbed a pound of hamburger from the refrigerator and set in on the counter, then began rummaging in the cupboard for a can of tomato sauce, cussing a blue streak as he found everything but what he was looking for.

Lizzy got busy browning the hamburger in the only relatively clean frying pan on the stovetop. She added salt and pepper, watching Tiny Tim out of the corner of her eye.

"Sons a bitchin' sonsabitches! Oh, here she is." He pulled out the can of tomato sauce, grinning like a fool, his forehead beaded with perspiration from becoming so flustered.

"Here, love." He set the can on the counter next to Lizzy, watching her brown the meat.

Lizzy grew uncomfortable under his scrutiny. She shifted from foot to foot, nervously, chopping and stirring the meat, cranking up the heat a bit on the stove.

Tiny liked her looks. She was just his size, and something about her screamed *excitement*. He placed his arms around her waist as she stirred the meat. Literally.

Lizzy went from slightly uncomfortable to very uncomfortable. When she felt his hands migrate to her hips, she tensed every muscle, anticipating the worst. She wasn't disappointed.

"Lizzy, Lizzy, Lizzy. What a beautiful girl you are." His hands moved fast–exploring the crotch of her blue jeans, rubbing, then her breasts, as he left a trail of sloppy kisses on her neck.

The telephone rang.

"Whew. Saved by the bell, huh love?" Tiny gave her a little squeeze, and then extracted himself to answer the phone.

Lizzy exhaled and tried to get herself together, as she listened to the one-sided telephone conversation with concern.

"Changed locations? No, no, don't worry. I'm alone." He looked at Lizzy and met her gaze, winking.

Foolish man. If only you knew. Lizzy smiled.

"Yeah, we'll be here all day." He looked into the receiver, frowning. "Yeah, I know it well. But… Okay. Yes, I'll meet you there. Yeah, I'll be waitin' for your call." He hung up the phone, looking miffed and confused.

"Anything wrong?" Lizzy dared to ask.

Tiny Tim looked at her briefly. "You could say that, love." He quickly left the kitchen.

Chapter 27

Maria was so surprised to see FBI Agent Peter Slade walk in that she almost choked on her coffee. "Jeez, there goes the neighborhood."

Joe stopped what he was doing and looked up. "What–" He stood as did Maria.

"Slade! What are you doing here?" Peter worked at FBI headquarters in Washington, D.C. Maria hugged him and Joe shook his hand vigorously.

"Beats the hell outta me. Colder than a witches–" He grinned. "Just wanted to see your beautiful face in person, Sanchez. Oh, and you too, Joe."

Joe smiled. "That's okay, I know you've always been in love with my wife."

Slade laughed. It was true. Why deny it. All three of them had been through a lot. He was happy to see Maria and Joe together. They were each other's destiny, but he would always hold a torch in his heart for Maria Sanchez.

"So, what are you doing here?" Maria motioned toward a chair, and Peter sat, letting out a loud sigh.

"Well, I told you I'd look into the two thugs who whacked Leo Gianelli in the sunshine state."

"Yeah, did you find something?" Maria leaned forward in anticipation.

"Gosh, I just love the way you get so excited, Sanchez."

"Peter, knock it off. Spill it." Maria could only take so much of his goofing around.

"Why not wait to spill it to those who count most." Chief LaSalle came around the corner, having heard most of the threesome's little exchange. It was enough to make her puke. Considering she had contacted FBI Agent Slade, it pissed her off that the first person he ran to was Sanchez.

"Chief LaSalle, I presume." Peter stood and extended his hand. He had spoken with her on the telephone several times, but it was somewhat of a shock to meet her in person, even though he had been forewarned by Maria and Joe. Her voice was so commanding, it belied her tiny stature.

Chief LaSalle looked at the outstretched hand, and slowly gazed up at the tall drink of water. He was quite handsome, with brown curly hair flecked with gray at the temples. The tweed jacket with elbow patches and tight faded blue jeans added to his boyish charm.

She decided to take his hand. "Peter Slade, I presume." She locked eyes with him and smiled.

"Nice to finally meet you, ma'am." He shook her hand vigorously, then stopped himself, not wanting to snap her teeny tiny bones.

"So, you have news?"

Slade nodded.

"Why don't we all retire to my office, where there's a bit more privacy." She frowned at Sanchez, chastising the lead detective with her eyes for allowing this open conversation.

Maria looked at Joe and rolled her eyes, behind the chief's back.

Peter caught it and grinned. "Yes, shall we?" He offered his arm to the petite woman, always the charmer, to the point of being too much.

LaSalle ignored the FBI agent, and led the way to her office, her bright red business suit and matching high-heels reminiscent of the devil.

The chief shut the door and motioned them to sit.

Maria sat between Peter and Joe, determined to keep her mouth shut.

The chief popped a piece of nicotine gum in her mouth, and leaned forward, engaging Slade in a stare down.

Peter Slade shifted, uncomfortable under her scrutiny.

She enjoyed making men squirm. Power was great, even though once she left this place it became short-lived. Hell, even her dog Fred didn't listen to her. "What do you have for me, Mr. Slade?" She did not smile, simply held his gaze for an honest answer.

Peter licked his lips, nervously. He didn't know how to act for some reason, felt like a chastised boy, reciting an answer to a difficult question in front of the entire class. "Well...I-I," he stammered, then seemed to regain some control.

"Remember I told you about the two thugs the FBI thinks whacked Leo Gianelli? The three of them were seen in Guido's Italian Eatery..."

The chief nodded, as did Maria and Joe.

"Well, Los Angeles agents have a definite ID on one of them–brought him in for questioning late last night." Peter tilted his chair back so it balanced on two legs.

"Please don't do that. So, what's his name, and what was his alibi? Is he still being held?"

Peter returned his chair to the floor, properly ashamed. Already he didn't like this woman. "Vincent Micelli. They still aren't sure about the other one. Vinny wouldn't talk. The only reason they got him was because the dumb fuck used his credit card to pay. They had to release him–lack of evidence. But his alibi was shaky according to the agents. He was scared, ready to bolt in any direction, despite the lack of information he divulged."

"Figures," Joe said.

"Well, that's more than we have. We have nothing on Stan's killers, not even a fuckin' name."

Slade was surprised to hear the F-word come out of that prissy little mouth, although he wondered why he should be, with her barracuda personality. "It sounds like there's a definite crack in Vinny Micelli's armor...I guess he was almost reduced to tears. Ever hear of a Mafia soldier with a conscience?" Slade grinned.

"That's great," Maria offered. "Work on that crack. We need all the help we can get. Too bad he wouldn't give up the name of his partner."

Peter shook his head. "But, they think he's close to giving up even more than that. Like I said, guy's on the edge. The L.A. agents are good. They have a plan and they'll get him to talk."

The chief kept her gaze on the FBI agent. "I've told Peter about our undercover agent."

Peter nodded. "I hope she can make her way to L.A. This whole operation is getting more and more corrupt. Mass quantities of drugs, so pure they are deadly, coming into Los Angeles. I'd say ninety percent of it is coming through Santini. Add to that his penchant for young girls–the underage prostitutes coming in from your fair city are keeping vice and narcotics very busy. Then there are the dead ones or those missing."

"Believe me, it's no fuckin' cake-walk here, either." The chief got a small twinge of satisfaction seeing the FBI agent flinch every time she said the F-bomb. "We've got a major bust in the works as we speak, thanks to our undercover agent. Heroin coming in through Flying Cloud Airport in Eden Prairie."

"Eden Prairie?" Slade was unfamiliar with Minnesota.

"A suburb," Joe offered.

Peter nodded. "Thought maybe...a prairie."

"The BCA is working with us as well." The chief turned her attention to Maria and Joe. "By the way, BCA Agent Bill Foley will be here after lunch, to go over some of the finer details of the case. They've put together some interesting facts. We must all work together on this." She knew Agent Foley was an ass, but he was an ass they had to work with, despite his arrogant ways.

Peter Slade grinned. "My buddy."

"Everyone's buddy," Maria added. She didn't care for him either. Never did. They had worked with the man many times over the years, and it never got easier. He was difficult to get along with, to put it mildly.

"Who's attending the Davis girl's autopsy?" The chief looked at her watch.

"Powders. I suppose I should make sure he left. He wasn't very keen on the idea." Maria stood.

"We're done here, anyway. Go ahead. Peter I'd like you to stay for a bit. There are some strategies I would like to go over with you on this case."

Joe and Maria left the FBI agent alone with the she-devil. They hated to do it, but didn't have a choice.

Maria shut the office door on their way out, giving Peter a sympathetic look that frightened him even more.

Chapter 28

Marco Santini was having a panic attack–or something similar. He did not like it when things didn't work out according to plan. It made him crazy.

Checking his watch for the hundredth time, he debated calling Stephen to tell him the latest. *Fucking cops. Fucking Vincent Micelli.* He should have taken him out when he first suspected disloyalty. Perhaps it was already too late.

Add to this, the worries of getting the fucking heroin into safe hands without incidence. Marco lit another cigarette. He would have to quit again. He smoked way too much these days. These latest stresses really played a number on him.

Steve rented an SUV much like the one he owned, not giving a shit about the cost of gas. It was snowing pretty good in this God-forsaken state, and since he had quite a distance to drive, the last thing he needed was to slip off the road and have an accident.

He had already called Tiny Tim and briefly filled him in. Now, on I-35, on the way to the airstrip in Owatonna, he made the call to L.A. Marco answered on the first ring.

In Los Angeles, Marco's heart skipped a beat when his cell sang a tune. He scrambled for it. "Yes."

"Marco, my man."

"Stephen. Thank God. Where are you?"

Steve heard the tension in the Boss's voice. "In the rental, on my way to pick up the goods. What the fuck is wrong now?"

Marco sighed. "Plenty. Fucking cops."

Steve felt a surge of adrenaline at the mention of cops. "Go on, no time for games, Marco. Spill it. Am I driving into a fuckin' hornet's nest?"

"No, no, no. Do not worry."

"Yeah, easy for you to say. What then?" Steve was losing patience. He hated this shit.

"No, it's Vinny...and Louie. Vincent was taken in for questioning on the murder of Leo Gianelli. They were all seen at

Guido's that night and fucking Vinny, the genius he is, paid by credit card. Then they whacked Gianelli, after advertising to the world."

"Fuck."

"He was released...nothing to hold him. But I do not trust Micelli. He is weak. Perhaps we should have taken him out when we had our initial suspicions."

"Fuck," Steve said again. "Take him out now."

"Believe me, I have thought of it." Marco took a long drag from his cigarette.

"Do it. Either you do it or have someone else. We don't want the fucker to talk."

"Stephen." Sometimes Marco felt he had to talk to his partner like a child. "It would cause suspicion to take him out right now, don't you think? *Hmm*?"

"You don't want him to talk. Hey, it's only our fuckin' necks in a noose if the fucker talks. You know what a fuckin' basket case he can be. Gutless."

"He won't talk," Marco said simply.

"How can you be sure? The fucker is soft–softer than a goddamn little girl."

"Trust me. I will be sure. He will be sure. We will all be sure, okay?"

Steve could tell Marco was smiling on the other end. "Okay." Marco obviously had something nasty planned for ol' Vinny. That appeared definite, however he couldn't help but wonder what threats would guarantee silence? He didn't doubt the Boss for a minute. Marco rarely shared his secrets, and Steve didn't really want to know.

"Now, have a safe trip. Let me know once you've retrieved the goods. I look forward to your return and trust everything will go smoothly."

"Yeah, easy for you to say," Steve said again, ending the connection.

Chapter 29

BCA Agent Bill Foley sat opposite Joe and Maria, bald head glistening under the bright fluorescent lighting. He looked up, frowning, as Agent Slade approached.

"Hey, you're in my seat." Peter smiled. "How's it goin', Foley?"

"It's goin'." Foley turned his attention back to the detectives, not wanting to deal with the FBI clown.

Peter Slade pulled up another chair, not taking offense at being ignored by the little bald BCA agent, who was known for liking no one. He listened with interest to the information gathered so far, then threw in the data he had gleaned on the L.A. connection.

"Let's move this to one of the conference rooms," Maria said, noticing Powders return from the autopsy.

"Why? My schedule is tight, Sanchez." Agent Foley glanced at his watch.

"Fine. Just leave us the information and you can be on your way." Maria wasn't going to let this guy call the shots.

Foley smiled snidely. "I have a few minutes, yet."

"Joe, why don't you take these gentlemen into one of the empty conference rooms. I'll find you. I want to speak with Tom about the autopsy."

"Sure. C'mon, guys." Joe escorted the two men to the nearest empty conference room.

Powders had just sat down at his desk, when Detective Sanchez came up behind him.

"So, how did it go? Thanks for attending. We really didn't have anyone else." Maria smiled.

Tom looked at her. "Fine."

"So, everything went fine?" This was so frustrating. She really wanted to shake the man to get some kind of response other than the perfunctory one-word responses. "What did you learn?"

"The usual." Tom turned around and rifled through a stack of files on his desk, smiling inside. He had the dumb-ass act down pat.

Maria didn't have time for this crap. "Okay." She went in search of Joe and the agents, hoping to get everything put together in one big picture, so they could determine exactly what they had to work with.

Maria found them in one of the smaller conference rooms on third floor. She thought of the old days and how Chief McCollough would have been in the middle of everything. Not the new chief, though. She had her own agenda.

"Hey," Maria said, entering and shutting the door.

"Hey," Joe and Peter responded together.

Foley just glared at her, impatient. They needed *him*, not the other way around.

"So, did you talk to Tom? How did the Davis girl autopsy go?"

"Well, he said it went fine. That's about all I got...for now." She looked at Joe and sighed.

Peter Slade laughed. "Oh, I remember that look. Detective Tom not one of your favorites?"

"He's fine," Maria offered, glancing at Foley who had begun drumming his fingers on the table. "Let's get down to business, shall we?"

"Please." Bill Foley sat up straight, passed Maria a pile of papers. "This is case files of runaways. Slade has cross-referenced some of them with the underage prostitutes who have been taken into custody in L.A. Correct?" He looked at the FBI agent.

"Correct. The girls we have information on are included in there." Peter nodded toward the papers. "What we need right now is something on Santini and one of his covert operations."

"Any news on the heroin shipment?" Maria asked Joe.

Joe shook his head. "Nothing yet. I spoke with the chief briefly just before you got here."

Agent Foley actually smiled. "Etina is good, but this is almost too easy."

Maria was surprised. She knew the BCA was aware of everything the Minneapolis Police Department did, but his comment indicated something a bit more. "You know Tina personally?"

Foley looked down at the table, avoiding eye contact. "I have spent time with her, yes."

Maria glanced at Joe and raised her eyebrows. Peter caught it.

"From what I've read about her, Etina Altmark seems pretty impressive. Perhaps that's an understatement." Peter Slade looked at the others.

"She's definitely an original," Maria offered.

They put together a rough picture–the who, what, and where of everything related. In a nutshell, they had one dead cop and one dead Mafiosi, underage runaways showing up dead either here or in Los Angeles, along with massive quantities of narcotics being brought in from outside the United States–probably Mexico–and the person responsible for all this ill fate was Marco Santini.

Twenty minutes later, they left the small room. Joe and Maria returned to Homicide and their desks. Slade went back to his hotel, and Foley headed to his office at the Bureau of Criminal Apprehension. Hope was pinned on the heroin bust, and a possible break in the case. They had a couple of positives: the knowledge of where the shipment was coming in, and optimism that Vincent Micelli would turn on the Family. Both were long shots.

Chapter 30

Steve saw signs for the Owatonna exit, and shifted the SUV into the right lane. He was ahead of schedule. According to Marco, the small Cessna would arrive at 4:30. Steve checked the clock in the SUV–4:07, and signaled for his exit.
He followed the signs to the airport, finding it with relative ease. The snow had picked up again, now coming down hard. It was almost dark outside.

The officers were told to stay at the airport in Eden Prairie until given the all clear. Patience wore thin as they spent part of the morning and all afternoon with nothing to show for it. It was almost 4:30 in the afternoon, and starting to snow. Drinking coffee to keep awake and warm, they waited.

Steve had been there ten minutes when he saw the Cessna approach. The airstrip appeared dead. No radio tower, only a small nondescript brick building that looked empty, dotted the landscape.
This is perfect. He got out of the SUV, feeling his coat pocket to double check for his piece. It was fully loaded, safety off, ready for action if necessary. He walked to the fence, watching the plane circle and land, skidding in the snow, then finally coming to a complete stop.
Precipitation came down in curtains of hard pellets, more ice than snow. Steve pulled up his hood, found an opening in the fence, and made his way to where the plane sat, engine idling. One hand cradled the gun inside his pocket. He was too important for this shit, but, if you wanted a job done right, you had to do it yourself.
The door to the plane opened and a tall, thin man emerged, looked in Steve's direction, and waved.
Steve returned the wave and kept walking toward the plane, a nervous smile plastered on his face. The icy wind whipped at his blue jean clad legs, exposed skin on his face tingled. *Who could*

live somewhere like this? How did you ever get used to this nasty shit?

"Hello," the tall thin man called over the howling wind, as Steve approached. A large box, sealed with shipping tape, sat at the man's feet.

The grip on his gun tightened. "Hello." Steve was a couple of feet away. He looked at the box, then the stranger.

The stranger held out a gloved hand in greeting.

Steve would have to remove his hand from the gun in order to shake the man's hand. He wasn't prepared to do that. Instead, he held out his other hand, forcing the stranger to switch hands.

The other man smiled, knowingly. There was no need to exchange names or get too friendly. They both knew the ropes.

Steve nodded toward the box. "That it?" he hollered.

The stranger nodded vigorously, and shouted through cupped hands, "Let's go to your vehicle."

This time Steve nodded, instructing the stranger, with hand signals, to pick up the box and follow. He looked up into the plane before he turned, and saw the outline of the pilot. The man watched them closely. Once again Steve thought, *I'm too important to do this shit...not the way I want to go down...in a drug deal gone bad.*

They made their way as quickly as possible to the SUV to get out of the arctic elements.

"Man, it's getting mean out there," the stranger said. He removed his hood, revealing a young, handsome face.

"Isn't it difficult to fly in this shit?" Steve asked.

"Yeah, can get a little tricky." He grinned.

Steve turned on the dome light and reached for the large cardboard box, setting it on the seat between them. It was labeled 'Text-books' and had a phony bookstore name. "Got a knife?"

The other man pulled out a pocketknife to cut the seal.

Steve opened the flaps, then removed a couple of books from the top to get to the goods. He pulled out a couple of textbooks from the middle, and flipped open the covers to reveal something much better than a history lesson.

He removed the blocks of Mexican heroin, unwrapped one and broke off a small piece. He crumbled it between his fingers, put it to his nose and sniffed, then placed a tiny amount on his tongue. Steve looked at the other man and grinned. "Good stuff." He turned off the dome light.

The man just looked at him, shrugging his shoulders. "If you say so."

Steve extracted a sealed envelope from an inside jacket pocket and handed it to the stranger. "It's all there–no need to count."

"Don't take offense–I was ordered."

This time it was Steve's turn to shrug his shoulders. He watched the other man open the envelope and thumb through the bills.

"Okay, nice doin' business with ya." He shoved the fat envelope into a jacket pocket, then held out his hand.

Steve glanced toward the plane, no longer seeing the outline of the pilot in the lighted cockpit. *Where did he go?* He quickly shook the other man's hand, suddenly wanting to get out of here.

The stranger opened the door, casting them in bright light. Glancing back at Steve, he grinned, seemed in no real hurry.

Steve saw the shadow of the pilot approaching the SUV and quickly removed his gun, aiming at the departing passenger.

The pilot stopped, appearing to think twice about their plan.

The man departing the vehicle saw the gun, and held out both hands in a *hey, we're cool* gesture, closed the door and joined the pilot. The two dark figures hurried back to the plane.

Steve followed them with his gun, inside the dark shadows of his vehicle, heart pounding, and blood rushing to his brain. He kept the weapon trained on them until they climbed up into the Cessna, now barely visible.

Putting the SUV into gear, he peeled out of the parking lot, onto the service road. He let out a sigh of relief, running his fingers through his long sweaty hair. Nervous sweat. *Even in this fuckin' cold.*

"Man, that was close," he said aloud, picking up speed, wanting to put distance between him and the drug runners. His heart didn't stop pounding in his ears until he reached I-35, bound for the Twin Cities.

The sloppy Joes were edible, but lacked *something*. Regardless, they were devoured. Tiara spent the afternoon with

Nick, behind closed doors. Tiny Tim sat by the phone, periodically picking it up to check for a dial tone.

Lizzy was cleaning up, hands immersed in soapy dishwater when the phone rang. Tiny had left his post to go to the bathroom. She dried her hands and moved toward the phone when Tiny came flying out of the bathroom.

"Got it, love." He grabbed it on the fifth ring, breathless. "Hello there."

Steve had nearly disconnected, thinking no one was home. He planned to board the Santini jet, bound for L.A. without looking back. Finally, the little dickweed picked up. "You almost lost out, Tim. Didn't think no one was fuckin' home."

"Sorry, sorry, sorry. Had to take a fuckin' leak and everyone else is...preoccupied."

"I'll be in Minneapolis in about an hour. Do you have some girls there?"

"Oh, indeed we do. A couple of fresh ones," he said, thinking of the two youngest. They would get top dollar on the streets of Los Angeles.

"Expect me around six o'clock, okay?"

"I thought you wanted to meet elsewhere."

"Changed my mind." No sense in having Tiny meet him if he was going to bring a couple girls back with him to L.A. Moreover, after his experience at the Owatonna airfield, he wasn't keen on meeting in strange places. He'd be in and out in a heartbeat–drop off the smack, pick out a couple whores and away he'd go.

"Good, good. Didn't want to go out in this bloody awful weather," Tiny said, excited that the second in command was coming here. "Six o'clock. We'll be waiting."

Steve disconnected, and concentrated on driving. He almost missed the Minneapolis exit because of the heavy snowfall.

Tiny Tim hung up the telephone and did a little dance. He grabbed Lizzy, dripping hands and all, swinging her around the kitchen floor like a ballroom dancer.

Lizzy giggled despite herself. "Why are you so happy? Good news?"

"Yes, love. Very good news. We are having a visitor–a very *important* visitor. Let's clean up this dump, shall we?" He left her to the greasy pan and walked though the apartment, clapping his hands to announce clean-up time, finding something for everyone to do.

Lizzy looked deeply into the dirty dishwater, thinking. *What is going on? Who is coming? Someone important.* She wondered if the heroin bust was a success. She wondered what would happen next, tried to prepare herself for whatever came her way. She was still a player in the game. She had to stay that way, and if possible make the stakes even higher.

Chapter 31

The police officers left Flying Cloud Airport with nothing to show for their efforts. Darkness had fallen and a full-force blizzard had grounded flights for the rest of the evening.

No heroin. No nothing.

Whoever had given this juicy little tidbit appeared to be full of shit. That was exactly what officer Todd Williams told the chief when she called to give them the 'all clear' and tell them to go home. It had been the wrong thing to say. She ripped him a new asshole.

A foul mood was had by all and the weather made it even worse.

Maria and Joe packed up to go home. They'd planned to stop by Peter Slade's hotel room, but with the nasty weather, promised him breakfast instead, before his flight back to Washington DC.

The chief was in a mood, and still worked diligently in her office, evidently with no plans to go home.

Maria voiced her concern to Joe. "Someone got back to the source–I just know it. Who in this department is working both sides of the fence?"

"That, my dear is the ten million dollar question." Joe shut his briefcase and grabbed his coat. "Are we ready?"

Maria still sat at her desk, deep in thought. "Can you wait a couple of minutes?" She stood and looked toward Chief LaSalle's closed door.

"Why?"

"I need to tell her about Powders." Maria looked at Joe directly. "What if he's the leak and we let this go?"

"Maria, we don't have any proof."

"Well, in the old days with Chief McCollough gut-instinct was proof enough. And let me tell ya–my gut tells me something is definitely not right with the man."

"Well, darlin', first of all these ain't the old days, McCollough's long gone, and second, knowing how Chief LaSalle

feels about you, your gut is not going to phase the woman."
"Well, at least I can say I tried." She stood and quickly walked to the chief's door, before Joe could say another word and she lost her nerve. She knocked once and entered.

Chief LaSalle had her high heels off, feet propped on the desk, and looked like she could eat glass for a light snack.

"Sorry to bother you," Maria said tentatively.

"What is it, Sanchez?"

"Well, ma'am. I debated saying anything, but considering this latest bust fell apart...well..."

"Well, what? For Christ's sake–spit it out." Chief LaSalle had no patience left in her today. Everything that could have gone wrong, did. Plus, she worried about Tina. Worried someone may have overheard their conversation when she called this morning. Perhaps that is why there was no dope–if that's the case, Tina's dead already. That last thought sickened her.

"Tom Powders–"

"What about him?" The chief interrupted, not in the mood for a tattletale.

"Well, he's in his personal e-mail an awful lot and his behavior is suspicious to say the least. Have you considered–"

Sandra LaSalle burst out laughing. "If you tell me you think *he* is our leak, I will shit a brick right here and now."

Maria looked at the other woman with contempt. How crude, and yes, she would pay good money to see the bitch shit a brick–hopefully it would do some major internal damage. She smiled, turned, and left the chief's office, quietly shutting the door on her way out.

Maria walked back to her desk, so angry she could barely see straight.

"Well–" Joe stopped, took one look at his wife, and knew the answer. "She didn't believe you."

"Not only did she *not* believe me," Maria offered in a shaky voice. "She outright laughed in my face, Joe. She is a rude bitch."

"Yes, yes she is, but Maria...she actually laughed?" Even Joe was surprised at this reaction.

"Laughed."

"I'm sorry, honey." Joe slipped on his coat. "Let's get the

hell outta here." He had grabbed Maria's coat while she was in with the chief and now held it out for her.

"I should've listened to you. I never should've said anything. Like you said, what proof do I have?"

"Maria, you've never listened to me before, why should now be any different?"

She slipped into her coat and looked at her husband somewhat exasperated. However, a small smile played at the corner of her mouth. "Let's go home, Joe."

The apartment was so clean you could practically eat off the floor. The girls were spiffed up, too. Tiny Tim went through each room, inspecting the corners for dust, then went over each girl, taking much joy in the process–touching their hair, their clothes, their bodies. He made sure the young ones–Dani and Shawna–looked especially fetching.

At six o'clock, everyone sat in the living room, soft music on the stereo, incense burning, waiting.

In strictest confidence, Tiny Tim told Nick exactly what was going on. Of course, Nick told Tiara, who told Lizzy, Kathy, and Beth. The only ones who didn't know were Dani and Shawna.

Lizzy wondered if only *two* runaways would be taken to California tonight. Then there was the heroin–the cops must not have found it, or else they changed the drop-off location. According to Nick, it was almost pure, Mexican heroin. *That should do some major damage.*

At quarter past six, a knock sounded on the door.

Tiny Tim sprang up, almost knocking over his drink. He ran his fingers through his stringy hair and took a deep breath before opening the door.

Steve Freyhoff stood in the doorway brushing snow off his coat, taking in his surroundings. "Hey, Tiny."

"Steve, buddy. You made it. Come in. Come in. Can I take your jacket?" Tiny Tim motioned him inside with a flourish.

"Can't stay long, Tiny. Just here to make a drop-off and a pickup. I suppose you have a house full?" he asked, hearing muffled voices come from the living room.

Tiny grinned. "Don't I always?"

"Yeah, yeah you do. Let's get this part taken care of. Here."

He handed Tiny several cellophane blocks of Mexican heroin.

"Oh lordy, lordy. This looks absolutely lovely." He held it up to his nose attempting to sniff through the cellophane.

Steve grinned at the dumb-ass doper. "It's wrapped pretty tight–kinda difficult to get a good a sense of smell. It's pure shit. *Really* pure. Get it?"

"Yes, I get it. I can hardly wait to give it a try, but that will have to wait a bit, I suppose." He unbuttoned his shirt and placed the blocks inside, buttoning back up. "If it's as pure as you say, we should do quite well on the streets."

"Yeah, make sure you get top dollar. And be careful."

"Careful is my middle name, boss. You know that." Tiny Tim blinked at the tall blonde man standing before him, somewhat insulted.

Steve shifted from foot to foot, anxious to get going. "So you got a couple girls for me to take back?"

Tiny Tim grinned, insult forgotten. "Oh man, do I ever. A couple of youngun's barely weaned off their mama's titty."

Steve grimaced. "You know me Tiny–I gotta pick. I don't want to baby-sit on the plane ride back home. Marco's not with me this time."

"They will be fine, but by all means–you're the boss, you choose. Everyone is in the living room." Tiny Tim led the way.

Steve entered the living room. "Hello, Nick."

Nick sat in a chair with a good-looking black girl on his lap. He pushed her off, then stood, and shook hands, having only met Stephen Freyhoff once before. It was an honor to have him in their apartment. If not for him, they wouldn't be here. He was surprised the man remembered his name. "Hey," he said, pumping the other man's hand.

"Are you going to introduce me?" He looked at Tiara. She was tall, almost eye-level with him and he stretched well over six foot tall.

Tiny scooted into the conversation. "Please, let me do the honors. We have Tiara, the most gorgeous chocolate creature alive." He went around the room, pointing to each girl and saying a little something about them. He introduced Kath as a party-girl, Beth as sweet and demure.

Steve tuned out Tiny Tim as his eyes rested on the little

blonde at the end of the couch. It was *her*–the girl at the airport.

Tiny introduced Dani and Shawna with much flourish, and finally came to Lizzy, noticing Steve already locked into her. "And here we have Lizzy. She can make some mean sloppy Joes."

Everyone laughed, and Lizzy blushed.

"I love sloppy Joes," Steve mumbled, unable to take his eyes off her. She was exquisite–tiny, with porcelain skin and large crystal blue eyes.

Tiny Tim didn't like the way Steve looked at Lizzy, but feeling the blocks of heroin in his shirt made it easier. It called to him. "I tell you what–sit for two minutes, get to know the girls a bit. Nick and I will be right back." He motioned the boss to the chair Nick had previously occupied.

Tiny and Nick escaped into one of the back bedrooms. Tiny had the fix kit out, cooking up a batch within a minute.

Steve sat, uncomfortably looking around the room. "So, who would like to go to L.A.?" He only wanted two of them, and knew who he wanted, but wanted to make sure they wanted it as well.

"Shit, we all do." Tiara spoke for all of them. "Except for the babies–can't speak for them," she said, nodding toward Dani and Shawna.

"We ain't babies," Danielle piped up. "And we wanna go, too."

Tiara laughed. "You don't even know what you're talkin' 'bout, okay? Shut up."

Dani looked like she might cry as she scowled at the older girl. Tiara was a bitch. She hated her.

When Tiny and Nick returned, they were flying high. Grinning like fools, they joined the group.

"I can only take two with me," Steve said, rising from the chair. "I'll take Tiara and Lizzy."

The two girls grinned at one another.

Nick and Tiny looked crest-fallen.

"I–I thought you'd want the young ones," Tiny stammered, not wanting to lose his Lizzy before he had his way with her.

"Tiara and Lizzy," Steve said again.

Nick reached out and slid his arm around Tiara's waist. "I'll miss ya, T." He looked sad.

Tiara hugged him. "I know, baby, but it's for the best. Remember what I told you?"

Nick racked his stoned brain. No, he didn't remember. He just stared at her, vacantly.

"My father?" T just looked at him, exasperated. "Drunk...crazy..."

Nick nodded, still confused.

Tiny accepted it without too much difficulty, already thinking about another fix. Besides, the young ones would be fun–once he gave them a taste of the H. Hell, it would be a party like no other. "Go gather your things, girls," he said to Tiara and Lizzy, wanting to move on with the evening.

The girls left the room, returning five minutes later with all their belongings shoved into backpacks, coats in hand.

Steve grinned. "Wow; that was fast."

"We travel light," Tiara said, anxious to leave. Didn't want to think about leaving Nick. "Let's go."

They said quick good-byes. Lizzy hugged Beth and whispered in her ear to *go home.*

Beth just looked at her, tears standing in her frightened eyes.

Tiara reminded Kathy again about the amount of shit she put into her body. Whispering the name of the now dead Melanie seemed to get through to her–for now, anyway.

Steve left with the girls. He was glad to see Lizzy climb in the passenger side next to him. He looked at her and smiled. "I've seen you before."

An alarm went off in Lizzy's brain. "No, I don't think so," she replied. "I would've remembered." She smiled nervously.

"At the airport, 'bout a week ago."

Lizzy just looked at him, fear in her eyes. He smiled at her– nothing sinister lurking in his kind green eyes.

"You look a little worse for wear. Must've been a rough week, huh?"

Lizzy looked down at the floor. "Yeah, kinda."

"Well, things will look up now. You'll like L.A."

"I'm sure I will." Lizzy looked at the handsome man and felt her heart skip a beat. *Whoa. Watch it.* She didn't go gaga over men. Ever. *What's going on?*

Once their guest of honor departed, Tiny and Nick brought out the H, and cooked up a batch. Only two needles, but they could share.
Let the fun begin.

Chapter 32

The roads were terrible and it took almost an hour to get home. Maria stayed quiet the entire way. Joe drove, attempting to cheer her up by keeping things light, but it was no use. Joe pulled into the driveway. "Finally. We're home." He squeezed his wife's leg. "You okay?"
Maria tilted her head and smiled. "Yeah, I'll survive. Glad we're home. It's been a day, hasn't it?"
"Yup. Sucked." Joe opened his door.
"Yes, sucked. That pretty much sums it up. Hope Tina is okay." Maria extracted herself from the Jeep and trudged through the snow to meet Joe on the other side.
"Me, too. Wonder what happened? We gotta try not to think about it. Don't do any good." Joe led the way into the garage and into the bright inviting warmth of the house.
Tess and Tony were down in the basement playing pool.
They grabbed a couple of beers and joined the kids, trying to put work out of their minds.
They played a foursome–Joe and Tony against Maria and Tess. The women won. Before long, work was temporarily forgotten and family took precedence over everything else.

Lizzy had one opportunity and she took it, at the airport. Tiara waited in the restroom–she had her period bad and needed tampons. Steve had given Lizzy a twenty-dollar bill and sent her into the airport shop to pick up tampons and a newspaper. He had spotted a Starbucks and was busy getting a latte.
A bank of three payphones lined the back wall, next to the small array of tampons and sanitary napkins. Setting the box of tampons down, she dug into her jeans pocket for a quarter, coming up with two nickels, a dime and several pennies. *Shit! Gotta hurry. Can't get caught now–I'm goin' to L.A.* She dug in her jacket pocket, saying a little prayer.
She pulled out a lifesaver covered with lint, a nickel, and a quarter. "Thank you, God," she muttered, deposited the quarter

and lifted the receiver. Punching in the sequence of numbers, she tapped her foot anxiously, waiting.

Chief LaSalle answered. "Hello." She listened. "Thank God you're okay. I knew it wouldn't take you long to get to California." Sandra waited. "Tina?"

Lizzy terminated the call.

"What are you doing?" Holding his latte in one hand, Steve stood behind Lizzy.

She hung up the telephone and checked the coin return, then proceeded to pick up the other phones, checking first for a dial tone, then the coin return. "Checking for freebies. Sometimes I'll come away with close to a dollar." She grinned at Steve.

"Let's go, okay?"

"Okay." Lizzy grabbed the tampons. Her heart pounded out a staccato beat from almost being caught, as she moved toward the cash register.

They walked to the restroom where Tiara waited, making small talk, friendly, easy-going. Steve waited outside the women's restroom while Lizzy hurried inside.

Lizzy looked under the stalls for her friend's feet, finding her in the last stall. "Hey T. It's me."

"Christ all mighty, girlfriend. 'Bout fuckin' time." Tiara reached under the stall and Lizzy placed the box of tampons into her outstretched hand.

"Sorry. The shop was busy," she lied. She looked at herself in the mirror while she waited for Tiara, thinking about Los Angeles and what lay ahead. Her mind went to Stephen Freyhoff. Once again, her heart did a little dance.

Tiara emerged, looking frazzled. "Can't believe there were no fuckin' tampons in the goddamn machine." She nodded angrily toward the dispenser on the wall. She had almost broken the damn thing trying to get it apart. "I miss Nick already."

"You'll probably see him again, don't ya think?" Lizzy looked at her new friend.

"Did you fuck Tiny Tim?" Tiara asked.

"No! *Eew.*"

"Yeah...I know. I can guarantee if you'd stayed one more night, you woulda had to."

Lizzy looked disgusted. "Yeah...that's what I figured. Glad

we got out of there."

"Me, too. It was only a matter of time before my old man caught up with me. I saw his fuckin' car a couple days ago. Did I tell you?"

Lizzy shook her head. "No."

Tiara nodded, washed her hands, then grabbed half a dozen paper towels. "Yup, saw him cruising in downtown Minneapolis. Fucker is on a mission."

"What happened...between the two of you?" She held the other girl's gaze. "Maybe you don't want to talk about it."

Tiara shrugged her shoulders. Catching her reflection in the mirror, she ran her fingers through unruly curls. "He's a creep–beat me, fucked me–I hate him. I wish him dead." He was the only father she had ever known. She had always *thought* he was her biological father. Her mother shattered the illusion the day she left. Said her real father died before she was even born...screamed it. T looked at the little blonde and wondered what Lizzy's story was.

"I'm sorry. That sucks."

"Yeah, sucks. Hey, girlfriend–we better split 'fore your new boyfriend leaves without us." Tiara grinned at Lizzy's surprised expression.

"*My* boyfriend?" Lizzy was shocked.

Tiara laughed, heading for the door. "Yeah. You both got that *look*."

Lizzy followed her out the door.

Steve leaned against the wall, and smiled when they approached.

Tiara looked at her with a 'See what I mean?' twinkle in her eye.

"You girls ready to fly?"

They both nodded, eagerly following the man who would change their lives.

Chapter 33

Marco mixed the first martini of the day and lit a cigarette, then returned to his desk and put his feet up.
He smiled, satisfied. The heroin was on its way. Everything had worked as planned. He had just heard from Stephen–they were taxiing down the runway, homeward bound as they spoke.
Marco's smile vanished as his thoughts went to Vincent Micelli.
He picked up the phone and dialed. "Yes, it's me. I would like to speak to Vinny within the hour. Yes, in person. In my office. Thank you."
Marco disconnected, took a deep drag off his cigarette, and squinted into the smoky air. He looked forward to the meeting, still unsure of the outcome for Vincent.

Once they reached altitude, Steve poured a drink and rolled a joint, breaking off a small piece of H from a compressed block. Crushing it, he sprinkled it on top of the pot in the folded paper, rolled it tightly, and twisted the ends.
Steve had given the girls a tour of the small plane before takeoff. There was a compact refrigerator stocked with juice and pop. Tiara sipped a diet Coke and Lizzy selected cranberry juice.
"Interesting choice," Steve offered, nodding toward Lizzy's juice. "Perhaps you'd like to add some vodka? Marco has top-shelf."
Tiara watched the exchange with interest.
Vodka was one drink that Lizzy could handle. As a full-blooded Russian, she'd practically been weaned on it. "Sure. Just a little, though."
Steve retrieved a glass and filled it with ice. He poured a shot of vodka and handed it to Lizzy, letting her add the juice. "Tiara?"
"No, nothing for me–thanks. I'm on the rag. Can't really handle my liquor when I'm bleeding like a stuck pig."
Lizzy laughed. T definitely called it like she saw it. She was

so 'out there'.

Tiara smiled at them. "However, I will partake in some of that." She nodded at the joint Steve had tucked behind his ear.

He removed the joint, flipping his long, blonde hair back into place. "What, this?" He grinned, placed it between his lips, and lit it. He coughed and choked. "Good stuff," he croaked, passing it to Tiara.

She took a toke and held it, feeling euphoria enter her system. She passed it to Lizzy who declined, using the vodka as an excuse.

"Wow," Steve said, as the plane encountered brief turbulence. "I'm fuckin' wasted."

Tiara giggled. "Me, too. Glad to be out of fuckin' Minnesota."

"Lizzy, why don't you come sit by me," Steve said, patting the seat next to him.

Lizzy glanced at T, who smirked. She downed the rest of her drink, then stood to join Santini's top man. She reminded herself why she was here, as the thought of sitting next to this man thrilled her. She didn't like this feeling. It scared her. And she didn't scare easily.

"Care for another?" He nodded toward her empty glass. He retrieved the vodka without waiting for an answer and filled her glass halfway.

Lizzy added the rest of her cranberry juice and raised her glass in a toast. "To us." She looked at Stephen, locking eyes and searching his soul.

Steve was under her spell. He couldn't look away. This girl held something special inside, he could see it in her eyes. He wasn't sure what or why, but looked forward to finding out. She was a runaway, too young, bad news–Marco would not allow it. "To us," he offered, touching his glass to hers, holding eye contact until she glanced away, a smile on her flushed face.

Chapter 34

They had just retired; lights out and almost asleep when the telephone rang shrilly on the bedside table. Maria picked up, wondering who would be calling this late. She hoped it wasn't another dead runaway.

She wasn't surprised to hear the chief. It sounded as if she'd been crying, and drinking. "Yes?" She turned on the lamp, a look of alarm on her face, which soon softened. "That's great news. Okay. Okay. Yes, you too. Have a good night, Chief LaSalle." Maria replaced the receiver, confused.

"Chief?" Joe inquired.

"Yes..."

"She called you after 10:00 p.m. to tell you to have a good night? The look on your face, honey..." He placed his hands on her shoulders. "Well?"

"Well, Tina is on her way to California. She's safe." Maria shook her head as if to clear this next thought. "Then she says, in a shaky, slightly slurred voice, this floors me..."

"You realize you're *exactly* like your daughter." Joe grinned at her.

Maria stopped mid sentence. "Am not!"

"Yes, you are. You beat around that same bush just like her."

Maria looked her husband in the eye. "Okay, Joe. The chief told me she would consider what I told her about Powders. She agrees his behavior is strange and that she'd been a bitch when I approached her on the subject earlier."

"Wow. She said that?" Joe was astonished. He didn't think the barracuda had it in her.

Maria nodded. "Yup."

Joe kissed her forehead. "And just for the record, I like the way you beat around the bush. It's an endearing quality."

Maria laughed. "Yeah, right! It drives me nuts when I talk to Theresa."

Joe smiled. "Yeah, I guess what they say is true–the apple doesn't fall far from the tree. Hey, it could be a helluva lot worse." He pulled the covers up to his chin still grinning.

Maria snapped off the lamp, then snuggled up against him. "Yeah, it can always be worse." She couldn't help but think of their son when Joe made the remark, 'The apple doesn't fall far from the tree'. *With his genetic history, what chance did the poor kid have?*

"And I love you for better or worse." He kissed her, slipping a hand over one breast.

"Yes, I know you do," she offered between wet kisses. "And I do you."

Joe groaned. "I like that–you *do* me."

Chapter 35

Vinny was nervous. *This isn't good. Nope, not good at all.* He took a final drag off his smoke, flicked it into the street, and entered Santini Realty.

Raoul, Marco's personal bodyguard, waited by the elevator to escort him up to Marco's posh office. Neither spoke a word as they rode the elevator.

Vincent Micelli followed Raoul down the hall, borderline panic surging through his veins.

Raoul knocked once, opened the door, and ushered Vinny inside. He smiled and left, closing the door quietly behind him.

Vinny stood just inside the door, waiting, shaking.

"Vincent, my boy. Please come in. Don't be shy." Marco sat at his desk, feet up, martini in hand, a smile on his face.

Vinny moved toward the man, remembering to have proper respect and wait to be seated.

Marco scrutinized him, thinking. *Little fuck. I should take you out right now.* He thought of the loaded weapon in the top drawer. The safety was off, the drawer open a crack. He could see a fraction of the handle. His mind whirled, thinking, planning.

Vinny extended his hand. It shook. "Good to see you, Marco. How are you?" He felt like he might cry. He noticed Marco inch the top drawer open farther.

A brief look of surprise flickered across Marco's features and he smiled, smoothing his groomed mustache and beard. Perhaps, the man was smarter than he looked. He closed the drawer. Politeness pleased him. He grasped the other man's hand.

"Good to see you as well. I am fine. And you? How are you, Vincent? Please, please have a seat." He pointed at the empty chair next to the man, and wiped his hand on his pants. Poor Vinny was slick with nervous sweat, from head to toe.

Relief flooded Vinny. He sat, nervously smiling, hoping he was somewhat out of the woods. Mopping his sweaty brow, he muttered, "Um...I'm okay...I guess." He thought of the cops and knew the Boss knew. No point in denying anything. "I didn't talk. The cops. I'm not stupid."

Marco frowned. "No, you are not stupid. However, you are not the brightest bulb in the pack either. Moreover, what I worry about is not your stupidity, but your cowardliness. You have a weakness, Vincent. Call it compassion for the under-dog. Call it whatever you will, but it cannot be tolerated."

Vinny didn't know how to respond, but knew he'd better think of something if he wanted to walk out of here. "I would never do anything that would hurt the Family."

"No, not intentionally," Marco countered.

Vinny looked down at his hands, clutched in his lap to keep from shaking. "What can I do to prove myself to you? I'll do anything you want, Boss. Anything."

Marco leaned back in his chair, and watched the man squirm, greatly enjoying himself at Vincent's expense. Finally, he smiled. "Okay."

Vinny's eyes darted back and forth. *Okay, okay, what? What does that mean?*

Marco stood, grabbed his empty martini glass, and popped the olive resting at the bottom into his mouth with flourish. "Care for a drink, my friend?"

Vinny stood as well, frightened at the sudden movement. "Sure," he said a little too quickly. "I'll have what you're having."

"Good choice, my friend." Marco mixed a fresh batch of martinis, shaking the mixture with crushed ice. He poured, added a large Spanish olive, and handed Vincent the drink.

Vinny grabbed the martini, self-conscious of his large sweaty hand in contrast to the small fancy glass. He looked at Marco, who seemed to have been born with a martini in hand. *Fancy.*

"To our newfound friendship, a *strong* friendship." Marco raised his glass.

"Friendship," Vinny said, raising his glass. Taking a sip, he tried not to grimace as Marco watched him very intently. He thought he pulled it off.

"Do you drink martinis often?" Marco smiled.

Vinny debated lying, then thought better of it, knowing the man could be set off at the smallest of lies. He thought back to several instances of soldiers who were no longer alive due to a simple twist of the truth. Marco Santini demanded honesty–and those who couldn't provide it to his liking were removed in a heartbeat. "Nah, not really. I'm more of a whiskey man."

"You should have said something. Stephen has several brands. It would not have been a problem."

"That's okay. Like to try new things." He took another sip of the drink and didn't grimace. "It ain't bad." He smiled.

Marco Santini returned the smile. "You are okay, Vincent. We will be in touch."

Just like that. *Whew! Dismissed.* Vincent set his glass on the bar. "Thanks, Marco. I promise I won't let you down."

"No, you won't. I promise." Marco walked to the large window, turning his back on the man, and looked out over Los Angeles. He smiled to himself as the office door quietly shut.

By the time the private jet landed in L.A., it was late and they were all exhausted and burnt out.

Steve took the girls to his apartment, surprised upon opening the door to find it clean. Then he remembered how he had worked like a woman, nesting. He grinned. "Home sweet home."

The girls looked around their surroundings, wide-eyed. It was gorgeous. Pale cream colors dominated the large room. A leather sectional occupied a good portion of the room, glass coffee tables in odd designs at each end were arranged around a beautiful oriental rug with intricate designs in earth tones. The only bright colors were the wild abstract paintings that adorned the eggshell white walls and several brightly colored floor vases. Simple, but elegant. A loft with recessed lighting glowed invitingly.

"Wow," Tiara said. "Awesome."

Steve yawned. "Thanks. I like it." He shrugged his shoulders. "I could do better, but I like it here."

Lizzy yawned, and set down her backpack.

"There's a loft where someone can crash, and there's here." He pointed to the sectional couch.

"I get the loft," Tiara said immediately, challenging Lizzy with her eyes, and grinning.

Steve looked at Lizzy. His bedroom was just down the hall. She could sleep in his bed. Maybe he'd invite her to join him.

"This is fine," Lizzy said, sitting. She smiled shyly at Steve.

"I'll go get some blankets," he offered.

When he left the room, Tiara moved next to Lizzy and sat down. Lowering her voice to a whisper she said, "He wants you. I would say you should use this to your advantage, girlfriend."

Lizzy looked at the other girl. She did not need advice from a sixteen-year-old runaway. "Whatever," she replied the standard response all teenagers used.

"I mean it," she said.

"We'll see," Lizzy offered.

Steve returned with a stack of blankets and pillows.

"I'm pooped," Tiara announced. "Gonna check out the loft." She grabbed a pillow and a blanket. "Nighty-night."

Lizzy frowned at her friend. "Good night."

"Night," Steve said.

Tiara shimmied up the wooden ladder like a squirrel, leaving Lizzy and Steve alone.

He turned to Lizzy. "Would you care for something to drink?"

Lizzy shook her head. "No, thanks. I'm tired. Think I'll just crash."

"Yeah, me too." He stood. "Well, if you need anything or get freaked out in the night, whatever, my room is right down the hall."

Lizzy grinned. "Don't worry, I do not have nightmares."

Steve detected a slight accent, and asked her about it.

Lizzy blushed, and had the lie ready, because she knew it was only a matter of time. In fact, it surprised her that he was the first one to ask. "Yes, my family moved from Russia when I was about ten years old. I guess a little bit of the old country still hangs on."

"How old are you? Sometimes the way you word things makes you sound older. Maybe it's just the Russian in you."

"I'm T's age. Almost seventeen." Lizzy looked him directly in the eye as she told the lie, not even blinking.

He stood. "Okay, I'm gonna crash. If you get lonely..." He left the statement hanging as he walked away, then called "Goodnight," before entering his bedroom.

Lizzy covered up, fell asleep almost immediately, and dreamt of the old country...and her mother.

Steve lay in bed, eyes open, thinking about the girl who slept in his living room. *Lizzy. Beautiful Lizzy.* He remembered he was supposed to call Marco when he arrived. "Shit," he said aloud. He picked up his cell from the bedside table.

It rang and rang. Marco finally picked up just before voicemail kicked in.

"Hope I didn't wake you," Steve said, knowing he didn't. Marco never went to bed before 2:00 a.m.

"No, Stephen. Are you home, safe and sound?"

Steve grinned. Sometimes Marco appeared sincere, almost motherly. "Yes, safe and sound. Got the goods and the girls."

"Good. We will distribute it tomorrow. Did you bring the girls to Darcy's this late?"

"Hell, no. I value my fuckin' life, ya know."

Marco laughed heartily. Darcy Love was in charge of the runaways, once they came to L.A. A force to be reckoned with, she called the shots–to a point. She and Marco had an *understanding* that went way back. He probably trusted her more than he trusted any woman. "Smart man. Any spitfires?"

Steve thought of Tiara and mentioned her to Marco.

"*Hmm*, sounds promising. Perhaps I'll pay her a visit. Beautiful, huh?"

"Yes, very…in an exotic sort of way. Very athletic."

"And I like chocolate." Marco grinned, feeling slightly aroused. "What about the other one? There are two, correct?"

"Yes. She's mine." Steve sounded like a little boy even to his own ears.

"Oh, she is, is she?" Marco laughed. "We'll see." He disconnected, leaving Stephen to contemplate his next course of action.

Chapter 36

Maria didn't know what to expect when she walked into Homicide, but it wasn't what she found. Chief LaSalle stood at Tom Powders desk, talking and laughing with the man as if they were old friends. She barely glanced at Maria when she walked by.

Joe had stopped in Narcotics to go over some details concerning the Melanie Davis case, so he wasn't privy to the auto-ignore Maria experienced.

They had taken Agent Slade out to breakfast as promised, and got him on his flight back to Washington, D.C. In turn, Peter promised to keep in close contact with the agents in Los Angeles, and keep Joe and Maria apprised of the situation brewing there.

Slade planned to make a trip out to California within the next couple of weeks to help make plans for a Mafia rendezvous with the agents there. It was only a matter of time before they made their move. He tried to talk Maria and Joe into meeting him there. They could turn it into a working vacation. Joe wasn't keen on the idea, since the last time he was there, he'd ended up in the hospital with multiple gunshot wounds.

However, they promised Slade they would think about it. Maria personally *did* want to meet Roberto Santini's nephew and Nicholas' brother. Working with the California FBI would prove advantageous as well since the Minneapolis Police Department had a vested interest in the outcome. They could also check on Tina.

Perhaps she'd work on Joe and they could go with the chief's endorsement. *Maybe...*

Maria spent the next half an hour at the white board, shuffling cases around because two detectives were out sick with the flu. Joe came through the door around the same time she finished reassigning duties.

She pulled him aside, into the small niche where the copy and fax machine resided. "Whoa, what a turn-around from last night." She noted his look of confusion. "The chief," Maria offered.

"Oh? Why?" She had piqued his interest.

"She was standing at Powders desk when I came in–talking and laughing like they were buddies from way back. She totally fuckin' ignored me. I mean for Christ's sake, she seemed almost human last night, on the verge of tears over Tina. What the hell is going on with that woman?"

Joe looked concerned, shaking his head. "I don't know, but I don't like it. Something seems odd."

"What do you mean?"

"Well, maybe I've been living with *you* too long." He grinned at his wife. "Maybe, she's just acting like his buddy, so she can get close and slam him."

"*Hmm*. Okay, but I know that's not what you were going to say."

Joe just looked at her.

"Spill it, mister."

"Maria–"

"Spill it!" She smiled to soften her demand.

"Well, it's just a thought now, so please don't read too much into it, okay?"

"Yeah, yeah, yeah, talk about beating around the bush."

"Sometimes I think she's hiding something...something sinister...corrupt. I don't know. I've caught her in situations where she scrambles to cover up whatever she's doing."

Maria frowned, leaning closer and lowering her voice to a mere whisper. "What was she doing?"

"Oh, just on the phone or going through files. Which in itself is not suspicious, but the way she'd act when I came upon her is what caused suspicion. Like I say, maybe it's nothing. I just find her behavior odd sometimes, that's all. And when you told me about the Tom thing...well." Joe stopped. The look in Maria's eyes told him to shut-up.

Maria had peeked her head out in the main office and saw the chief approaching.

"Well, well, well–what do we have here? Meeting of the minds?" The chief looked from one to the other, as she approached the fax machine.

Maria grabbed a stack of paper someone had mislaid. "Nope,

just making copies. The damn machine was acting up again. Joe fixed it."

"Well. Way to go, Joe." The chief turned her back to them, fed paper into the fax machine and waited for an incoming report. Glancing over her shoulder, she added, "Well, I can certainly think of better places to converse than right here. Okay?"

"Yes, ma'am." They quickly left, passing Powders' empty desk on the way to their own. The screen-saver displayed on his PC and a stack of files teetered on the corner with a half-eaten powdered-sugar donut balancing on top.

Maria shook her head. "Wonder where the heck he is now–probably on a *special* errand for the chief."

"Who knows."

Maria looked at her husband. "Don't worry–I'll let it go. For now."

"Yeah, for now. That's what I worry about–for now."

Maria grinned. "Let's get to work."

Chapter 37

Lizzy finally found the bathroom. She was getting worried. She had to pee really bad–the cranberry juice and vodka had built to a crescendo. Even the bathroom was gorgeous. A pale mauve marble floor, with matching pedestal sink, and a claw foot bathtub. *Oh, to take a bath in here...bubbles up to my neck.*

Standing in only a T-shirt and panties, she looked into the mirror, then closed her eyes. *I am Lizzy. I am a runaway. I am desperate. I would do anything for money.* She opened her eyes, gazed deeply into her soul. *I am Etina. I will do anything to bring down the Family and get results. Anything.*

She shook her head, coming out of her reverie. Washing her hands, she splashed cool water on her face, then returned to the living room.

Dawn was just beginning to break. She stood for a moment by the window, looking out on the sleeping world. She wondered what her friends in New York were doing. She couldn't tell them the truth–had only mentioned going out of town for a week or two. It was for the best. Who knew if she'd ever return. It was anyone's guess and possibly only up to God.

Etina was spiritual, despite the incredibly awful things she had to do in the line of duty. It became her salvation. Without God in her life, she couldn't do the things she needed to do in order to get results. Drugs, sex, undesirable actions were required sometimes to complete her job. She wondered what would be taken into account when she met her maker. Possibly a one-way ticket down below–a risk she knowingly took–the highest possible cost.

She turned, intent on climbing back into her bed and dozing for another hour or two. Stephen stood behind her, a short distance away. She jumped a little, startled.

He took in the sight before him. She was beautiful–short platinum blonde hair, heart-shaped face, pale and thin but shapely legs, perky breasts with nipples erect.

"Sorry, didn't mean to scare you. I heard you moving around

in here and realized I never showed you where the bathroom was." Clad only in boxers, his long blonde hair tangled around his rugged, handsome face. Muscular arms crossed his bare chest. Steve felt slightly uncomfortable with his lack of clothing as he watched her take in his body. *I've never been shy a day in my life. How odd.*

Lizzy's breath stayed caught in her throat, as her eyes took in the beautiful man standing before her. "I-I found it...the bathroom," she stammered. Taking a much-needed breath, she added, "Sorry if I woke you."

"Nah, you didn't wake me. I always wake up at this time."

Lizzy smiled. "Me, too. Internal alarm clock."

Steve grinned. "Do you drink coffee?"

Lizzy lied. "Sometimes. I'm getting used to it–let's put it that way." In reality, she'd grown up on it, but most kids in America didn't like the bitter taste and she had to think like a kid, not an adult.

"I have sugar. I'll make a pot of my favorite–hazelnut."

"*Hmm*, sounds interesting." Lizzy followed him into the kitchen, and watched him pour beans into an electric grinder.

"I hope Tiara is a sound sleeper." He grimaced, and pushed down the lever to engage the grinding action. Measuring water, he carefully poured it into the reservoir and flipped the switch. "There, we'll be good to go in about ten minutes."

They sat on Lizzy's makeshift bed and talked while the coffee brewed. Steve told of growing up in California. He talked a little about his family–about an older brother no longer with him, who he missed very much. He talked briefly about Marco Santini. She got the impression his relationship with Marco was tenuous at best. He never asked about her life, for which she felt extremely grateful. She hated to lie even though it was an integral part of her job to do so. He probably figured many runaways didn't want to discuss their past–that's what they were running away from.

Steve wondered when he should make his move on this beautiful girl. He was falling for her and hoped she felt the same way. He thought she did. He excused himself for a moment, and returned with a tray and two cups of steaming aromatic brew, complete with cream and sugar.

Lizzy normally took her coffee black, but went through the motions of doctoring it up properly with cream and sugar, as any teenager would do.

Steve turned the stereo on low, and they resumed conversation, sipping coffee and softly laughing. He slipped an arm behind her and felt her soft hair tickle the back of his hand.

"Can I ask you something? You don't need to answer if you don't want to?" She hoped she sounded innocent enough. "What do you do for a living?"

Steve looked at her, a smile on his handsome face.

"I mean, look at your apartment. You must have a good job."

Steve laughed. "Yeah, you could say that, babe."

Lizzy returned the smile. She liked it that he called her babe. She looked at him questioningly.

"*Hmm*, let's see–how do I answer that. I wouldn't say it's really a job. More an investment. An adventure."

"An investment? Like in property?"

"Yeah, something like that. Real estate, let's say." That's all the girl needed to know. "You know what they say?"

Lizzy looked at him, eyes wide. "What?"

"Curiosity killed the cat."

Now he showed a side that was a little frightening. She knew he had to have one. "Okay. I get it." Lizzy looked away.

"Hey, I'm kidding." The hand being tickled by her hair, rubbed her neck softly.

A shiver raced through her involuntarily.

He noticed. "Are you cold?"

"Maybe a little."

Steve flung the blankets over their bare legs. He wrapped his muscular arms around her, enveloping her in a hug. "I've wanted to do this since the moment I laid eyes on you." He lowered his mouth to hers, exploring and tasting.

Lizzy felt a stirring inside, as his warm lips touched hers. She parted her mouth slightly for him to enter. What started out as a soft kiss, soon became passionate. She wrapped her arms around his neck and pulled him closer.

He stopped for a moment, looking at her and letting out a groan. "Oh, man. I'm in trouble."

Lizzy put a finger to his full lips and shook her head, then laced her fingers around his neck and pulled him to her. She felt something akin to love for this man, if that was possible. Her feelings confused her, and could definitely prove to be dangerous.

Chapter 38

Tiny Tim wasn't prepared to deal with this shit. *Fuckin' Kath. Fuckin' doper.* The stupid chick never knew when to stop. Now he had a possible mother-fuckin' OD on his hands and where the fuck was Nick? They'd been up all night partying, well, for most of the night, anyway. Tiny fell asleep and Kath just kept on going.

Tiny was beside himself. Dani and Shawna were no fucking help. Beth had left–said something about going back home.

He thought of Lizzy often–the cute little blonde, just his size. And of course T. He missed her and her smart-ass black girl comeback lines. He wondered how they were doing in California. He wished they were here to help him right now.

He stood Kath up, which wasn't easy, considering she was bigger than him–both height and weight wise. "C'mon Kath. Walk girl. Walk. That's it, you can do it." She stumbled along with him. He had given her cold coffee earlier–cup after cup. It looked like she had wet herself. He didn't give a shit, and wasn't about to go change her. He would have pawned her off on the young ones, but Shawna and Dani were in wasteland, too. They all were. *Except for Nick. And where the fuck was he?*

He dragged the girl around the living room to the beat of Van Morrison–Moon Dance. *How appropriate.* She seemed to be perking up a bit. "Can I just have one more moon dance with you, my love," Tiny sang along with the stereo. They waltzed around the living room. He dropped her only once. She moaned and cussed at him. *A good sign.*

When the song finished, Tiny poured more cold coffee down Kath's throat and propped her up on the couch next to Dani and Shawna. "Now, watch her you two. Understand?" He grabbed their chins, saying again, "Understand?"

"Yeah," they said in unison, pulling away from him.

Kath passed out again. At least she was breathing.

"Try to keep her awake if you can." Tiny walked into the kitchen.

"Yeah, right," Dani said looking at Shawna. Both girls giggled, not knowing how to take care of themselves, let alone someone else.

Tiny picked up the telephone and dialed Nick's cell. He should have been back by now. He was delivering a considerable amount of H to one of their best sellers. He'd left more than two hours ago. Tiny hoped nothing had gone wrong. He didn't want to deal with the fall-out all alone, or worse, with two babies and an overdosed runaway. He started to freak.

No answer. He left another message. "Fuckin' Nick," he said aloud, slamming down the receiver. "Sonofabitch."

Dani had lightly slapped the older girl's face a couple of times when her head tilted their way. She looked funny and had drool coming from one corner of her mouth. When Kath started dry heaving, the girls called for Tiny.

"Oh for fuck's sake. What the fuck now?" He grabbed a towel and placed it on the sick girl's lap. "What are we gonna do?" he asked the babies.

They just looked at him, glassy eyed.

"You're no bloody help, are ya? I guess I'm on my own with this one." He didn't want another dead runaway. Steve warned him if it happened again, it might be the last time.

He grabbed Kathy's coat and bent her arms to get them into the sleeves. "We're going bye-bye, girlfriend," he said. He struggled to get the damn coat on.

Dani laughed and Tiny backhanded her. Laughter turned to tears.

"Shut-up. Both of you. Sit there and don't move. I shall return."

With that, he left, half-dragging, half-carrying Kath out the door. *Maneuvering steps should prove to be a challenge.* He shut the door, and locked up behind him, contemplating the stairs.

They had definitely reached a pinnacle in the case, although a small one. The day began tenuous at best, with nothing but negatives surrounding the detectives.

The Minneapolis Police Department received a phone call mid-morning from Hennepin County Medical Center. A teenage girl, reported missing almost a month ago, had been dropped off in the ER. Staff had found her passed out in one of the chairs. It was questionable if she'd make it until evening.

On a positive note, the wooden bead found at the Bauer crime scene appeared to be part of a necklace. Several strands of hemp rope found inside the bead, had been traced to a local shop that dealt in hemp clothing and jewelry. The store had received ten necklaces, and with six still on the shelf; they only had four purchases to track down.

BCA Agent Foley offered to follow up with the store clerk. He'd been in an odd mood since he found out Etina had made it safely to California. He knew she could do it. Knew she could do anything. She was really truly *all that*.

Maria and Joe were in constant contact with the hospital. If the girl woke, they would be notified. It didn't look good. She remained in guarded condition, and there had been no improvement so far. They planned to visit later in the afternoon. The parents hovered at her bedside.

Peter Slade contacted Homicide when he made it back to Washington, D.C. He reported the California agents were closely watching Vincent Micelli. Vinny was a possible candidate for a wire. It depended on what they could use and make stick to get the fucker to do what they wanted. So far, they were working on intuition and hunches.

Chapter 39

Marco thought he would pay his friend a surprise visit. It was a rare occasion when he did. He awoke earlier than usual feeling especially *alive*.

He telephoned Stephen, about ten minutes from his apartment.

Steve stepped out of the shower. Lizzy still lay sleeping in his bed. She was amazing. The best sex he ever had, but he wouldn't tell her that. Not yet anyway. His cell was singing in the bedroom. Wrapping a towel around his waist, he got to it before voicemail kicked in. "Yes."

Marco grinned into the phone. "Stephen, hope I did not wake you."

"No, man, you're up early," he said, checking his watch on the bedside table.

Lizzy rose up on one elbow, yawning and stretching.

The sheet fell to her waist and Steve lost his thoughts. "What's that?"

Marco repeated he was about five minutes away from his door.

Steve slammed his phone down on the bedside table. "Shit, get dressed. The Boss is coming…in a few minutes."

Lizzy scrambled out of bed and slipped on her T-shirt, hunting for her panties. Finding them buried under the quilt, she wondered where her jeans were. *Living room.*

She ran into the main room, found them folded neatly, exactly where she'd left them last night. She slipped into them, just as Tiara came down from the loft, clad only in a thin white T-shirt and bright hot pink panties.

"Mornin', sunshine," Tiara called as she made her way down. "So, how was your night?"

Lizzy blushed. "Hey, girlfriend–I'd love to tell you all about it, but you may want to get dressed–"

The doorbell rang. "Goddamnit," Steve said, zipping up his pants. "Sorry, girls. Can't keep the man waiting." And he couldn't. There was nothing Marco Santini hated more than waiting. It would surely put him in a sour mood and Steve didn't want that, considering things were a little crazy right now anyway. He wished he could've smoked a joint before having to deal with the little fucker.

The doorbell rang again.

Tiara had just reached the bottom rung and considered scooting back up, but realized she'd be caught halfway. She self-consciously tried, to no avail, stretching her T-shirt longer as Steve opened the door.

In walked Marco Santini.

Marco first noticed the darling little blonde cleaning up. She was adorable. Then his gaze fell on the most gorgeous chocolate covered creature he'd ever laid eyes on. She stood by the wooden ladder leading up to the loft, clad in a thin white T-shirt, her darkened nipples showing through easily. But what got him right where it counted was the panties–hot pink silky panties. The bright color next to her dark, smooth skin drew his attention and he couldn't look away.

Tiara smiled at him, a twinkle in her eye.

Lizzy noticed the exchange and worried. T had no idea what she was getting into. Lizzy shot the girl a warning glance.

Tiara saw it, but chose to ignore it. "Hello there," she said instead.

Marco smiled, seemingly in a trance as he approached. He took her hand and kissed it softly.

Steve introduced them. "Marco, meet Tiara."

Marco still held her hand. "Beautiful...my pleasure."

Tiara looked down at the man–he was considerably shorter. She felt like an Amazon.

Lizzy joined the group when Steve motioned her over.

Steve placed his arm around her narrow shoulders. "And this is Lizzy."

Marco came out of his reverie, released the black girl's hand, and turned his attention to the little blonde. "Lizzy, nice to meet you." He reached for her hand, which she reluctantly offered.

Steve cleared his throat. "So...wow, man, what a surprise. I planned on coming in to the office today." Steve became nervous having the man on his home turf. He could count on one hand the number of times Marco had come over.

Marco laughed. "Perhaps I shall visit more often. I never realized you were hiding such lovely things from me."

"Not hiding, just got home." Steve rubbed his whiskered face, wishing he'd had time to shave.

"I know, I know. So, where is the...stuff?"

"You girls wait here, okay?" He led Marco into the kitchen, opening the pantry for him to see.

"You unpacked it." Marco ran his manicured fingers over the stacks of heroin.

"Yeah...last night. Took up too much space."

"Where are the hollowed out textbooks?"

"In my bedroom closet. I'll burn them tonight in the fireplace."

"No mistakes, Stephen. We made it this far." Marco frowned at his friend.

"No shit. Don't worry." Steve looked at the smaller man. "I will burn them tonight. I would've last night, but it got too late."

"I understand."

"I'll bring the shit to Louie this afternoon for distribution to the street vendors."

Marco checked his Rolex. "Already taken care of."

"What do you mean?" He didn't like this. He was in charge of the H.

"Do not worry. I do not mean to step on your toes, my friend. I am only trying to be of assistance. Louie will be here in twenty minutes to pick up the goods. I figured you had your hands full...what with the girls and everything."

"Louie?" Fuckin' Marco always had a way of making perfect sense, but it still pissed him off. Steve scratched his head. "Whatever, man."

"You have been a very busy man, no?" Marco looked at Stephen, begging him to disagree.

"Yes, Marco. Very busy. Jet-lag big time," he offered.

"See? I am only trying to help." Marco patted his back in a friendly gesture. "Now, what about the girls?"

Steve looked at him cautiously. "What about them?"

"Are you taking them to Darcy today?"

Steve seemed to contemplate the idea, although he had

already decided. "Ya know...since it's almost New Year's Eve it'll be crazy over there. You know how Darcy goes all out for the holidays. I think I'll just let them crash here for a couple of days, let 'em get used to the climate so to speak...for a while."

Marco laughed, stroking his mustache.

"What? What's so damn funny?" Steve grinned, too.

"Careful. Don't let pussy think for you." He still smiled. "Perhaps I'll join you to ring in the New Year this year."

The doorbell rang, as Steve registered what the other man had just offered. He wasn't sure if it was good or bad.

Chapter 40

"Louie...come on in." The girls were up in the loft, giggling, thankfully. *Keep them as far away from this shit as possible.* "Where's Vinny?"

"Don't know...haven't seen him yet today." Louie followed the under-boss into the kitchen. "Nice place ya got here."

"Thanks." Steve wasn't happy. He didn't like anyone to know where he lived. Not good for his health in this business.

"Marco! Didn't know you'd be here." Louie hugged the man.

"I just wanted to make sure things went smoothly. We had some problems earlier." Marco smiled charmingly.

Louie set the duffel bag down, unzipped it, and spread it wide. "Big enough?"

Steve eyed the bag. "Yeah...think so. Don't make no stops in between."

"Hey, not to worry. Done this many times." Louie looked to Marco for affirmation.

"Yes, Louie can be trusted. Not to worry."

They filled the bag with all but one block of the heroin. There was room for a T-shirt and a towel placed over the top. Perfect.

Marco escorted Louie outside to his car, and watched him drive away. Returning inside, he sat at the table opposite Stephen. "Good job. I mean that. I know you had some issues from early on. You deserve something extra, which is why I will look the other way while you have your fun with the little blonde."

Steve frowned, but kept his mouth shut.

"Personally, I like her friend better." Marco smoothed his well-trimmed whiskers, smiling. He slipped his hand into an inside pocket and pulled out an envelope, then slid it toward Stephen.

"What's this?" Steve opened the envelope, fanning many hundred-dollar bills.

"Just a little something extra. I wanted to show my

appreciation. You can have most of the block, too," he offered, referring to the block of heroin he'd removed from the stack before packing it.

"Thanks," Steve said, setting down the envelope. "I don't need that much H, though. I only *smoke* it occasionally. I'd feel uncomfortable with that much."

"Fine. I'll take most of it with me–keep it in the safe."

"There ya go. That way we can get to it if we need to. Hey, I asked Louie about Vinny. He said he hadn't talked to him for a while."

Marco smiled. "Didn't I tell you? Vinny and I had a little chat." He pursed his full lips and frowned, shaking his head. "I don't know…I think perhaps, I may have gotten through to him."

"I find it hard to believe you didn't take him out," Steve said, cocking an eyebrow.

"So do I. Maybe I'm getting soft in my old age, huh?"

Steve looked at the other man, and said nothing. He knew there was nothing further from the truth and wondered just what *special lesson* Marco had in store for Vinny Micelli.

Vinny knew he took his life into his own hands by meeting Anthony Rossi. He was in way over his head, not sure where to turn for help. Fuckin' cops were definitely *not* the answer. He'd be a dead man going that route. But as it stood, he'd be a dead man if he stayed in his current situation. Anthony Rossi was a long-time rival of the Santini family. The families had fought for control over the Los Angeles drug traffic for more than a decade.

The bar was empty, save for a man chatting with the bartender when he arrived.

They both looked up when Vinny walked in, and the man yakking it up, rose reluctantly to his feet. He towered over Vinny by about ten inches. "Micelli?"

Vinny nodded.

"This way." The large man strode to the rear and down a darkened hallway, with Vinny following. They came to a closed door. The man knocked, opened it, and stepped inside, motioning for Vinny to wait.

While he waited, Vinny wondered what the fuck he was doing here. *Is this a mistake? Too late now.*

The large man stuck his head out. "Boss will see ya now."

Vinny entered the small smoke-filled room, his heart hammering in his chest. Behind him, he heard the large man leave and the soft thud of the door closing.

Anthony Rossi sat, immersed in paperwork, fat cigar always a permanent fixture in his mouth. He was in his mid-fifties, overweight–almost to the point of obesity. He looked up from the mountain of paperwork, squinting through a stream of smoke rising from the large stogie. "Micelli, right?"

Vinny nodded, and extended his hand. "Mr. Rossi, sir."

"Have a seat," Anthony Rossi croaked.

Vinny took the proffered chair and wondered again what the hell he was doing here. What did he hope to accomplish? Could this man give him the protection he needed or was this just another mistake, possibly his last?

"What can I do for ya?" Rossi reluctantly removed the cigar and placed it in the ashtray, then gazed across the large desk at the other man.

Vinny Micelli had rehearsed what he'd say in his head, but now drew a blank. "Um...well...not sure where to even begin, to tell ya the truth."

Anthony Rossi just looked at him, waiting. He didn't have all fuckin' day. Micelli appeared nervous, scared. He could smell the man's fear. "You work for Marco Santini, right?" He thought this might help get the conversation flowing.

Vinny nodded. "Yeah, that's part of the problem I guess you could say. Man, that fucker...he's a loose cannon." He wrung his hands together, feeling his armpits drip with perspiration. *Man, this is hard.*

"Yeah, that he is. He's a man without a conscience and that's what makes him unpredictable."

"Well, I know I'm in trouble–on a sort of probation I think. I wasn't included in the H shipment that just came in. Wouldn't have even known about it if not for Louie."

Anthony Rossi lit a fresh stogie, thinking. He'd heard the talk on the street. *There was a trust issue involved here...ol' Vinny had too much of a conscience, rumor had it. Associated himself real close with a fuckin' undercover narc, for fuck's sake.*

Vinny waited, not sure what else to say.

"Tell ya what." Rossi blew a cloud of blue smoke over their heads. "I got a job you could help me out with. It would benefit both of us and possibly give you some satisfaction at one-upping Santini."

Vinny smiled, liking the sound of it already. "What?"

"You said Louie was dropping off some H? How much?"

"A lot by the sound of it. Louie left a message on my cell. Said something about a large duffel bag full of blocks."

Anthony Rossi grinned. "Perfect. I know who he'll be delivering to, and as luck would have it, he owes me...big." *I'll buy half of the shit and cut it, then resell. Make considerable cash on Santini's deal. The little fucker thinks he can rule the roost in everything–thinks he owns L.A. Has the market on the three main profits–drugs, credit card fraud and prostitution.* Rossi's grin got bigger. *This'll be fun.*

Vinny breathed a sigh of relief. Maybe for once in his miserable life he had made the right decision. This would be easy. Shit, he was already acquainted with the street vendors who distributed the dope.

Anthony Rossi explained what Vinny needed to do in order to ingratiate himself with him and his people. He didn't trust this frightened man–fear made a person weak–but he'd use him for a while. He'd play it by ear. Hopefully gain further insight into the Santini organization. And if it didn't work out, the hit would be easy enough, the blame placed where it belonged–back on Santini.

Vinny left with a fistful of cash. His escort took him all the way to the door leading outside.

"Thanks for coming," the large man said, smiling, as he held the door wide.

Vinny wondered if the guy had listened to every word they said.

Two agents in a surveillance van watched Vincent Micelli exit the bar on Sunset Strip. Vinny paused, looking up at the sky, and grinned broadly before climbing into his vehicle.

"Someone seems a little lighter on his feet than when he arrived."

"Yeah, must've gotten good news, huh?"

The agents pulled out a couple minutes after Micelli, staying back far enough not to cause suspicion. The thug wasn't going anywhere without them knowing about it anyway. The tracking device placed on his vehicle's undercarriage took care of that.

Chapter 41

Marco stopped to talk to the beautiful black girl before leaving. She waited for him. She wanted him. He could tell. Her nipples stood to attention as they spoke. He could not take his eyes off her. She was gorgeous.

Lizzy watched the body language between Tiara and Marco Santini with mounting concern. She tried to tune in to what he said. Something about New Years Eve tomorrow night. Tiara had stars in her eyes.

Lizzy was shocked when Marco leaned forward, stretching, and T bent down to offer him a kiss. Not passionate, but a kiss nonetheless.

She tried to appear busy when Marco passed by, on his way out, but he didn't miss a beat.

"Good-bye, Lizzy. Lovely meeting you."

"Likewise," she said politely, feeling shivers race down her spine. She smiled shyly.

Marco smiled. "Beautiful girls." He gave Stephen an approving nod, adding "Tomorrow," and departed.

Steve had some errands to run, and left shortly after Marco, leaving Tiara and Lizzy alone in the apartment. He had the hot-tub running and told them to make themselves at home.

As Lizzy lowered her body into the hot bubbling water, she watched Tiara, who was in her own world, eyes closed, deep in thought. T had a look of satisfaction on her face. Lizzy let out her breath and immersed herself up to her chin.

Tiara opened one eye and smiled. "Sweet, huh?"

"Yeah, sweet."

"I wonder how the girls are doin'."

Lizzy's thoughts lingered on Beth and Kath as well. "I don't know, I worry."

"Yeah, me too. Wish they coulda come with."

"Maybe they're better off where they are." Lizzy closed her eyes, thinking. She hoped Beth went back home as she'd suggested. As for Kath–she had a bad feeling in the pit of her guts. Kath and heroin didn't mix.

"Why do you say that? I think we're doin' pretty fuckin' good, girlfriend."

Lizzy opened one eye. "Careful what you wish for."

Tiara looked at the other girl. "You should talk. I know you fucked Steve last night."

Lizzy felt her stomach lurch. "I recall you telling me to."

"Since when do you listen to me?" Tiara countered.

"I do listen to you, T." Lizzy sat upright. "And I want you to listen to me right now, okay?"

Tiara met her friend's passionate gaze. "Okay," she said softly.

"Marco Santini is no one to fuck around with. He is a very dangerous man, Tiara. You have no idea."

The tough side of Tiara bristled. *How dare this little nothing of a girl try to scare me.* She saw the brass ring and she was gonna grab it. "And how do you know?" she asked.

Lizzy looked away. "Stephen," was all she said.

Tiara studied her, squinting through the steam. "I'll be careful. He likes me. He's rich...can give me what I deserve."

"Or more than you bargained for."

"Ya know, I could give you the same advice. Do you really think Steve is any better? They're partners for Christ's sake. I think we're both makin' the right moves."

How could Lizzy argue and not sound like a hypocrite, as well as cause suspicion? "Just be careful. I will too."

"Deal. We'll cover each other's ass." Tiara held out her hand.

Lizzy reached across and grabbed Tiara's hand, squeezing it. "Deal."

The contrast of colors–black and white wet glistening skin–made both girls smile. They needed each other.

Chapter 42

Maria and Joe entered HCMC, a dismal outlook surrounding their presence.

The hospital had telephoned the police department twenty minutes ago. Kathy Spencer had deteriorated even further. She wasn't going to make it. They also reported another girl in the waiting room asking questions about the Spencer girl.

Maria went to the nurses' station, while Joe scanned the waiting room, looking for the other girl. It was a hectic afternoon and the hospital appeared short staffed. Maria waited for five minutes before the harried receptionist acknowledged her.

Joe joined her side. "No sign of the other girl."

"Shit. Figures."

After showing proper identification, they were given Kathy Spencer's room number. They had a chance to speak with the admitting nurse who had discovered Kathy in the waiting room. No one had seen who dropped her off, which was their first question. At that time of the morning, the waiting room had been empty.

The girl's condition had been downgraded further, and only immediate family members were allowed to see her. They asked the nurse about the other girl who inquired about Kathy's condition. She sent them back to the receptionist.

"Oh, let's see." The receptionist scratched her head. "I've seen so many people already today. She was average height, I'd say, a little chunky. Brown hair. Kinda long, mousy." She shrugged her shoulders, looking at Maria and Joe.

"What was she wearing?" Maria asked.

"Blue jeans I think...and she had a pink coat on. Yes, I remember that–a pink jacket." She smiled at them, then turned her attention to a new arrival.

Maria and Joe rode the elevator up to Kathy Spencer's room in Intensive Care. They waited outside the door while the doctor tended to his patient. A man and woman in their mid-forties clutched each other, gazing down at their daughter.

As the doctor exited, a look of defeat on his face, Joe stopped him, flashed his badge. "Hey, Doc. Minneapolis Police Department. Can we have a minute of your time?"

"Sure." The young doctor turned his attention to him.

"How long does she have?"

"Not long. We've done everything we can. Her organs are shutting down."

"Has she woken up at all? Said anything?"

The doctor shook his head. "No. She's been comatose since she arrived. We've stabilized her, but once the organs start going, there is nothing more to do. The heroin has already won. She never had a chance. Sad."

Maria thought her job was rough at times. *It can always be worse. How do you leave the senseless death of a young girl at the office when you go home at night? Sometimes it's hard to turn off.*

They saw no point in invading the Spencer's privacy, and left Intensive Care. They scanned the waiting room again for the brown-haired girl in the pink jacket. Maria checked the women's restroom, but saw no sign of her.

Deep in thought, they entered the parking lot, got into the jeep, and headed back to City Hall. Snow had begun falling and gray skies cast a somber glow on the afternoon. Conversation was sporadic as Joe maneuvered the vehicle through congested traffic.

Chief LaSalle had her head together with the BCA agent when Maria and Joe entered Homicide.

"There you are. How did it go? How's the girl?" Chief LaSalle shot at them, as soon as they entered the room. "Let's go into my office, please."

They filed in after her. Joe shut the door.

"Okay. Let's share." The chief sat down at her desk.

"Kathy Spencer won't make it another twenty-four," Joe offered quietly.

"Shit." The chief popped a piece of nicotine gum into her mouth. "Shit. I'll have to deal with the mayor before he hears it somewhere else." She looked at her audience and realized she said it aloud. *Too much on my fuckin' plate.* She chewed the gum furiously, thinking.

"Well, on a lighter note I have a name to go with the wooden bead found at Stan Bauer's crime scene," Agent Foley said, standing by the window, watching the snow fall in the rapidly darkening sky.

"Really?" Maria asked, impressed. It certainly didn't take long to track down a name.

Agent Foley turned around and faced them, feeling smug. He had lucked out. Out of the four customers who had purchased a necklace, two were female, one was from Wisconsin, and their main suspect–a young male, resided in the heart of the city. The girl at the counter remembered him because he hit on her and told her his name. "Yes, Alex Carlson. He's got a rap sheet. Small-time thug a couple of years back. Looks like he graduated to the big-time."

"Well, let's get on it," Maria said. "Bring him in for questioning."

"Way ahead of you, Sanchez," Agent Foley said snidely. "If we could find him, we would. Seems to have left town."

Maria just looked at the BCA agent and his condescending stare. "Bummer." She glanced at the chief who had begun snapping her gum, which Maria had learned from experience, meant she had something to add.

"Well, we'll find the little fuck–by nook or by crook." LaSalle grinned, feral. "Now...I have news." She looked at each of them. "About Tina."

"Is she okay?" Agent Foley showed his concern for the Russian cop plainly on his face.

"Yes, she's better than okay. She has managed to finagle her way much deeper than we ever dreamed."

"What do you mean?" Maria asked with interest.

"Tina is...*hmm*...how should I say this?" She looked at Agent Foley with something like sympathy, sprinkled with a hint of amusement. "She is *with* the under-boss."

They all took a moment to soak in this information. Maria and Joe understood perfectly.

Foley seemed to be having a difficult time grasping the situation. He paced back and forth the length of the small office, clenching and unclenching his jaw. Finally, he turned to the chief. "*With* the under-boss?"

"Yes. That's all I will say." She smiled. "I think it's

enough." She changed the subject. "Let's keep tabs on this Alex Carlson character. Keep someone watching his place–nab him when he returns."

"*If* he returns," the agent said, looking like he'd lost his best friend.

"Yes, *if* he returns. Give your findings to Maria and Joe. We'll stick someone from Surveillance on his apartment building. Can't hurt."

They filed out of the chief's office, filled with too much information–none of it very useful.

Maria had never liked Agent Foley, but her heart felt for him. He was obviously in a lot of pain. "Ya know," she offered as he hurried past. "It's just part of her job...and she does her job very well."

"Gee, thanks, Sanchez. I'll try to remember that." He shut the door a little too hard, leaving at a brisk pace.

Maria stood there a moment. *I was only trying to help.* Exhaling loudly, she headed toward her desk and the mountain of paperwork that waited. She felt a pair of eyes following her.

Glancing around the office, her gaze came to rest on her ex-partner, who quickly looked away. She studied his profile as he suddenly busied himself with a folder on his desk. *What is your story, Detective Powders?*

Beth emerged from the third floor restroom and checked the hallway for the two cops. She saw the man show his badge to the doctor who took care of Kath. That's when she hid.

Kath was really bad. Dying. *Fucking Tiny Tim.* He knew what she was like. Beth had tried to stop them, but they laughed at her and pushed her away. Told her to go home to Mommy.

That's exactly what she did. Funny thing, her parents never even missed her...or so it seemed. No one was home when she arrived, and the key to the front door that normally hung in the garage, had disappeared.

Beth had nowhere to go, so she rode the bus for most of the night, getting off at a stop near Tiny Tim's apartment.

She was debating between climbing the long metal staircase and going back when the door flew open and Tiny stumbled out, dragging Kath behind him. Beth knew immediately what had happened, and knew where he'd take her. She remembered Melanie, how he had tried to help her, but she died on him. So, he dumped her.

She caught the next bus to HCMC.

Beth cautiously looked up and down the hall–no sign of the cops. She returned to Kathy's room, peeking through the small window. Her mom and dad had left for a little while–probably to get coffee or something.

She quietly opened the door and snuck inside, tiptoeing to the bed and Kathy, who lay motionless under the white blanket.

Hot tears slid down her cheeks, as she collapsed into the chair next to the bed. "Kath," she whispered. "Hang on." She grabbed the lifeless hand of her friend. It felt cool to the touch. She stroked it and put it to her face.

Beth thought of Kath and her outrageous behavior. *Party-girl. Tiara*–everyone–had called her. *Don't know when to just say no.*

Where was Tiara now? And Lizzy? She missed them, and it made her cry even harder, still holding Kath's hand to her face.

Kathy Spencer watched from above her hospital bed. *Poor girl–heartbroken and all alone.* Kathy felt so bad for her friend. She reached out to her.

Beth felt Kathy's hand move, softly squeeze her own. "Kathy? Kath?"

The machine monitoring Kathy's heart abruptly flat lined, sounding an alarm at the nurse's station.

Beth felt the life drain out of her friend, as the hand she held went limp. She muffled a sob that escaped from deep within as she slowly stood, registering what happened.

Stumbling backward out of the hospital room, she ran haphazardly down the hall, almost knocking down a pair of nurses hurrying from the other direction.

They didn't even notice her.

No one ever did.

Tiny Tim was pissed when Nick arrived home mid-afternoon. "Where the fuck have you bloody been?"

Nick threw his leather jacket on a chair, surprised at the attitude. "You know where I've been. Getting the stuff distributed." He took in Tiny's appearance. "What happened to you?"

"What happened to you?" Tiny mocked, pacing the kitchen. "What the fuck *didn't* happen? You were certainly gone long enough."

Nick walked into the living room. Dani and Shawna lay passed out on the couch. He knew Beth had left earlier, upset. *Let's see—who's missing? Where is party-girl?* "Where's Kath?"

Tiny glared at his roommate, ready to slap him despite their size difference. "Kath is in the hospital. Either there or in the bloody morgue." Tiny smiled at the look of shock on Nick's face.

"What happened?"

"Oh, come on now, you bloody well know what happened. She did way too much smack. The shit is *too* fucking good."

Nick shook his head.

"What? Do you think you could've handled her any better? At least I dropped her off in the emergency room this time. *This time we made it.*" Tiny sat down, holding his head. He thought of Mel who had died too soon. He'd had to get the body out of the car. He had totally freaked.

Nick walked into the kitchen, picked up the phone, and dialed.

"Who're you calling?" Tiny called from the living room.

"The hospital. You took her to HCMC, right?"

Tiny Tim flew into the kitchen, ripped the phone out of the larger man's hand, and slammed down the receiver. "You are bloody well *not* calling the fucking hospital. Are you a fucking *moron* or what?"

Nick looked at him as if he was crazy.

"They have caller ID you know. They may be just looking for someone…anyone to tie her to. I guarantee the fucking cops will be looking for someone's neck to put in the noose."

Nick shrugged his shoulders. "Whatever, man." He walked into his bedroom and shut the door.

Tiny Tim joined Dani and Shawna on the couch. "How are my girls doing? Are you hungry?" he asked with fatherly concern.

Chapter 43

Vincent Micelli was ordered to wait until early morning–after bars closed, but well before sunrise–before visiting Jacko, the main dealer, and who Louie would surely visit first. Supposedly, Jacko owed Anthony Rossi a big favor. Vinny didn't want to know what the favor was–the less he knew, the better.

He hoped he'd made the right move. For now, he had to play both sides of the fence, which could be deadly. He popped a couple more antacids into his mouth, on the way back home. His stomach had been nothing but a churning mass of irritable guts the past couple of weeks, ever since he took part in whacking Leo Gianelli. He felt ill just thinking about it. "I'm in the wrong fuckin' business," he said.

Vinny put on the turn signal and took the next exit, not noticing a pale blue van, lagging several cars back, taking the same exit.

The FBI agents planned to set up shop somewhere in the vicinity of Micelli's house. Something big was cooking. Paying a visit to the Santini family's long-time rival wasn't a coincidence.

They slowed and hung back as Micelli made his way through residential streets to his modest home.

Steve didn't exactly check up on Louie. More like following his part of the deal through to the end. He didn't care what Marco said. There was a lot of smack at stake and he went through major bullshit to pick it up.

His mind was set at ease–Louie did, in fact, deliver it. Jacko held all the H–and thought it would all be sold by end of the week.

Not entirely satisfied, he decided to call Minneapolis and check on the situation there. Tiny Tim answered on the first ring, sounding uptight and nervous.

"Hey. It's me. What's wrong?"

Tiny Tim felt his heart lurch to his stomach. "Mr. Freyhoff! What a pleasant surprise," he lied, trying to get his panic under control.

Steve frowned at his cell phone. "So, is everything okay? You sound...strange."

"Oh, sorry, man. Making macaroni and cheese. Wouldn't you know–I didn't put in enough water and burnt the damn noodles." He was so good at lying. Scary.

Steve felt there was more to it, but let it go, instead asking how the H had been moving.

Tiny Tim informed him Nick had taken care of it this morning. He didn't think it necessary to mention the girl in the hospital. If she died, then he would have to tell. Perhaps she'd pull through. He held his tongue for now. He knew to do anything else might end his free ride and his accustomed lifestyle. Tiny wasn't stupid.

Chapter 44

Maria and Joe huddled together, going over the case. After receiving another update from Slade, concerning Vincent Micelli, they filled him in on the Minneapolis side of it, and the BCA agent's smug attitude at uncovering a lead.

Peter laughed. "Ouch, I bet that hurt. I know how you feel about Foley, the cocky little bastard."

"Nah, he's going through his own private pain." Maria filled him in on Tina and the new plan concerning her recent kudos.

"Love sucks," Peter said when she told him of Foley's obvious affection toward the beautiful Russian.

Maria laughed. "Yeah, sometimes it does," she said, looking over at Joe. "And sometimes it is our salvation, the thread that tethers us to the rest of the world."

"Deep, Sanchez." Peter sighed. "Let me talk to Morgan."

She shook her head, and handed the telephone to her husband. He must've mentioned the trip to California, because she heard Joe say L.A. wasn't one of his favorite places.

Tom Powders didn't like being kept out of the loop. Everything was hush-hush. The chief told him not to take it personally. Sanchez and Morgan knew the case better than anyone. That's the *only* reason they were working it together.

He looked over at the bitch. He had her number, as did the chief. Chief LaSalle had told him, 'Tom, I don't like Sanchez. I'd like to see her transfer. Husbands and wives shouldn't be allowed in the same department.' Technically, Joe Morgan wasn't in the same department. His title was Special Investigations, but they worked closely together, so he frequently jumped the fence.

Tom checked his e-mail one last time to see if a response to his last inquiry had come through. Nothing. He'd have to check again as soon as he arrived home. Chief LaSalle had left hours ago. He wanted to keep an eye on the 'Dynamic Duo', but it cut into his drinking time. *Time to call it a day.*

Powering down his PC, he grabbed his coat, slyly watching his archenemies. They'd get their just rewards in good time.

Chapter 45

The hot tub zapped every ounce of strength they had, so Tiara retired to her loft and Lizzy climbed between the sheets in Steve's bed. He had told her that's where she belonged...no more sleeping in the living room.
Once alone, she made a quick phone call to the chief and filled her in. Chief LaSalle was ecstatic, but worried, and cautioned her to tread slowly, to be extremely careful.
Lizzy snuggled down deep into the blankets, feeling completely out of her own skin. She knew where her duties lay, what her job required, but this new intense feeling she felt for Stephen overrode all else. Although she sensed wrongness, a feeling of contentment washed over her every time she thought of him, of the two of them together.
Closing her heavy lids, her breathing evened out and soft slumber took her away from all worries.

Steve was glad to be home and felt satisfied that the deal had been seen through to the end. The heroin was all properly distributed. Cash would start rolling in and everyone would be happy. His thoughts went to the beautiful little blonde who hopefully waited for him. She was almost too good to be true. He half-expected her to be gone when he opened the door.
Locking the car, he made his way into the apartment building thinking the year would end on a positive note. It had been a very successful year for the organization. Very profitable. Tomorrow was New Years Eve. *Marco.* "Shit," he said aloud. He didn't want Marco Santini in his apartment tomorrow evening. Perhaps he'd suggest they go somewhere else–anywhere else.
Retrieving the mail, he took the elevator up to his floor, whistling as he unlocked the door. He pushed the door open.
No sign of the girls. He walked into the kitchen and placed the mail on the counter, then walked into the sunroom where the hot tub was located. They had been in it. Wet towels lay in a heap. He made his way back through the living room, then stuck

his head into the bathroom. Empty.

Steve removed the holstered gun from his belt and walked into the bedroom, where he found a sleeping angel. He stood over the bed, watching her.

Beautiful girl. Those eyelashes, that face. He found himself smiling. He was falling in love–head over heels in love.

Steve set his gun on the bedside table and disrobed. Quietly, he slipped under the covers next to Lizzy and spooned.

Lizzy shifted slightly, feeling a rush of passion at his closeness, in her half-asleep state. She yawned.

Steve wrapped his arms around her, whispering in her ear. "Oh, baby, I'm really falling for you."

She stuck her butt out and rubbed against him, molding to his body. "Me, too," she whispered, feeling forces inside her tear ever so slightly.

He slowly entered her from behind, deliberately taking his time as their bodies melded as one. Every crash sent her to oblivion, consumed with a passion she'd never felt before. She moaned in pleasure with each thrust, wanting more of the same.

Switching positions, Lizzy straddled him, riding him through wave after wave of ecstasy, until they collapsed with exhaustion.

They fell asleep, still wrapped around one another; her head nestled in his armpit, legs entwined. He softly snored. She felt more content than ever before in her lifetime.

Marco left another message on Micelli's cell phone. The little fuck wasn't answering. Anger coursed through his veins, all consuming. *I should have brought him down.*

It was just a feeling, but feelings such as this had proved successful in the past. *Vinny was up to something.* The man was on borrowed time. Micelli knew it. There was no other reason Marco could think of why his calls were not being returned.

"Perhaps I should pay Vincent a visit," he said aloud. "See first hand what he is up to." If he didn't hear from him in the next twenty-four hours, that's exactly what he'd do.

Chapter 46

Maria and Joe were exhausted, physically and mentally, by the time they finally arrived home. They had received a phone call from HCMC just before leaving Homicide. The Spencer girl had passed away.

As they entered through the garage, Maria noticed Tess' car was gone. "Anyone home?" she called, walking through the house. Tony was in his bedroom, loud music blaring.

Maria knocked on the boy's door, then turned the knob.

The door was locked. She knocked louder, beginning to get mad. "Tony, open the damn door, please."

The kid still didn't hear her. *What the hell...* She walked back into the kitchen, and found Joe standing by the counter, going through today's mail.

"Hey, Tess left a note. She ran to Mike's...left a Spanish–" Joe looked up.

Maria was so mad, she could hardly speak. "Tony."

"What? Isn't he in his room?"

"Well, I don't know. I think so. He's got the door locked and the fuckin' music so loud he doesn't hear me knocking, or doesn't want to."

"We'll see about that." Joe set the mail down and stormed down the hall to their son's bedroom. He knocked loudly. "Tony! Open up!"

Nothing.

Joe looked at his wife from narrowed eyes. "Be right back."

He jogged into the kitchen and retrieved a long narrow screwdriver. Returning, he slipped the pointed end into the center of the lock, then turned the knob.

The door opened to reveal no Tony.

Maria searched under the bed, in the closet. No kid. Then she noticed the screen off the unlocked window.

Joe joined her side. "Should we lock the goddamn window?"

Maria smiled slightly despite her anger. "Now, wouldn't that just burn him?"

"It would force him to come in through the front door," Joe offered, totally serious.

Maria shook her head. "No, let's not play games with him. He might decide to not come home."

"Maria, we have to stand our ground. He's at a very difficult age. We gotta show him who's boss."

Maria disagreed and told him so. She reminded Joe how Tony was different from other boys due to his violent childhood. *Seeing your mother murdered can affect the rest of your life.* At fifteen, Tony appeared to be a normal teenager, but appearances could be deceiving. Especially at this age.

"Well, what do you suggest we do? Wait for him to climb back through the damn window and pretend nothing happened?"

"No. I didn't say—"

At that moment, the window opened and a blue jean clad leg came through, followed by a dark head. Tony looked up, saw his parents, and froze. "Shit," he said.

"Yeah, shit is right," Joe replied.

Tony pulled the rest of his body inside, shut the window, then turned to face his accusers.

Maria kept a check on her anger, with some difficulty. "Well, young man. What do have to say for yourself? Where were you?"

Tony looked from Joe to Maria, down at the floor, then back to Maria. "Stepped out to get some air..." He knew it sounded lame, but wasn't about to tell them what he was really doing.

"To get some air?" Maria asked, shaking her head. "Through the window?"

"You know most people use the door," Joe said. "Are we supposed to accept that as an explanation?"

It sucked having parents who were cops. He hated it on a daily basis. *Fuckin' pigs.* "Okay, I stepped out to have a smoke, okay?"

"You smoke?" Maria asked, surprised. "I've never even smelled cigarettes on you before. My God, Tony!"

"Jeez. Don't stroke out. It's not that big of deal. I didn't want ya to know," Tony offered, looking guilty.

"Don't smoke, kiddo. It's so damn dumb," Joe said. "And even though you think it's cool now, soon you won't be able to quit."

"I know, I know. I don't smoke much. It's just...once in a while." Tony looked lost and alone. He figured he had the look down pat.

Maria hugged him. "We love you, Tony. That's why we care. We love you, okay?"

Tony hugged her back. "I know. Me too. I'm sorry."

Joe hugged the kid as well, patting his back. "Next time use the door, okay?"

Tony just smiled and looked away as his parents left, softly shutting the door on their way out.

He let out the breath he had been holding. *Jeez–gotta be more careful. That was close and didn't I reek? For cops they aren't very smart.* He smiled. He kind of told them the truth. He smoked, but not cigarettes. The special delivery had finally come through a friend of a friend. He had to try the stuff out. He wasn't disappointed, he was wasted.

Tony felt he won round one.

Chapter 47

Vincent Micelli looked at his reflection in the mirror, convinced he was doing the right thing. After his visit with Anthony Rossi, he came home and took a nap, wanting to prepare himself. He wasn't used to carousing around in the wee hours of the morning. Things had to go off without a hitch.

When he picked up his cell to clip to his belt, he noticed two missed calls from Marco. Mustering all the courage he could, Vinny returned the man's call, thanking God he didn't answer. He explained on voicemail how he hadn't been feeling well and had been sleeping, trying to sound convincing.

He slipped on his leather jacket and checked the pocket for his piece, then grabbed the car keys, and headed out the door. He had the wad of cash Anthony Rossi gave him to buy the heroin and a handful of antacids. Everything *had* to go smooth–his life depended on it.

The two FBI agents watched Micelli's garage door open and then his car slowly pull out of the driveway.

"Well well well, odd time to be going anywhere. And away we go," said the agent behind the wheel. He started up the van and pulled out into the street a few minutes after their target left.

The other agent picked up his cell to call yet another FBI agent, who waited for the word. "Hey. He's gone. Safe to go in." He disconnected and gave his partner a thumbs up. Agents were going in to bug Micelli's house.

The driver slowed in order to stay back and not cause suspicion. "Wonder where we're going?" They watched the dancing dot on the video monitor that was Micelli's car.

Vinny popped a couple more antacids to help settle the ham sandwich he'd scarfed down before departing. He'd thought he should have something in his stomach. Now he wished he'd forgone the freakin' sandwich. He burped again, this time tasting bile. "Ooh, man."

He finally reached his destination. Vinny parked outside Jacko's place, sitting for a moment, listening to Red Hot Chili Peppers on the radio. He loved their music. He loved California.

Vinny wanted to get this over with. Anthony Rossi had told him to purchase the H, then sit on it for several hours. At exactly nine o'clock in the morning, he was to return to the bar. Someone would be awaiting his arrival. Probably the same big bruiser.

The song ended. Vinny removed the keys from the ignition, and took a deep breath.

He said a little prayer, entering Jacko's building. He hoped against all odds he would be in and out within a matter of minutes.

Chapter 48

Lizzy opened her eyes in the darkness, confused for a moment. She had no idea where she was. She felt movement next to her and every muscle tensed, then she remembered. *Stephen. What the hell am I doing?* She looked at the clock–3:25 in the morning–and quietly slid out of bed. She slipped on her T-shirt and panties.

She was surprised to find Tiara in the living room, sitting in the dark, her knees tucked under her. A pipe lay in an ashtray on the table next to her.

Lizzy stood for a moment in the darkness, not wanting to startle her friend. She wondered what the girl had been smoking. She got an answer soon enough. She cleared her throat and T's head jerked toward her.

Tiara was wasted and deep in thought, thinking of the future with hope, looking forward to the New Year. Her glassy eyes took in the little blonde standing in the middle of the living room. She smiled. "Liz," she whispered.

"T, what up?" The teen lingo had become second nature. She looked into the other girl's eyes with concern, then pointedly at the pipe on the table.

Tiara looked at her blankly, then patted the seat next to her on the sectional.

Lizzy sat down, looking closely at her friend. Her face was wet, eyes red-rimmed–she'd been crying. "Anything wrong?"

Tiara shook her head. "Not any more, girlfriend."

Lizzy picked up the pipe. "Whatcha smokin'?"

Tiara grinned. "Ahh, just a little weed…a little H."

Lizzy turned to her. "Heroin? Where did you get it? Stephen?"

T laughed softly. "Don't worry, didn't get it from your boyfriend."

Lizzy felt her stomach flip-flop. *Boyfriend. Stephen Freyhoff–my boyfriend.*

"Tiny Tim slipped me a little before we split. I was thinking of the girls...wonder how they're doin'. Kath is probably sleeping with Nick. And Beth..."

"I've been thinking about them, too. Don't worry about Nick. He only has eyes for you. Do you miss him?"

Tiara rubbed her hands over her face. "Yeah, a little." She looked at Lizzy. "Okay, more than a little."

Lizzy put her arm around the girl's shoulders. "You really liked him a lot."

"Yup. A lot." She got a defiant look on her face. The drugs were wearing off, somewhat. "But it's a new day, right?"

"Yes." Lizzy smiled. "Don't smoke no more of that stuff–heroin. Pot's okay, but the H is bad shit."

Tiara frowned and crossed her arms. "I don't need no babysitter. I'm not Kath."

"I know, but you don't know what that stuff can do to you."

"Sounds like ya know from experience," Tiara countered.

"Maybe I do." Lizzy looked directly at the other girl, and told the truth about this one small facet in her life, one that had molded and shaped her into wanting to clean up the streets. "I had a brother who died using the shit."

Tiara leaned forward. "Really?"

Lizzy nodded, thinking of her only sibling with regret. Shortly after their mother was murdered, her brother started using drugs. Her father had never been in the picture, liking vodka and women better than his family and all their issues.

"Sorry." She sighed. "I'm not a user, though."

Lizzy nodded toward the pipe. "Yes, you are."

"That don't count. Smokin' a little don't hurt. It's when you shoot." She picked up the pipe, clutching it in her fist.

Lizzy tried not to sound too motherly. She was supposed to be a teenager, not a twenty-eight year old who'd seen it all. She shrugged her shoulders. "Whatever."

Tiara stood and stretched, yawning. "Think I can sleep now. Burnt out. Later, girlfriend." She headed for the loft and slowly ascended the ladder, almost missing a rung, but recovering.

Lizzy watched her go, thinking about the situation. She was falling in love with a man she needed to take down. Deeply in love, she reminded herself. She shivered involuntarily. She also felt responsible for Tiara's safety, but would have to put it aside if it interfered with her duties. *My duties.* She tried to focus on the reason she was here. There were many bad people in the world. It was her job to eradicate some of them—she owed it to her brother. She didn't want him to have died in vain. It happened years ago, but she remembered everything, every detail. She had been only fifteen years old. He was nineteen. The difficult lesson of what life was really about forced her to make a choice—be strong, or curl up and die. She grew up quickly after that.

So, it didn't matter how she *felt*. It didn't matter if she had finally met the love of her life. *It just didn't matter.* This analogy went against her true belief: Everything matters; it's what makes us who we are. *The trick is, learning not to care so much.* In the end, she knew she would do what was right. She always did.

Chapter 49

Vinny approached the door with trepidation. Jacko was an ex-biker, about 6'6", 350 pounds, nasty scars. A nice enough guy, but his outward appearance was daunting to say the least.

He took another deep breath and pushed the buzzer. Vinny peered at the peephole, knowing he was probably being watched.

A minute later, the door opened and Jacko loomed in the doorway, towering more than a foot over Vinny.

"Vinny! What the fuck? C'mon in, man."

Vinny grinned, hoping for this reception. *So far, so good.* He had to play everything just right. "Jacko, how the hell are ya?"

Jacko shut the door and led the man to the living room, offered him a drink.

Vinny declined the drink, knowing his stomach would not appreciate it, even if his nerves did.

"Hey, I was surprised not to see you with Louie when he made the delivery. You two are usually attached at the fuckin' hip." Jacko grinned, making the puckered scar on his left cheek look like a half-moon, complete with craters.

"Oh, wasn't feelin' good." A rush of panic sliced through him. *Now what? Why would I want to buy H.? I'll say it's for someone else. But where did I get the money? I had the money. I'm not a schlep.* Vincent Micelli answered his own questions, wanting to get this over with. "Feelin' better now and *um...*"

Jacko took a swig off his drink and eyed the smaller man with suspicion. He seemed nervous. "Yeah?" he prompted.

"Well..." Vinny fidgeted. "I wanna buy some back. It's not for me. A friend. A girl."

Jacko grinned. "Ahh, I get it. Got a chick willing to do anything to get her fix? Nothing quite like it, is there?"

Vinny forced a laugh. "And I mean anything. A babe, too."

"Say no more, but I'm surprised you're coming to me. I mean Marco–"

"Marco and I aren't seeing eye to eye these days. You know what he can be like." Vinny closed his mouth, not wanting to reveal too much. When he got nervous, he ran at the mouth.

Jacko looked at him and nodded. "Yeah, Marco can be a real trip. Not someone you want as an enemy. Hey, no questions asked, okay? How much ya want?"

Vinny removed the wad of rolled up bills he got from Rossi and laid it on the coffee table in front of them.

Jacko picked up the money and thumbed through it, calculating in his head, then went to get the heroin.

Vinny waited on the couch, feeling the comforting weight of the gun in his jacket pocket. *Almost done. You're doing fine.*

Jacko returned with the drugs, handing Vinny a sealed package. "This'll do ya. Enjoy."

Vinny unzipped his leather jacket, placed the goods in an inside pocket, then stood a little too quickly. "Thanks, man. I really appreciate this."

"Sure, no problem. Hey, ya don't have to run off right away, do ya?" Jacko genuinely appeared to want his company.

"Sorry, man. Gotta run–you know, pussy awaits." Vinny grinned and headed for the door, anxious for the safety of his car.

"Sure, I understand. Good luck." Jacko let the man out, then picked up the telephone, and dialed.

The other party answered on the first ring.

He told of his unexpected visitor, knowing he'd get flack for not calling while Vinny was there. "Sorry, man. Tried to keep him here." He hung up, thinking, poor stupid bastard.

Jacko knew which side his bread was buttered on. It was necessary to make the call to Stephen. The man had been concerned enough to pay him a visit earlier. There *was* cause for concern.

The FBI agents waited for a bit. They could have taken him right now, but there was no point in alerting Jacko. They had bigger fish to fry. They'd get Micelli on his home turf, convince him to see their side of things. He'd be more than willing to cooperate.

Chapter 50

Tiny Tim couldn't sleep. Worry made him antsy, so he packed up the girls and drove around for a while. Needing answers, he finally sent Dani to check on Kath at HCMC. She came back looking confused.

"She's not here." Danielle said, slipping into the back seat with her friend.

"What do you mean, Dani? She's here. I brought her here. She was very sick." A surge of panic washed over him.

"That's what the nurse told me. She said, she's not here anymore, honey. That's all I can tell ya." Dani shrugged her narrow shoulders.

"Well, bloody hell. What the fuck's going on?" Tiny was starting to worry.

He headed back to the apartment, making a mental note to get the morning paper and check for any dead runaways in the daily news.

Beth still hadn't made it back home. Hanging out at the Block E complex left a little to be desired. The enclosed block of fun included an arcade, a movie theater, ice cream parlor, a dueling piano bar, and a nightclub with a multitude of other specialty shops.

She remembered Kathy telling her she'd been to a Rave party at the nightclub a few weeks ago. She'd met some guy with really good weed, a gram of coke and a really big... She blushed just thinking of how the party-girl talked.

Still, she missed her.

Walking the city streets, she didn't know where to go. It wouldn't be light out for a couple of hours. Visions of Kath in her final moments occupied her brain. Cold, hungry, and lonely, she stood in the doorway of a closed restaurant, arms wrapped around her, the thin pink jacket barely keeping her warm. She didn't want to go back to Tiny Tim's, but didn't want to go home either. *Where to go...where to go?*

A city bus roared by, spitting out diesel fumes that clouded the cold night air. *Wish I was in California with the girls.* She felt a hot tear slide down her cheek. *You're too fat. They don't want you...nobody does.*

She walked toward the shelter of the bus stop, thinking of riding the bus again for a while. At least it was warm.

Tess had fallen asleep at her boyfriend's house. She left him softly snoring, grabbed her Spanish book, and headed home. She slowed down, noticing the girl in the pink jacket waiting at the bus stop. The girl was no more than fifteen or sixteen years old and looked cold.

Picking up her speed, she kept driving, despite wanting to stop to see if the girl needed anything. Her mother always told her she was too kind to perfect strangers—one of these days it would be her undoing.

Tess looked in the rearview mirror. The bus had pulled up and the girl got on. *She'll be fine. Mom will be proud of me when I tell her.* She smiled to herself, hearing her mother's voice of reason. *You can't always be picking up strays, Theresa.* Ever since she was a small child, she had always wanted to help those weaker—whether it be dog, cat, or human.

Theresa's smile quickly faded as thoughts turned again to the girl at the bus stop. *Where was she going and where had she spent the frigid night?* The girl in the pink jacket had looked like a runaway.

Tess pulled into the driveway, and shut off the motor. Looking up at the full moon still visible, she felt a small amount of peace settle over her. The moon had a calming effect...always had. "She'll be okay," she whispered in the frosty air, and walked into the house.

Chapter 51

Vinny had been home for about half an hour. He'd just made a phone call to Anthony Rossi, relaying his success. The boss was mad he had telephoned and woke him up. Vinny thought he'd be doing Rossi a favor by letting him know it's *a go* for later. He poured himself a bowl of Cap'n Crunch and watched an old episode of some long ago cancelled sitcom. *Why do I always fuck up? Destined to be a fuckup.* Crunching resounded in his head as he thought of his many mistakes.

The two FBI agents now had orders to wait until morning *before* Vincent Micelli made the delivery to Mr. Rossi. They'd surprise him–an 8:00 a.m. wake-up call. They planned to bring down Anthony Rossi–one king pin down, one to go. "A good way to end the year," the agent behind the steering wheel offered.
"Not for Anthony Rossi."
They laughed, drank coffee, watched, and waited.

Steve received the phone call from Jacko around four in the morning. He rolled over, expecting to find Lizzy, but found an empty bed. Grabbing the singing cell, he flipped it open. "Yeah." He listened to the fast talking ex-biker.
"Well, why the fuck not?" He listened, frowning. "Okay, okay. I get it. Glad you called." Steve closed the phone, tossed it on the bedside table, and swung his legs off the bed.
"Shit, fuck," he said aloud, slipping on his boxers and a T-shirt. "Fuckin' Vinny Micelli. Marco should've taken him out. I told him."
He walked out into the living room and adjoining kitchen.
Lizzy was making a pot of coffee. She smiled upon seeing him. "I didn't think you'd mind." She stopped, coffee scoop in mid-air, taking in the storm clouds that brewed in her lover's eyes. "What's wrong?"
Steve wrapped his arms around her and breathed in her scent. "Nothing now," he lied. "I woke up and found our bed empty."

Our bed. Lizzy couldn't help but catch the phrase. Standing on tiptoe, she planted a kiss on his rough, unshaven cheek. *Our bed.* Gosh, she liked the sound of that.

"Baby, I think I'm falling in love," he said looking into her eyes. He'd deal with fuckin' Vinny Micelli later.

Lizzy locked eyes with him. "Me, too."

Chapter 52

Alex Carlson looked out the window, hot Miami sun already baking waves into the air above the pool. JJ was still sleeping in the other room. Marco Santini had called them personally. They were to stay put–not go back to Minnesota. The cops were onto him. They'd found *something* at the scene.

Alex scratched his head. "What the fuck?" he asked himself. Marco seemed pissed, but didn't go into detail. Only told him his place in Minneapolis was being watched; he might never be able to go back or else risk jail time.

Money was on the way to pay for expenses–more than enough to make them comfortable. Still, the thought of *never* being able to go back to Minnesota weighed heavily on his mind. He had family there.

Alex thought back to whacking Stan Bauer. He grinned and thought, *snitch got what he deserved*. He turned serious, racking his brain, wondering what he could possibly have left at the scene.

He walked to the closet. Pulling out the jacket and boots he had on the day Bauer was killed, he turned over the boots, inspecting the deeply tracked soles. They appeared relatively clean. He looked inside. Nothing.

Next, he picked up the jacket, checked out the zipper, the pockets. The nylon material slid from his hands and fell to the floor. Picking it up again, he noticed something on the carpet.

Rolling the small wooden bead between two fingers, he was momentarily at a loss where it came from. He checked both pockets again, this time digging deep and came up with several wooden beads from the necklace he'd broken more than a month ago. He remembered tossing it into the trash, but a few stray beads must've remained. "Fuck."

"Hey, man, whatcha doin'?" JJ came out into the main room, rubbing his eyes.

Alex jumped. "Shit, do ya hafta sneak up on a guy?"

JJ barely acknowledged him, going to the mini fridge to retrieve a juice. "Hey, when I got up to take a piss, saw ya on your cell." He uncapped a bottle of orange-pineapple juice and chugged half. "Who were ya talkin' to?"

"Marco."

JJ almost choked. "Santini?"

"Yeah, only Marco I know." He couldn't help but be a smart ass. It was the only way he knew how to cover-up his fuck-up. "We're supposed to stay put. He's sending more cash." Alex looked at his partner and wondered how much he should divulge. *Nothing*, he decided.

"Cool. For how long?" JJ didn't notice Alex had his winter coat out. It was eighty degrees outside.

"Don't know. A while. Cops are thick in Minneapolis."

JJ accepted it, going back to bed, tossing the empty juice bottle into the garbage on the way. He still had at least six more hours of tequila to sleep off if he wanted to party tonight–New Years Eve.

Chapter 53

Maria and Joe slept later than usual.

Maria wanted to go in to Homicide, although it was Saturday and New Years Eve day. She wanted to add more information to the case file and get the ball rolling on the autopsy for Kathy Spencer.

She planned to ask Tess if she wanted to ride along, while Joe hoped to take Tony ice fishing on one of the area lakes. The kid didn't know it yet and probably wouldn't be thrilled, but *he was gonna have fun if it killed him,* as Joe put it.

Maria poured a cup of coffee and stood at the kitchen window, looking out at the snow-covered ground. It was subzero, but the forecasted high was supposed to reach above freezing later today. *Spring thaw.* She shivered involuntarily.

Joe came up behind her, startling her out of her reverie. He slid a hand under her T-shirt, cupped a breast, and kissed her neck. "Happy New Year, baby."

"Happy New Year." Maria turned and kissed him full on the lips, wrapping her arms around his strong neck.

He picked her up off the ground and held her to him, rocking back and forth.

Maria laughed. God, she loved this man. They fit so well together, in every aspect.

"Jeez, you guys," Tess said, coming into the kitchen. She averted her gaze, but smiled.

Maria and Joe disengaged, both grinning.

"I'm simply wishing your mother Happy New Year," Joe offered, looking guilty.

"Wow, so that's how you wish people Happy New Year, huh?"

Maria laughed.

"Not people, only your mom." Joe shook his head, grinning.

"Hey, I'm gonna run to City Hall today. Just need to tie up a couple loose ends. Want to ride along? I'll take you to the new Chinese restaurant."

"Sure, sounds like fun—especially when you throw in one of my favorite restaurants." Tess grabbed a cup, filled it with coffee. "I'll jump in the shower. Be ready to go in...half an hour." She headed for the bathroom.

"Okay," Maria called to her retreating figure, reading Joe's expression before he opened his mouth.

"Half an hour...my ass. That girl has never taken less than an hour to get ready."

She wrapped her arms around his neck again and pressed up against him, moving back and forth in a slow dance. "Guess we have a little time to kill then. *Hmm.* What should we do?"

Chapter 54

Vinny hadn't slept well at all. He sat on the edge of the bed. Morning sun streamed through the bedroom window. He checked the clock on the bedside table. He was due to meet Anthony Rossi in a little more than an hour. His heart did a couple of sick palpitations at the thought. "Oh well, just gotta get it over with," he said. That seemed to be his mantra lately.

Vinny walked into the kitchen, clad only in boxers. Picking up the bag of coffee beans, he decided against it, already feeling his guts start with their daily churn and burn. Instead, he opened the cupboard, retrieved a large bottle of antacids and popped three into his mouth, then headed for the shower.

FBI agents listened to Vincent Micelli come to life, talk to himself and finally head for the shower. Listening devices had been strategically placed in every room, except the basement, so they heard *everything*.

The two agents got out of the van and made their way to the back of Micelli's residence.

Once inside, they patiently waited for Vinny to finish his morning routine. The two agents made themselves comfortable, one stationed on the living room sofa and one in the bedroom.

Vinny stepped out of the shower and toweled dry. Clearing off a steamy spot on the mirror, he squinted at his reflection. He discovered a scared man–deer in the headlights stare–returning his gaze. Taking a deep breath, he told himself everything would be fine. Opening the door, he walked across the hall to his bedroom, to retrieve a clean pair of underwear.

He rifled through the top drawer of his dresser, trying to find a pair of boxers that didn't have shot elastic. He slipped on a relatively new pair.

Vinny had no more than pulled them up to his waist when the man hiding behind the door made himself visible.

"Vincent Micelli. FBI." The man came toward him with a pair of handcuffs.

Vinny felt his heart lurch violently to his stomach, his balls crawled up to his guts. He spun around, staring at the stranger. "What the–"

"Good morning, Vincent." Another man appeared at the bedroom door. "FBI." He showed his badge. "Shall we talk? I'd say it would benefit you greatly if you answered yes."

Vinny looked back and forth between the two agents. "O-okay." He visibly shook. *Fuck, fuck fuck. Now what?*

"You look a little nervous. Perhaps you'd like to have a seat," the first agent said, showing his credentials. "I'm Rudy, this here is Larry." He nodded toward his partner. "We're looking for cooperation, that's all," he offered, placing the handcuffs on the dresser in a show of peace.

Vinny sat on the edge of the bed, focusing on his trembling bony knees. He was scared. Really scared. "Cooperation in what? I don't know nothin' about nothin'."

"Oh, I think you do," Larry countered. "Would you excuse me for a moment, please? There's something I obviously need to prove."

"Certainly," Rudy said smiling, then turned to Vinny. "I'll keep our friend company."

Vinny tried to think, think, think, but couldn't manage to string two coherent thoughts together. Panic turned his blood to ice, made him shake even more.

"A little chilly in here," the FBI agent offered.

Vinny tried to control his internal vibrations, but wasn't having much luck. He knew he looked as frightened as he felt. No more tough-guy persona–too late for that. *I'm in deep shit now.*

The other agent, Larry, returned with Vinny's leather jacket and a frown on his face. "This your jacket, bud?"

Vinny groaned in answer. *Too late.* He was *so* busted. *Fuck.* He'd spend the rest of his miserable life behind bars for all the heroin riding in that fuckin' coat.

"That's what I was afraid of." The agent pulled the substantial package of heroin from the inside pocket.

The other agent eyeballed the package, and shook his head. He looked Vinny in the eye and whistled. "Whew! That's a lot of smack you're carrying around there, son. Enough to *never* see daylight again."

"It ain't mine. It ain't mine. I'm just the fuckin' go-between. Please, man." He started crying.

Vinny would be willing to do anything they wanted. All they had to do was ask.

The agents smiled. Life was good.

Steve wasn't sure what to do. He *had* to tell Marco about Vinny. Something was going on. Jacko's call clinched it. They had to move before it became too late. They had enough on their plates and he hated to add to it, but... Minneapolis seemed the hub of many issues lately. Good thing they sent Alex and JJ south. The cops had found something. He knew it. Marco said things were handled, not to worry. He still worried.

Then there was the frantic message left on his cell from Tiny Tim. Something else had happened in Minneapolis. When he returned the call, no one answered.

He kept telling himself not to panic, but knew what the Boss' reaction would be when he discovered they had a definite turncoat. Marco would go ballistic, make drastic demands, but wouldn't be surprised. He'd had Vinny's number from the beginning. *Drastic times call for drastic measures.* He could already hear the little Italian in his brain.

Lizzy joined him in the living room after she showered and dressed. "I forgot to tell you..." She leaned over and planted a kiss on his lips. "Happy New Year."

Steve grabbed her, bringing her down on his lap. "Jeez. How could I forget? Happy New Year, baby."

"So what are we gonna do tonight?" Lizzy looked at him excitedly.

Steve scratched his head, thinking about the kind of mood Marco would be in by this evening. He had made reservations for a private room at one of the local clubs, which was much better than having the New Years Eve celebration at his apartment. "Party till the cows come home."

Lizzy smiled at the expression. "Sounds like fun."

"Well, as much fun as is allowed considering the company we'll be keeping."

Lizzy raised an eyebrow. "Why?"

"Marco...well, never mind." Steve shrugged his broad shoulders, realizing he didn't need to vent to her about the Boss.

"You don't like him very much do you?"

He looked at her.

"Marco..."

"I know who you're referring to. I wouldn't say I don't like him. I do. Let's just say I respect him more than I like him, if that makes sense."

"Yes, it makes perfect sense. He is your boss, right? That is the smart way to be...how does the saying go? 'Keep your friends close and your enemies closer.'"

He grinned. "Yes, that saying is very apt, concerning Marco Santini. But, in answer to your question. Yes, *we* will have fun. We won't hang out long. Make an appearance, then come back here and celebrate the New Year our own way." Steve wrapped his arms around her and buried his face in her clean hair.

"Well, we should stay a while. We wouldn't want to offend. I take it he is a man who may be easily offended."

Steve laughed. "Oh, man. Is that the understatement of the year. Yeah, guess you could say that."

His cell rang and Steve looked at the ID window, surprised Marco would be up this early. His ears must've been burning. "Shit. Speak of the devil. Literally. I gotta get this, babe." He flipped open his phone. "Steve," he said. Walking out into the misty morning air on the balcony, he shut the glass door, drowning out all conversation to Lizzy's ears.

Lizzy watched the man she loved sit down, place one leg on the chair opposite him. His lips moved, then a stern expression came over his face as he waited for a reaction. He obviously got it. She watched him pull the phone away from his ear, return it, and talk some more.

Steve was on the receiving end of Marco's rant and it wasn't pretty. He'd just told him about Micelli and the purchase of the heroin from Jacko.

Marco finished screaming, and was now laughing.

"What the fuck is so funny?" Steve asked, shaking his head. *What a mind-fuck.*

"Of course." Marco offered an explanation between bouts of laughter. "You know who is behind this, do you not?" He sighed, waiting for Stephen to catch up.

Steve thought about it a minute, then nodded. "Why yes, yes, I do. Now that I think about it. Rossi."

"Very good. You are learning, my friend. Slowly, but surely. Yes, Anthony Rossi thinks he has pulled one over on us." He chuckled. "We will see."

"What about Micelli? Do you want me to make some arrangements for the little fuck to have an accident?"

"No, I want to handle this personally. I will take care of him, once and for all. There will be no body so there will be no questions–or perhaps I should say there will be no answers, therefore no problems. Time to test some other loyalties within the Family as well."

Steve wondered what the hell he had planned, but didn't want to know bad enough to ask. He decided to wait on telling him about more possible problems in Minneapolis. After all, until he talked to Tiny Tim, he was in the dark. No point in adding to Marco's mood. "Are we still on for tonight? The club?"

"Yes. I wouldn't miss it for the world. Bring the chocolate-covered beauty. Good-bye, Stephen." Marco ended the connection.

Steve looked at his phone. "Chocolate-covered beauty." He grinned, then thought of Vincent Micelli and frowned. *The guy will be lucky if he sees the first day of the new year.*

Chapter 55

Maria and Tess stopped at City Hall, rode the elevator up to Homicide. No Tom Powders this time, much to their relief. Maria called the morgue and got one of the assistants. Dr. Lang wasn't around this weekend. The body of Kathy Spencer lay in storage. Maria got the assistant to pencil in an immediate date. She was especially interested in the toxicology reports.

Maria powered up her PC while Tess wandered around the empty office, reading the white board and checking out the small conference rooms down the hall.

She brought up the file on Melanie Davis and the autopsy report. Powders had said it was routine and it appeared to be so. Cocaine overdose. The preliminaries done on the most recent victim, Kathy Spencer pointed to heroin.

It's what they had feared. The failed interception from Tina's lead, slapped them in the face. Somehow, their knowledge had leaked back to the source of the dope, the original flight plan had been altered. Now it was New Years Eve and bad shit circulated the city streets. High-grade heroin. It could prove to be a rough night for Narcotics. There were more officers out in both St. Paul and Minneapolis due to the recent massive influx of drugs...and the holiday.

Maria stared off into space, thoughtfully. *Who in their midst was a traitor of the worst caliber. Nothing stinks worse than a bad cop. Could it be someone not in Homicide, but one of the other divisions? Anything's possible, but who?* She shook her head, coming back to the computer screen.

"Let's cruise, Mom. I'm hungry." Tess appeared at her side.

"Okay, sweetheart. Just give me a minute." She printed off the report and made a note to follow up on the tentative autopsy on the Spencer girl.

Maria had promised to take her daughter to their favorite Chinese restaurant on Nicollet Avenue. It turned out to be a beautiful day on the last day of the year. For once, the weatherman was right. Sunny, pale blue skies made the thirty-degree weather feel like spring.

They drove to the restaurant, passing the bus stop where Tess had seen the girl earlier. "There's quite a few runaways around this area, isn't there?" She told her mother about the girl in the pink jacket. How sad and lonely she looked. "Just kinda lost, you know?"

"Did you say pink jacket?"

Tess nodded. "Yeah, why?"

"Well, a girl in a pink jacket was seen at HCMC inquiring about the latest OD victim. Can you describe anything else about her?"

"Stringy brown hair, average height, slightly overweight. Fifteen, sixteen years old." Tess had an eye for detail much like her mother. She smiled at her mother's look of surprise.

Maria would have the officers patrolling the area tonight keep an eye out. She'd at least like to talk to the girl. Perhaps it was a simple coincidence. There were a lot of girls in pink jackets, but maybe, just maybe....

Chapter 56

Vincent Micelli was ready for his rendezvous with Anthony Rossi. The two FBI agents had him wired, offering a couple tricks to appear calm, cool, and collected. Vinny knew his life depended on it. He would act to the best of his ability.

He had a sick feeling deep inside. His days were numbered anyway–no matter what happened.

He got into his car, buckled up, then pulled out of the driveway. Looking into the rearview mirror, he watched his new friends pull out and follow at a leisurely distance.

Vinny turned onto the street where Rossi's bar resided and his heart trip-hammered at the sick excitement moving him forward.

His cell rang. "What the fuck?" he asked aloud. Looking at the display, he recognized the number–Louie. He flipped open the cell as he slowed, looking for a place to park. "Yeah?"

"Vinny, my man. How the fuck are ya? Long time, no see."

"Hey. How's it going?" Vinny knew his side of the conversation was being recorded and he didn't want to involve his friend. The cops knew nothing about Louie…yet.

"Haven't seen you in forever, man. What the fuck's up? Whatcha doin' tonight for New Years?"

"Um…don't know. Probably just stay home. Watch the ball drop."

"Oh, c'mon, man. Live a little. How about putting a small amount of excitement in your miserable fuckin' life. I'm goin' to a party. I'll swing by, pick ya up."

Vinny couldn't help but laugh just a little. *Excitement.* He had plenty of that lately. "Maybe–I'll see."

"Tell ya what. Meet me at Angelino's around six tonight. We'll hook up, have some good food, maybe a little fun. I won't take no for an answer, and remember you owe me." With that, Louie disconnected.

Vinny closed his phone and parked the car. He did owe Louie. He would've been dead meat several times over if not for him. Louie had lied and given Vinny credit for whacking Gianelli, so Vinny could save face with Marco.

Depending on how things went...If he was still alive and free to walk the streets, perhaps he would meet his friend at their favorite Italian restaurant.

He got out of the car. As instructed, he didn't try to locate the hidden agents. When the deal was done, he had been told to depart as quickly as possible, and return to his residence to wait for further instruction. They assured him for now of his safety.

As expected, the big bruiser, from the previous visit, once again waited.

Vinny thought he handled himself quite well, so far. At least he wasn't shaking like a timid schoolgirl. Get this over with and get the fuck out, he told himself, as he approached the door to Anthony Rossi's office.

The big bruiser knocked and entered, instructing Vinny to wait outside the door once again.

A minute or so later, the guy returned and ushered Micelli inside. Vinny wondered how they would get past the big guy. The element of surprise, no doubt. *God help me through this.*

Anthony Rossi sat at his desk, a large cigar protruding from his mouth, as was customary. "Vinny," he said, talking around the stogie. "Have a seat, have a seat." The older man smiled a sardonic grin.

Vinny sat. "Well, I got the stuff." He unzipped his leather jacket and removed the package, placed it on the man's desk.

Anthony Rossi picked up the package, turned it over in his large, meaty hands, and grinned. "Wait here." He stood and waddled to the door, pausing briefly before opening it to look back at Vinny. He didn't trust him.

He shut the door, and summoned his bodyguard. Passing the package he said, "Check it out, then we take care of our friend."

Vinny felt panic surge through him, yet was too scared to move. *Why did Rossi leave him alone? Where are the agents? What the fuck's going on?* He didn't like this sudden panicky urge to flee. *Something is wrong–terribly wrong.*

He heard a crash outside the office door, followed by loud voices. A gunshot rang out, then another.

Vincent Micelli wet himself.

* * *

Louie paced the small living room. Pissed. "Should've known fuckin' Vinny would get himself in this predicament. Stupid fucker, and now it's up to me to prove myself loyal to the fuckin' Family. This sucks!"

He stopped his pacing for a moment, and looked out the window at the bright sunshine. Such a beautiful day and such a nasty task. Marco wanted no evidence. No body.

That meant it would get messy, but he already had a plan.

Louie had a spare set of keys to his brother's butcher shop. His brother, Russ, had locked himself out once a long time ago, when the wife was off visiting her damn sister, three hundred miles away. Russ had lost major money by being closed on a Saturday. A lot of people wanted fresh meat to grill for picnics or whatever, and the butcher shop was known locally for having some of the best cuts at reasonable prices.

Louie definitely had his work cut out for him. The only thing still unclear to him was what to do with the body once he had it all chopped up. *And the head...*

"Figure it out," he told himself, scratching his own head, thinking. He gathered some large black lawn bags, a pair of rubber gloves, and a rain slicker that came down to his knees, making a small pile in the middle of the living room floor. He wanted to be able to dispose of whatever he wore. *No mistakes. Not even a fuckin' option.*

He dug out an old pair of rubber galoshes from the small storage closet, worried he'd never find them. Moving a large cactus out of his way, he had an epiphany–*the desert.*

He could bury Vinny–or what was left of him–in the fuckin' desert, or some other remote location. There were plenty of places in the hills. He could even scatter him around a bit. "I'm a fuckin' genius," Louie told himself, grinning. He could do this. Yeah, it sucked, and Vinny was a friend, but matters had to be dealt with. He'd been *chosen* to do the task for a reason.

He *had* to succeed. There was no other alternative.

One agent caught a bullet in the leg, and all hell broke loose in the back hallway of the bar. It required three of them to take down the huge bodyguard. He now sat handcuffed in the back of a LAPD cruiser.

Anthony Rossi had put up a good fight, but was no match for men much younger and in better physical condition. He lay sprawled on the floor with a broken nose and black eye, moaning about a lawyer and lawsuits.

"Shut up," one of the agents said, handcuffing the man. He dragged him outside, and struggled to get him into another cop car waiting at the curb.

Rudy and Larry opened the office door and found Vinny still sitting where he'd been told, a wet patch spread across the front of his pants.

"You did good," Rudy whispered, patting Vincent's back.

"I wanna go home. You promised," Micelli pleaded, with tear-filled eyes.

The agents looked at each other. Larry shrugged his shoulders and nodded.

"Okay. But here's what we're gonna do," Rudy offered, pulling handcuffs out of his back pocket.

Vincent Micelli's eyes got huge. *What the fuck?* The agent said something, but he couldn't hear anything past the roar of blood in his ears.

"Vinny? Vinny, can you hear me?" Larry looked concerned.

Vinny tried to focus. The agent named Rudy was telling him to breathe evenly. In, out, in, out. *Okay. I'm gonna be okay.* Rudy told him he was gonna slap the cuffs on him just for show. So no one would think nothin'...for his own good. *Okay.* Vinny nodded and exposed his wrists for the iron bracelets. Hearing the click freaked him out. He couldn't help but wonder if the FBI agents would hold up their end of the bargain.

"Okay, we ready?" Larry led the way out of the bar into the bright California sunshine.

Chapter 57

Tiny Tim ignored the ring of his telephone. He needed to think right now. Kath hadn't made it. The big boys would be pissed. He never should've called and left a message when he freaked out.

Tiny didn't want to lose the trust he'd worked so hard to gain. But, he also knew the time had come when he had to fess up. To get caught in a lie would be worse. Ol' Stevo had pointed that out numerous times. Deceit would not be tolerated.

He decided the next time the phone rang, he would answer it and take his medicine like a real man.

Needing fortification for the evening ahead, he dug out the fix kit and proceeded to cook up a batch. *Happy New Year.* He closed his eyes as he plunged the needle into a vein...taking a ride somewhere over the rainbow.

Beth decided to try going home again. This time her parents were there, actually seemed kind of glad to see her. Her mom even hugged her. Her step dad only smiled, but maybe things weren't so bad here. Kath was dead. What choice did she have? She hated Tiny Tim's without Tiara and Lizzy.

She lay on her bed, thinking. For now, she would stay here, but maybe if things got bad again, she'd catch a bus or hitchhike to California. There are always options. That's one thing she learned on the streets. Life is full of options–and consequence.

Marco Santini sent over expensive dresses and shoes for the girls.

Tiara was ecstatic and already prancing around in a light pink off-the-shoulder satin clingy sheath and matching high heels.

Lizzy smiled at her friend. She looked gorgeous. Her toned light brown skin glowed.

She looked at her own dress. It was beautiful as well, and her style–a simple black, spaghetti-strap. It fit perfectly. She had tried it on, but removed it immediately. Mr. Santini had good taste and seemed to be able to judge a woman—at least her size—quite accurately. 'Remember to watch that man like a hawk,' Maria had told her. 'Makes his uncle look like a lamb,' Joe had added. She looked over at T and frowned. The girl was sucked in by all the material things this man could offer. Young and impressionable, she was an easy target.

How can I let this happen? Wrapping her arms around herself to warm the chill within, she walked to the window and gazed outside. *Because, in order to make a dent in the big picture, sometimes you have to sacrifice.* She remembered the great advice her trainer in Quantico Bay had taught her. She'd used it on many occasions since. *It's not a job for the weak of heart or mind,* he had also said.

"Hey, you okay, girlfriend?" Tiara stood behind her.

"Hey, yeah." Lizzy smiled. "You excited for tonight?"

Tiara laughed. "How can you tell?"

Lizzy glanced at her friend, then turned her gaze back to the window, feeling like a traitor.

"What?"

"Nothing." Lizzy looked briefly at the girl, and lowered her voice. "Just remember what I told you. Be careful."

Tiara shrugged her shoulders. "Don't worry 'bout me. I'll be fine. Been takin' care of myself since I been thirteen years old. Case you haven't noticed—I's a big girl." She grinned.

Lizzy hoped she was right, but had a feeling neither of them had met anyone quite like Marco Santini.

Chapter 58

Vinny finally felt more like his old self. The agents had kept their side of the bargain–he was back home, with Rossi and his thugs behind bars.

In his mind, the worst was over. Even his stomach had calmed down a bit.

He cleaned himself up and changed clothes, throwing the urine soaked pants in the garbage.

Checking the clock, he debated whether he should go to Angelino's Restaurant to meet Louie or just go to bed. "It's New Years Eve," he told himself, feeling he should stay up a while. *Maybe I'll go, eat some pasta, go home early. Shit, don't have to even go to the party.*

Louie had everything packed into the trunk of his car. He sat with the engine running in the parking lot of Angelino's Restaurant, thinking and waiting. Planning.

He didn't have to wait long. Vinny pulled into the parking lot, sliding into the space next to him, looked over, and grinned.

Louie just thought of something he hadn't even considered until now–Vinny's car. What would he do with the car? *Leave it here. What's the difference? We've been seen together a million times.*

Vinny walked over to the driver's side window and watched it slide down halfway.

Louie grinned. "Hey, partner. Wanna cruise to the party?"

Vinny put his hands into his jacket pockets and looked at the darkening sky. "Don't know yet. Maybe. Let's get some chow first–starved."

Louie turned off the car and got out. "Yeah, guess I could eat."

They walked into the restaurant side by side like best friends or brothers.

The soldier Marco requisitioned to tail Louie watched the

two men walk into the restaurant almost holding hands. He lit a cigarette and turned up the radio. He'd wait all night if necessary. He finally had an assignment that was exciting, a way to prove himself. He almost hoped ol' Louie would wimp out, then he could take them both out. Maybe he would anyway.

He almost missed them. They weren't in the restaurant very long. *Must've just had a drink or something.* He watched them get into Louie's car. Crazy Jimmy, as known to his friends, followed at a safe distance, but kept them in his sight.

Where the fuck are they going? Oh well, he had nothing better to do. Just when he thought they'd go another fifty miles, the car ahead slowed, then turned off onto a winding gravel side road.

He followed a good five minutes behind, slowing down considerably then doused his headlights. He didn't want to miss them or scare them off.

Louie had talked Vinny into going to the party—except there wasn't a party. Well, maybe a farewell party. He headed away from the city and outlying residential area.

"Jesus, Lou, where the hell is the party? Fuckin' Nevada?" Vinny cracked the window a bit, feeling a little carsick.

"Whatsa matter? You ain't gonna get carsick on me again are ya?" Christ, this guy was so fuckin' high-maintenance. It wouldn't be the first time he had to pull over when Vinny rode shotgun.

"Nah, I'll be okay. Been a little stressed lately, that's all." He opened the window a little more and breathed the evening air deeply.

Louie looked at his friend of several years. Poor Vinny wasn't cut out for this line of work. He should've had an office job or something equally safe. "What's been goin' on?"

Vinny laughed. "Oh, man. That's a loaded question. You don't wanna know. Believe me, you don't wanna know."

"Try me."

Vinny looked at his friend. And that's what Louie was, a friend. He had helped Vinny out numerous times in the past. Covered his ass. Still, how much could he really trust him? "Let's just say um...I fucked up once again."

Louie shrugged and kept his eyes on the road ahead. "Okay. Well, can't say I'm surprised."

"Hey, thanks a lot, man." Vinny looked out the dark window at the night flying past, and closed his eyes, stomach flip-flopping.

Louie drove, deep in thought. *Fuckin' Vinny was so predictable.* Just as he hoped, the guy felt queasy and now had his eyes shut. Hopefully he'd fall asleep.

His wish was granted. Vinny snored softly.

Louie figured the best bet would be a quick shot to the head. He slowed, then pulled over to the side of the deserted road. No houses, no cars, no nothing. Darkness reigned.

Turning off the engine, he sat for a moment, watching Vinny sleep like a baby.

This was almost *too* easy. He pulled out the gun and put it to his friend's head.

Vinny opened his eyes and looked at Louie, a moment of confusion, then acknowledgement, then resolution crossing his features.

"Get out," Louie croaked.

Vinny just looked at him, eyes becoming saucers in his face. Suddenly he appeared wide awake. "Louie, don't do—"

"Get out of the fucking car. Now!" He pressed the gun against his friend's temple.

Vinny did as he was told, sliding out. Louie pushed him, the gun steady, following close behind.

Standing next to the vehicle on shaky legs, Vinny had to lean on the car for support or he'd fall. Louie was his friend. Had been there for him through so much. How could he do this? "Please, Lou. Let's talk. Please."

"Sorry, man. Afraid it's too late for talk. You know how it works. I have orders." He pulled the trigger. A muffled *pop* resounded in the cool California evening.

Vinny's mouth remained open, ready to protest and attempt to reason with his friend. Too late for words, his head jerked back, then he collapsed into a heap on the ground. Only a small amount of blood oozed from the single bullet hole.

Situating Vinny back into the car was relatively easy. Thankfully, he wasn't a big man. Louie had placed one of the trash bags he'd brought along over the man's head, to catch any blood that might leak out onto the car seat. He buckled Vinny in and shut the passenger door, then looked up at the night sky, breathing deeply.

Louie had just opened the driver's side door when a car suddenly came out of nowhere. He was too surprised to move.

He discovered what it felt like to be an animal caught in the headlights of an oncoming vehicle, losing all sense–of direction, of everything. Panic took over–*what the fuck?*

Louie realized too late the dome light was on as he held the car door open, making the body of Vincent Micelli, in the passenger seat, appear bright as day for the rapidly approaching vehicle.

Too late. The man in the passing car, stretched his neck, slowing down to almost a stop, then waved or whipped Louie the bird, or something, and sped off.

Louie snapped out of his trance, adrenaline suddenly pumping, blood pounding in his ears. *What if they call the cops? How fuckin' odd. Did the guy wave?* The more he thought about it, the more he realized the probable situation. Marco sent someone to make sure he did the job. *Fuckin' Marco.*

In case he was wrong and the cops were already on their way, he whipped a U-turn, heading back out to the main highway, homeward bound.

Setting cruise control, he put in one of Vinny's favorite CD's, in honor of his dead friend, then went through the rest of the plan in his head.

For a minute, Louie thought he'd left the keys to the goddamn butcher shop at home. Searching his jeans again, he pulled out the ring that held his brother's spare key. He exhaled a sigh of relief.

Louie unlocked the back door, then opened the large double doors on the ramp for deliveries. After backing up his vehicle to the large doors, he dragged Vinny's body onto one of several metal carts lined up along the cement retaining wall.

Throwing all his supplies from the trunk on top of Vinny, he wheeled everything inside, then returned to move his car, parking it in the far, darkened end of the parking lot.

Louie checked his watch. *Plenty of time.* Something about

the nasty task sliding over into the New Year bothered him. Entering the shop, he shut and locked all the doors. Any shades that could be pulled, were.

Louie wheeled the laden cart over to the TorRey tabletop band saw. He had helped his brother many times, so he knew how to operate all of the equipment.

Donning his rain slicker, galoshes and rubber gloves, Louie went to work. He undressed Vinny, piling his clothes on the floor. He hoisted the dead weight up onto the stainless steel table, which was a job in itself. Sweat trickled down his back, making his skin crawl under the slicker.

Flipping the switch, the machine roared to life and Louie took a deep breath, mentally preparing himself for the task at hand.

The first several cuts were the most difficult–both physically and emotionally. Maneuvering the body of his friend against the resistance of the saw blade took every ounce of strength Louie possessed. After the first attempt, he stopped and actually cried. "What the fuck," he grunted. Finally, he managed to hold the body steady while the band saw did its work, almost taking his own arm off after the resistance to bone gave way.

"Holy Fuck," he said aloud. The blood, especially when dividing the torso, took him by surprise. He must've hit an artery because he was sprayed directly in the face, striping his hair bright red. Wiping the other man's blood from his eyes, he deposited the smaller chunks of meat into the double lined trash bags, gagging only twice before getting his excess saliva under control.

Taking another deep breath, he finished the torso without too much difficulty. Louie quickly did the arms and legs, feeling like a pro.

Vinny's head was the only part left, staring up at him, amidst a river of blood pooled on the shiny metal table. Louie stood, hands on hips, dripping blood onto the floor.

"Fuck that, I ain't gonna wrestle the fuckin' head." He picked it up, almost dropping it from the slippery blood coating it. Rubber gloves gave a little extra grip. He hung onto it by the ears. "Bye, bye Vinny." He held him eye-level, debated planting a kiss on the bluish lips, then decided against it. He deposited the last of Vincent Micelli into one of the three trash bags.

Louie glanced around the room—it looked like a scene from a horror movie—and felt something shift inside. He shrugged it off, thinking maybe he should go into business with his brother after all.

Turning on the water, he hosed down the table and blades thoroughly, then went to work on the floor. A central drain in the middle of the small room washed the rest of Vinny away.

Removing gloves and slicker, he deposited them into a bag, along with Vinny's clothes. He'd burn everything later.

Louie proceeded to wash himself in one of the big basins. He scrubbed his face and hair with antibacterial soap, watching pink suds and body chunks swirl down the drain. Taking half a dozen paper towels, he patted dry and wiped around the sink.

"There." He looked around the spotless shop. Piling the bags of Vinny on the metal cart, he added the supplies he had brought in.

Parking the cart by the large double delivery doors, he jogged across the empty parking log to retrieve his car.

Louie made another quick check in the meat-cutting room. *Clean as a whistle.*

He unloaded the cart, placing everything neatly into the trunk of the car. Scooting the cart back to its rightful place against the wall amongst the other carts, he spotted a couple drops of blood. "Shit. Cover your tracks, man." He didn't want his brother asking *any* questions.

Retrieving a bottle of spray cleaner and a handful of paper towels, he returned to the cart, sprayed it down, then did the doorknob as an afterthought. Wiping everything in sight down a second time, he finally felt satisfied.

"Okay. Now, we're ready to roll." He shut the doors and locked up.

Louie climbed into the car and let out the breath he held. Turning the ignition, he repeated what his old man used to say when he was a kid—"And away we go...." Jackie Gleason's famous words. His old man had loved Jackie Gleason. The Honeymooners was his favorite show. *The good ol' days,* his old man used to say.

He felt a tear slide down his cheek and brushed it away. "Sentimental fool," he told himself. Louie put the car into gear, heading for the country. He knew a perfect place to lay his friend to rest. *Remote, peaceful...if only we could all be so lucky.*

He checked the clock. He made it.

Chapter 59

Maria and Tess brought home supper. They planned to stay in for New Years Eve. Tess' boyfriend, Mike came over to play pool and hang out. Tony still sulked about getting caught climbing out his window to smoke cigarettes. He begged off going ice fishing with Joe–claimed he was coming down with a cold...maybe.

Joe decided to cut Tony's Internet time down to one hour per day. It seemed to be the end of the world to the kid. Their line was always busy and things had to change. *New Year, new you*, became Joe's standard response whenever Tony put up a stink.

Peter Slade called to wish them Happy New Year, and told them about the Anthony Rossi bust. He figured they could use a little good news. Vincent was willing to *cooperate*. They finally had some leverage against the Family. He reported contacting the chief, who appeared less than thrilled, which he thought odd.

As the evening progressed, Maria couldn't help but wonder if another OD from the pure heroin on the streets would be a statistic for this year or next.

When Maria and Joe were alone, she whispered, "One down, one to go."

Joe wrapped his arms around her. The kids remained downstairs playing pool. His hand groped a breast.

She shook her head. "You only have one thing on your mind. Always."

"Anthony Rossi." He kissed her neck.

She giggled. "You're thinking of Rossi while kissing me and feeling my breast? Whoa."

"No, I'm saying I was listening. One down, one to go– Anthony Rossi. Santini is next." He sat up. Talk of Mafia killed the mood.

"Sorry," she offered. "Vincent Micelli is key to our success."

"Let's not forget *our guy*."

"If by *our guy* you're referring to Tina–she just got there. I don't think she's even swimming with the sharks yet."

"Well, she's swimmin' with one of 'em–Stephen Freyhoff. The only one more dangerous is his boss." Joe whispered as well. They were always careful to keep conversations directly related to work, private.

"But it's Santini who calls the shots. I hope she knows what the hell she's doing. I wouldn't want to be in her shoes. I'm afraid for her, Joe. I do hope we'll see her again, but I have my doubts." Maria looked at her husband, shaking her head.

"I know, darlin'. Me, too. Me, too."

They sat together, wrapped in each other's arms, thankful for everything they had, knowing things could change in an instant.

Blissful peace. That was what he felt. Sweet, sweet contentment. Dani and Shawna, they liked the euphoria. He gave them only small amounts at a time. He had to be careful. Oh, so careful.

The ringing telephone finally registered in Tiny Tim's addled brain. "Ooh, ooh, bloody ringy-ding." He stumbled into the kitchen and reached for the telephone. "Tiny's residence," he said into the handset.

No response.

"Hello, hello. Don't be shy."

"Tiny! It's me, Steve Freyhoff. Where the fuck ya been?"

"Steve, Steve–"

"You leave this cryptic fuckin' message, then leave me hanging. Don't do that. What's up?"

Tiny Tim's blissful peace turned into confusion, then panic. "Ooh, Stephen, um. Another girl...another girl OD'd." Tiny started shaking uncontrollably, thinking of Kath. He missed her.

"Dead." It wasn't a question. Steve had a feeling it was something like this.

Tiny Tim started crying.

"Jesus Christ. That's just fuckin' great. I'll get back to you." Steve disconnected. Things just kept getting better and better. Now there were two dead girls. Not cool. Should he tell Marco, or keep his mouth shut?

"Thank you. You did well." Marco placed the phone on his desk. *That was easy.* Louie actually came through for the Family.

No more Vincent Micelli to worry about. No more Anthony Rossi to worry about.

He picked up his cell again, punched in numbers, and waited for Stephen to pick up.

Steve had just finished making love to Lizzy. He reached for his cell and looked at the caller ID. "Shit." He looked guiltily at his girl. "Sorry, babe. Gotta get this."

Lizzy knew the rules already. It was Marco. She needed to hear this, but... She rolled her eyes. "I'm gonna jump into the shower...get ready for tonight. Can I use your bathroom?"

Steve nodded and answered the phone. "This is Steve."

She slowly made her way into the adjoining bathroom. Closing the bathroom door, but pressing an ear to the wood, she strained to hear the one sided conversation.

"Hey, Marco. Really, what's that?"

Marco told him the news.

"No shit? Good. Micelli had to go. A good way to end the year, huh? Especially with Rossi out of the picture. Yes, tonight." Steve grinned.

Lizzy turned on the water and the fan, then stepped into the shower. *Micelli, Micelli. Must be Vincent Micelli.*

She stuck her head under the curtain of hot water. She would need to find out more before contacting the chief. Perhaps later tonight the talk would turn to their accomplishments.

Chapter 60

The girls looked beautiful. They were meeting Marco at the private club. Steve locked the apartment, and they rode the elevator down to the garage, then climbed into his SUV.

Tiara sat in the back seat, and stared out the window, thinking of Marco Santini. She was totally consumed with thoughts of him and his dark, Spanish eyes that spoke volumes. They had a definite magnetism...chemistry. *What would it be like to make love to him?* She smiled to herself. *Make love? C'mon, girlfriend, love has nothin' to do with it.*

Lizzy looked over at Steve and felt her heart flutter. She turned her attention back to the road and prayed God gave her strength to do the right thing, to put her personal feelings aside. A single tear slid down her cheek, and she quickly brushed it away.

Steve tuned in a radio station, then placed his hand on her knee, glancing at her periodically. "How ya doin', babe?"

"Good." She smiled, placing her hand over his. "You?"

"I'm fantastic." He grinned. "I met this great girl."

Lizzy laughed and patted the hand that migrated up her thigh, then nestled in her crotch.

Tiara leaned forward. "Hey you two, three's a crowd." She laughed and leaned back, returning her gaze out the window.

The private club was huge, looked extremely fancy. Tiara unbuckled the seat belt and smoothed her dress as Steve slowed down and turned into the parking lot.

Upon entering the club, a tuxedoed host greeted them. He informed Steve that Marco waited their arrival. They followed the man through a bustling bar, past waitresses scantily clad in tiny blue sequined outfits. Music blared from a live band while throngs of people periodically screamed and blew party horns.

Entering one of several rooms, the maitre d led them to the table.

Marco sat with another man and woman, laughing. His attention immediately diverted to Tiara, visually devouring her long lean body from head to toe. He smiled appreciatively, and motioned to the seat on the other side of him.

Steve held out a chair for Lizzy and then sat as well. A bottle of five-hundred dollar champagne waited, chilled and ready to be uncorked.

"Would you please do the honors, Stephen?" Marco nodded toward the champagne.

Steve obliged. He pulled out the icy bottle and wiped it on a napkin that lay over the bucket. With much flourish, he presented the label to all members at the table.

Lizzy giggled. He was charming in a completely opposite way from Marco. He appeared to ridicule all the fancy stuff, but was lighthearted in doing so. Santini smiled, as did everyone at the table.

"Ah-ha, 1975, a very fine year indeed." Steve pointed the bottle away from the table and popped the cork, smoke cascading from the opening. He poured, filling everyone's glass.

Marco held up his glass in a toast. "Happy New Year. Here is to much prosperity." He looked at Tiara, locking eyes. "And to beautiful girls." One eyebrow went up and he smiled, clinking glasses with the black beauty, then the rest of his guests.

"Happy New Year," everyone mumbled, touching glasses.

Steve kissed Lizzy, and whispered, "Happy New Year, babe."

"Happy New Year," she replied softly, self-consciously glancing around the table. Marco was watching her and held out his glass.

Lizzy met his eyes, which seemed to turn serious as they touched glasses.

Marco looked at his friend, Stephen, wondering how far he planned on going with this young girl. He appeared totally *whipped*.

Food arrived at the table shortly after they sat down. Starting with appetizers–jumbo shrimp cocktail and caviar. The main course was prime rib and lobster.

Tiara ate all she could. She'd never eaten food this delicious. If this is what it was like to be rich, she wanted it. All of it. It was worth anything she had to do to get it. Growing up on pancakes, macaroni and cheese, and bread and peanut butter–the main food groups–she knew this side of the fence existed, but had never experienced it first-hand. She'd eaten three rolls and had another on her plate. Maybe she'd slip a couple in her purse for later. *Always the scavenger, that's me. Way to look like a total loser.* She refrained from pocketing any food.

Dessert was a rich chocolate torte with a curl of dark chocolate on top and more champagne. Coffee was offered as well.

Conversation loosened up a bit as the evening wore on. The couple to the right of Marco, Jon and Sarah Jordon, had a successful real estate business in the L.A. area as well. Marco had known them for years. They departed shortly after dessert, offering the excuse of teenagers left home alone.

Once they left, Marco turned his complete attention to the beauty occupying the seat next to him. He touched her face, running a finger along her jawbone. "You are an exquisite creature," he said, loving every angle of her face, her eyes, her lips. He had fantasized about her since the moment they'd met, and told her so.

Tiara felt hypnotized by this man. His gaze held hers as she watched the candlelight dance like small moons in his deep brown eyes.

"I dreamt of you last night," he whispered, an inch from her ear. "My tongue was inside you, your back arched in ecstasy." He flicked his tongue in her ear and saw the effect he had on her. *Those eyes.* He could fall into those dark pits of desperate desire. "We devoured each other." He licked his full lips, then slipped his hand under the table and ran it along her long leg, the silky material of her dress riding up as his hand slid back and forth.

Tiara felt her insides melt at his touch. *Who is he? The devil?* She couldn't look away, didn't want to look away. She wanted to kiss him, wanted to feel his hands all over her body.

Lizzy watched Tiara out of the corner of her eye. The girl appeared lost in the moment. Santini knew all the tricks. God, she hated him and everything he stood for. It would be worth any price she had to pay to take this man down.

"Hey, babe. What do ya think?" Stephen asked.

She came out of her reverie and looked at her new boyfriend. "Sorry, what?"

"You're a million miles away. What are you thinking

about?"

"Oh, nothing, just what the new year will bring." She smiled.

"Good things." Steve grabbed her hand and put it to his lips. "I promise," he whispered, kissing her fingertips.

The waiter brought another bottle of chilled champagne in a bucket of ice.

Marco opened the bottle and poured the bubbly liquid into the four glasses as the clock approached midnight. "Another toast," he said, raising his glass. "To this evening. May it be everything we wish for." He locked eyes with Tiara, not seeing anyone else at the table.

The clock struck midnight and they could hear the party horns and cheers coming from the main area of the club.

"Happy New Year," Marco whispered. Leaning forward, he softly kissed Tiara's full lips.

She responded, feeling drunk by just being near this man. The kiss lasted a full minute. It was the best kiss she'd ever had.

Chapter 61

Louie knew where he'd bury the parts. It was perfect–remote countryside, but close enough to make it an easy jaunt. He turned down the winding dirt road and followed it deeper into the hills.

After about twenty minutes of driving, he pulled over as far off the road as possible, and turned off the ignition.

Removing the bags of Vinny and a shovel from the trunk, he trekked deeper into the woods, struggling and breathless, until he came to a small clearing. Louie had grown up in this area. Wine country. Vineyards spotted the rolling hills beyond the woods.

He had walked quite a distance but had a good sense of direction and wasn't too concerned about getting lost in the middle of the night. "Okay, how we gonna do this?" He set everything down and tried to catch his breath.

"Yessir, yessir, three bags full." He picked up the shovel and dug one hole. The ground was relatively soft, making the work surprisingly easy. *It's a good thing, after dragging the bags of Vinny*, he thought, muscles aching. Moving to another spot, he dug another hole. And then another. One hole for each bag.

By the time he finished digging the holes, exhaustion had set in. He sat on a log to rest, gazing up at the night sky. The half moon was luminous and stars glowed brightly in the inky blackness. No city lights to spoil God's nighttime picture.

Taking a deep breath and exhaling, he stood. "Let's get this over with." He placed one bag at each hole, and proceeded to dump the parts in; deciding the chunks of meat would become one with Mother Earth sooner without double-lined plastic trash bags to delay decomposition.

He covered each of the first two holes, packed the dirt, then shoveled leaves and pine needles over the fresh earth.

Getting to the last hole, he opened the final trash bag. Vinny looked up at him. He stepped back for a moment, freaked out. "Whoa. Okay man, you can do this. You can do this."

Glancing up at the sky again, he wondered, in what form of Hell he would fry for eternity. He shrugged his meaty shoulders and approached the final task with a vengeance.

A thought crossed his mind as he prepared to cover Vinny's final remains. Marco would want proof. This was a test of loyalty. Louie wasn't stupid. He knew his own life was on the line if he couldn't 'do' Vinny. Now positive it had been a hired tail checking things out after he whacked Vinny. He'd fuckin' bet on it. *Fuckin' Marco.*

Louie pulled out his pocketknife and knelt down. Vinny's head rested in the center of the guts, his two large ears protruding from either side. He remembered the hairy mole on the right ear. "That'll do," he said, quickly whacking off the ear and wrapping it in a piece of plastic cut from a trash bag. He placed the ear into his pocket for safekeeping, then covered the last hole.

Standing in the middle of the clearing, he admired his work. "Not bad." Gathering the empty bags and shovel, he trudged back toward his car. Total exhaustion had set in, and he found himself stopping every few minutes to catch his breath, heart pounding.

Exiting the woods, he panicked for a moment when he didn't see his vehicle. The moon flitted out from behind a bank of clouds and he spotted a flash of chrome from the bumper a short distance down the road.

He stumbled toward his destination, bone weary, almost tripping over his feet. "What a fuckin' night."

After opening the trunk and tossing the shovel and empty bags inside, he looked around his surroundings, committing them to memory. The large Redwood ten feet from the road would mark the spot in his mind forever.

Getting into the car, he felt his pocket for the lump of ear. "Good to go." He cranked the ignition and did a U-turn, heading home to bed and a good night's sleep.

Picking up his cell phone, he made the call. "It's done. Yeah. Happy New Year. I've got a little something for ya. A token of Vinny's appreciation you might say." Louie grinned into the phone. "Okay, thanks, Boss."

Chapter 62

The girls had taken a bathroom break and Lizzy tried to talk some sense into Tiara. The girl appeared totally sucked into Santini's plan, *whatever* it entailed. Head over heels. Would do *anything*. Talking a mile a minute.

Lizzy made an effort to remove her feelings from the situation, but it was becoming more and more difficult. She also realized she could use information gleaned from Tiara. She didn't want another dead girl. That's why she was here–too many dead girls already. Too many drugs on the streets. A multifaceted situation and if they didn't find enough to hold him, Santini would walk as he had in the past. He was a major factor in what was *wrong* with Los Angeles.

"C'mon, girlfriend. Let's get back to our men." T grinned and sashayed back to the table with Lizzy following.

Marco was on his cell phone, chuckling, as they approached. He then flipped it shut, severing the connection. "No more Vinny," he offered quietly to Stephen.

"'bout time," Steve mumbled, looking up as his girl returned.

Lizzy looked at Stephen and Marco. Both appeared satisfied with whatever news Marco had just received. She played the conversation back in her head–*No more Vinny. 'Bout time. Vincent Micelli.* She'd need to find a way to make a phone call tonight. Things were heating up. She watched Marco and Tiara. An inch from one another, they appeared deep in conversation, or sex-talk, or whatever he used to wrap her tightly into his toxic web. It made her ill. *How long before she is dead?*

Marco stood, as did Tiara. "We are leaving. Going to my place," Marco offered. "You are welcome to stay as long as you'd like. I've paid for the entire evening."

"Okay, we may be heading out pretty soon, too. Have fun." Steve grinned. Tiara looked to be a foot taller than Marco.

"Oh, we will." He looked up at Tiara, a smile dancing on his lips.

Lizzy watched them walk away and felt her guts clench. She

looked at Steve and wondered how much she could trust him. More importantly, how much would he trust her? She refilled their champagne glasses. "To us," she offered.

Steve raised his glass. "Us." He kissed her long and hard.

"Will she be okay?" Lizzy asked when they parted.

"Who? Your friend?"

Lizzy nodded. "I don't want anything to happen to her."

Steve shook his head. "Well...not sure how to answer that."

She sat up straighter. "I think you just did. He is dangerous, isn't he?"

Steve gazed at the beautiful girl sitting next to him. She looked so young and innocent. He didn't want to scare her away, but he didn't want to lie to her either. "Yeah, he is a dangerous man, Lizzy. But, he likes your friend. She'll be okay. For now."

For now. Lizzy thought about how Tiara sometimes let her mouth get her into trouble. She had witnessed it first hand.

"Don't worry, okay? Let's go home. C'mon." Steve stood.

Home. She wondered how he'd feel if he knew the truth–he was sharing his bed with an undercover agent. *He'd kill me in an instant.* She answered her own question. The man did not get as far as he did by having even an ounce of compassion.

Tiara followed Marco through the underground parking garage. His Mercedes kept company with a twenty-year-old Corvette and a Porsche. Riding the elevator, he watched her intently, smiling.

Upon entering his apartment, she was taken aback by the richness. Everything was decorated in deep earth tones. Very masculine, yet not. Large vases with fresh flowers adorned intricately carved tables here and there.

"Please, make yourself comfortable." Marco nodded toward the living room, then strolled into the kitchen to open a bottle of wine. "Are you hungry?" He didn't see how she possibly could be, but after observing her ravenous appetite at the club, thought it polite to ask.

A half wall separated the two rooms. "No, not for food, anyway." She watched him uncork the wine, letting it breathe. He looked at her and smiled.

Marco walked into the living room where she stood admiring

a painting on the wall. "Not for food? *Hmm*...well, we'll see if we can remedy that." He took her hand and led her further into the living room. They stopped in front of two voodoo masks. "What do you think?"

Tiara looked at the ugly masks and felt the hairs on the nape of her neck stand to attention. "Don't like 'em. Fuckin' freaky."

Marco laughed. "They are meant to be fucking freaky." He grinned up at her, eyes traveling over her body, wanting to taste every inch of her.

"Can I use your bathroom?" She hated to break the spell.

"Certainly. Follow me."

Tiara followed him down the hallway, peeking into the huge bedroom with the gigantic bed. She thought of him alone in the large bed, then immediately thought that was probably a rare occasion. He liked women too much. She had a feeling he was an expert at the art of lovemaking.

"There you go." He opened the door.

The bathroom amazed her. The entire room was black marble, from the sink, commode, and hot tub, to the floor. The walls were mirrored and inlayed with black marble. She grinned. "I see you like black."

"My favorite color."

"It's not really a color, you know."

Marco smiled. "I will leave you to your business." He quietly closed the door behind him.

Tiara lifted her dress and pulled down her panties, sitting on the toilet. "Wow," she said softly, unrolling a length of toilet paper and taking in her surroundings. "Unfuckinbelievable."

She flushed and washed her hands, then on impulse opened his medicine cabinet and peeked inside. Just average stuff–razor, shave cream, toothpaste. Shutting the mirrored cabinet gently, she checked her makeup, then went to join Marco.

The lights had been dimmed, candlelight now the predominant lighting, when Tiara returned to the living room. Marco sat on the leather sofa, two half-filled glasses of wine perched on a nearby table.

She joined him, sitting relatively close, but not touching him.

"You look beautiful in candlelight. You look beautiful in any light."

Tiara smiled. "Bet you say that to everyone."

"No, no I don't. Only those who are deserving of the compliment."

Tiara picked up her glass of wine and sipped it. "You are a very successful man, aren't you?"

"Yes in matters of business, anyway. In matters of the heart...well, let's just say I've had my share of heartache." He looked away, feeling a tear come to his eye.

Tiara touched his leg. "I'm sorry. Sometimes life can be a real bitch, can't it?"

Marco looked at her, then threw back his head and laughed. "Yes, yes indeed. It can be a real bitch." He returned her touch. "May I kiss you?"

"Yeah...yes." She turned and leaned toward him.

Their lips met and parted, tongues probing. His hands became suddenly very busy as one groped for a nipple through the front of her gown, while the other softly stroked her crotch. The kisses became hot and she pulled away, suddenly needing air.

"Are you okay?" he asked softly, concern as well as insatiable hunger in his dark eyes.

"Yes, just need...a....a breather." She took a sip of wine, feeling overwhelmed. This man was so much older, so much more experienced. "Do you have a cigarette?" She was actually shaking.

"Oh ho, I can do better than that. If you want, that is." He stood, and walked leisurely across the room. Lifting one of the smaller pictures on the wall, he revealed a small safe.

Tiara laughed. "Just like in the movies."

Marco quickly opened the combination lock. "What's your pleasure, little lady? Got a little weed, a little H." He was glad he decided to bring half the block of heroin to his home rather than keeping it all in the main office. He never wanted too much of anything in one location.

"How 'bout a little of each?" Tiara raised both eyebrows, noticing a huge stack of cash, along with a bunch of papers on one side, drugs on the other. She needed something strong enough to loosen her inhibition. He was a man of the world. Who was she? *Nobody*.

Marco brought the drugs and paraphernalia back to where

she waited, laying everything on the table by their wine. "Oh, and here are your cigarettes." He reached under the coffee table and pulled out a full pack of Marlboros.

"You're the magic man, aren't ya?"

He smiled, handing her a pipe with a small bud of marijuana in it. "Try this." He busied himself getting the fix kit out, preparing a small amount of heroin for injection.

Tiara watched him. *Did he do the shit?* She had never hit up, didn't really want to, but realized she would do it if he did. She lit the pipe, held in the harsh smoke, then exhaled a large cloud and coughed.

Marco prepared the syringe. "Ladies first." He readied her arm, tying the tourniquet and expertly hitting the right vein.

Tiara felt the euphoric rush and laid her head back, closing her eyes. "Oh, wow."

Marco smiled, watching. She was so beautiful. He prepared another syringe, but had no intention of putting anything into his own veins. Instead, he placed it on the table. He removed the pipe from her hand, put it to his lips, and lit it, holding the hit in his lungs. Pot always made him so horny.

Tiara looked at Marco and smiled. "You are very handsome. There's something about you. I can't quite put my finger on it, but you have a…a presence."

Marco raised one eyebrow. "A presence? I will take that as a compliment."

"Yeah, that's how I meant it." Her head fell back against the sofa, spinning, as the heroin traveled its course through her system.

Marco smiled. "You look absolutely exhausted. Lay down." He helped take off her high heels, massaging one foot and running his hand up her long leg, feeling every muscle and contour.

She moaned and smiled, then scooted down and laid her head back on the armrest.

He pulled her legs over his lap and licked her toes, working his way ever so slowly upward.

Her dress came off. He finished what he had started, taking his time slowly nibbling her ankle, inside her knee, her upper thigh. His tongue found the center of her, devouring, until she shook with pleasure, finally exploding in waves of ecstasy.

They made love all night to a heated rhythm synchronized to one another, moving from one room to the next, feeling a mutual passion neither had ever experienced before. A feeling unique to only them.

Chapter 63

Lizzy silently slid out of bed after disengaging Steve's long legs from her body. He snored softly, a smile on his face. *Must be having pleasant dreams.* She tiptoed out of the bedroom.

She needed to make a phone call. Tiara still wasn't back from Santini's. She hoped the girl was okay. She had decided Tiara would not be another statistic on Marco's list of dead girls. *Not on my watch.*

Lizzy had gotten Steve to open up a bit more about his boss. Tamara Wood had been strangled in a fit of jealous rage. Deanna someone met the same tragic end. There were several others as well, according to Steve that he *knew* about. *How many more that he didn't know about?*

Santini apparently had a rough time when it came to relationships. He seemed to be finished trying with women his own age. He'd moved on to younger, less experienced, more expendable targets. These girls wouldn't be missed when they disappeared–most were already missing for some time before encountering Marco Santini.

She picked up the cordless phone and climbed the ladder to Tiara's loft, looking for privacy just in case Steve woke up.

Lizzy crouched in a far corner and dialed the phone card number committed to memory, so charges wouldn't show up, then punched in the chief's private number. As always, her contact answered immediately, despite the hour. "It's me."

"Tina, thank God. You alright?"

"Yes. A lot is happening I think."

"Yes. There is. Don't know how much you know. Anthony Rossi was busted–he's a rival of Santini. Vincent Micelli helped bring him down. We have–"

"Vincent Micelli is dead." Lizzy interrupted her boss.

"What? Dead? You sure?"

"Yes, I heard Santini tell Stephen. I have concerns for a young woman. I think she is next on the list of dead girls. Speaking of which, Marco killed Tamara Wood, and a Deanna someone–perhaps one of your Jane Does. There are more who are nameless. We need to move on this, before it is too late for Tiara."

"Shit...fuck. No more Vinny Micelli. Get as much info as you can. We'll arrange for a rendezvous in a week or so. I'll send my people in for backup and we'll work with the FBI to bring the fucker down for something. We gotta make the charges stick this time, though. Hang in there Tina and call me in three days."

"Okay."

"*Three* days. Understand?"

"Yes, Mother." Lizzy ended the connection, and sat in the dark, thinking. She thought about the man she'd grown to love, lying in *their* bed, as he referred to it. She thought about Tiara, who was currently at the mercy of Santini and had no idea the world of hurt she was about to experience. Tiara Jackson acted tough, but was definitely out of her league. Way out of her league. She'd never survive.

Lizzy made her way down the ladder and slid the phone back into the charger on the kitchen counter. Stopping to gaze out the window at the half moon and smattering of stars on this first day of the New Year, she wondered what fate held in store.

Chapter 64

Maria woke early on New Year's morning despite the late night. She had just started a pot of horrendously strong coffee when the phone rang, startling her. She snatched it up quickly before it could wake anyone up. "Hello."
"Maria, Chief LaSalle here."
"Chief. Anything wrong?" Maria asked, expecting trouble.
"Well, when you think about it–what isn't?" LaSalle paused a moment before speaking again.
Maria waited, ready to hear another teenager had overdosed or something equally disturbing.
"I heard from Tina a while ago. Vincent Micelli, who was cooperating with the L.A. FBI, is dead. Marco Santini has his claws into another girl. Tiara Jackson. We got a 'for sure' on the Tamara Wood murder and a possible name for our Jane Doe. *Hmm*, let's see what else."
Maria heard the sound of ice clinking in a glass. Was the chief drinking this early in the morning, or still partying from the previous night?
"Oh, Deanna, that's the name of our Jane Doe. Maybe. Anyway, Sanchez–I'm thinking of sending you and Morgan out to L.A. Tina may need backup and I don't completely trust the FBI." She snorted, took another drink from her gin and tonic, and continued. "I shouldn't say that. I do trust them. Sort of. But Tina is one of us now. We gotta look out for our own. I want us to be part of the operation and see this shit come to a well-organized end. I want them all behind bars with no fuckin' way out."
"Yes, I agree. Funny, Slade had just mentioned a trip out there." Maria felt excitement at the thought of going, despite the knowledge Joe would be less than thrilled. So much for a working vacation. It would be anything *but* a vacation.
"Perfect. Peter Slade can coordinate with the agents out there. Be ready to go in a few days. Things may heat up sooner than we think." LaSalle disconnected.

Maria looked at the phone, listening to the dial tone. She hung up. "Didn't even say goodbye." She leaned against the counter, deep in thought, trying to absorb everything the chief had said. *Vinny Micelli dead. Marco was killing young women and his drugs were killing even more. Tina's in danger. I knew it. In over her head.* Maria grabbed a cup and poured from the steaming, spitting pot.

We're going back to California. She shook her head trying to dislodge the memory of their last trip there, almost ten years ago. They were lucky to walk away that time.

Maria couldn't help but think, *Maybe this time, we won't be so lucky.*

Chapter 65

Tiara woke up and wondered where she was. She looked at the balding middle-aged Italian man gently snoring next to her in the huge soft bed. *Marco Santini.*

It was still dark outside. Sitting on the edge of the bed, she tried to remember where the bathroom was. She had a bitch of a headache.

Marco reached out to her.

"I'll be right back, baby. Gotta pee."

Tiara made her way into the bathroom, again awed by the black marble room. "I could live in this fuckin' room," she mumbled, finished her business and washed her hands. Catching her reflection in the mirror, it startled her. She looked rough. "Fuckin heroin." She shook her head. She knew better...was one of the smart ones when it came to drugs.

She remembered her promise to Lizzy. She could handle herself. "Yeah, right," she whispered, feeling her heart beat faster at the thought of the man waiting for her in the next room.

Taking a deep breath, she returned. Marco appeared to be sleeping again.

Tiara slid in next to him and molded to his back, her long thin body becoming one with his. She felt herself become aroused again. She never realized how intense her sexual appetite could be. She'd had multiple orgasms last night. She'd never experienced anything like it. Ever. It was addictive.

Disengaging herself, she turned the other way, hoping to fall back to sleep. They could sleep for hours yet. She closed her eyes, feeling her head pound in her ears.

Marco rolled over and tossed one arm over her narrow hips.

She felt him against her and smiled. Crouching down a bit, she rubbed up against him.

He hardened at her slightest touch. This girl was different– she really did something to him. He caressed a bare breast and kissed her neck. "Do you love me?"

Her first response was to laugh and say, *I hardly know you,* but she didn't. Instead, she said, "I think so."

"Me, too." He slipped inside her and before long they were making love, moving to the rocking beat in their souls. He was a master at the art of pleasing a woman. He stopped and rolled her over, kissed her stomach, moving his tongue in small circular motions, finally reaching his destination.

She had never known anything like this–it was out of this world. She concentrated on what he did to her, feeling as if she'd explode. He knew exactly what to do. Her back arched as she cried out in pleasure that bordered pain, it became so intense.

They made love until the sky lightened, moving together as if they'd been lovers a very long time, but with the newness of perfect strangers.

Tiara rubbed her tired eyes, as they lay sprawled on the living room sofa, both exhausted, as if they hadn't slept at all.

"Coffee. I will make coffee," Marco offered, raising his head ever so slightly. He slapped her beautiful ass and stood, stretching.

What a gorgeous man. He had a perfect muscular little body. Not an ounce of fat. Moreover, his manhood sent her mind reeling. *I will never get enough of that.*

He caught her eye and smiled. "I do love you." He left her to ponder that last statement and strolled into the kitchen to start a strong pot of special coffee.

Tiara hugged herself, feeling incredibly alive and content inside. *What a wonderful feeling. Better than any drug and a true high. I hope it never ends. I love him so much. Oh, my God. So much.* She was under his spell, completely and totally consumed by passion. All inhibition was lost in the throes of their lovemaking. They did things she didn't realize could be done.

She dozed in the living room, a smile on her face while Marco started breakfast. The more he thought about her, the more he wanted her. He imagined her here with him...*always.* Perhaps this time, it will work, he couldn't help thinking.

Marco flipped the bacon. He was a very good cook. In fact, he was good at everything he did.

He thought of Stephen and the blonde. For some reason he didn't trust her. He wondered why. He shook his head, happy Stephen had not taken the girls to Darcy's place, as was customary. He thought of all the runaways who filtered through there...used up whores. Tiara was different...from anyone he'd ever encountered. She would stay with him from now on, he decided. By the looks of things, Stephen was planning the same.

Once again, the thought of Lizzy sent unease through his guts. Instinct was a good part of what he acted on.

Marco would talk to Stephen about some things–some very important things.

Chapter 66

Maria let Joe sleep for as long as she could possibly stand. Finally, she walked into their bedroom, third cup of coffee in hand. "What the heck, ya gonna sleep all day?"

Joe rolled over and grinned. "Jeez, woman, how long you been awake? Did I hear the phone ring in the middle of the night?"

Maria sat on the edge of the bed, next to her husband. She looked at the clock. "A long time ago, but no, not middle of the night. Early this morning. I was up making coffee." She tousled his thick, messy hair making it even messier. She loved to make it messier.

"And? Who was on the damn phone that early?"

"Chief LaSalle."

Joe propped himself up on one elbow. "What's up now?"

"Lots. She heard from Tina. Vincent Micelli is dead. We have confirmation that Marco killed Tamara Wood as well as one of our Jane Does and possibly many unknowns. He has another one...Tiara."

"Tiara Jackson." Joe recalled the picture the girl's drunken father had given them, included in their files. A beautiful black girl. Her old man was devastated and looked as if he'd been beaten up. Joe could understand why some of these kids ran away. Their home lives became unbearable, but the streets were deadly, especially these days. It was worse than ever before.

"Anyway, how does sunny California sound?" Maria asked, interrupting his deep thoughts.

Joe looked at her, frowning.

"The chief wants us there. We're taking Santini down, for the second and final time. Chief LaSalle is setting everything up. We'll be working closely with the L.A. agents."

"Slade be there, too?"

"Yes. We'll help coordinate everything. Peter doesn't know about it yet. He'll be surprised. I'm sure the chief called him soon after we talked this morning, and let's just say, she was a little tipsy." Maria smiled.

"Really?" Joe laughed. "She makes him so damn uncomfortable anyway. Bet that conversation was interesting."

Maria turned serious for a moment. "How do you feel about all this? About going back to L.A.? About everything?"

Joe shrugged his shoulders. "What does it matter? Part of the fuckin' job." He swung his legs off the bed, and sat next to his wife.

Maria ran her fingers through his wild hair again and shook her head. She looked into his piercing blue eyes and saw the determination. She loved him. More than *anything*, she loved this man. They had been through a lot together. Soul mates.

"I'll survive, darlin'. We'll survive." He put an arm around her and turned her face up to his, placing a kiss in the center of her forehead.

Chapter 67

Beth left home. She couldn't do it anymore. Her stepfather had showed up in her bedroom again. He'd awakened her with his disgusting touches.

She was riding the freakin' city bus once again.

Beth must have slept for a little while, because she dreamt she was suddenly falling down the narrow metal staircase that led to Tiny Tim's and Nick's apartment. In her dream, the night was pitch-black, with only the occasional glow of eerie moonlight flitting out behind clouds. Tiara, Kath, and Lizzy were there.

Beth jerked awake.

Coming out of a sleep-induced fog, she recognized the neighborhood, and pulled the cord to get off at the next stop. She wondered what the heck she'd do when she got there.

It was reasonably warm out for January. Twenty degrees sure beat the usual below zero temperatures.

Stepping off the bus and preoccupied with thoughts of where to go, she almost missed Nick walking on the other side of the street. She called his name.

He stopped and looked, then crossed to her side of the street. "Beth? What are you doing here? Thought you went home." He had been out walking for some time, needing to get away from Tiny Tim and the girls.

Beth shoved her hands deep into the pockets of her dirty pink jacket. "Did. Left again."

"Why?"

She looked at the ground, uncomfortable at discussing it, or even thinking about it.

"Never mind. It doesn't matter. You need a place to stay?"

She looked at him and wrinkled her nose. "Don't know if I wanna go back to yours. Tiny creeps me out. And Kath...."

"Yeah, I understand." Nick shifted from foot to foot, trying to keep warm. "Hey, I'll buy ya a hot chocolate and we can talk about it, okay?"

Beth grinned. "Okay." As they walked, Beth asked if he'd

heard from Tiara and Lizzy."

"No. Wish I had. Have you?" He looked at her, a ray of hope in his eyes.

She shook her head.

"I really miss her. Big time." He walked faster and Beth almost had to run to keep up.

"Me, too. I'm thinking of maybe making a trip."

Nick slowed down. "Where? L.A.?" He laughed, thinking she was kidding.

"Hey, what's so funny? Why not?" Now it was Beth's turn to be hopeful. "I stole some money from my mom's purse. Got almost two-hundred bucks. She just got paid." She looked down guiltily, then shrugged her shoulders, and glanced shyly at Nick. "We could go together."

He stopped and looked at her, then continued walking at a more leisurely pace, saying nothing, but thinking. He had money, too. His take of the drug money, and he had saved quite a wad.

Beth felt heat rise to her cheeks despite the cold, realizing the way that must've sounded. "I don't mean *together*, I just meant we could catch a ride together, ya know?"

He touched her arm. "Don't worry, Beth. I know what you mean. I have a car, ya know."

"You do?"

"Yeah, the old beater Tiny Tim tools around in. It's mine."

"*Hmm*, I thought it was his." She kind of remembered now Tiara mentioning Nick had a car. She congratulated herself for maybe playing it right for once. She wanted to get out of here. Out of Minnesota. Beth hated her stepfather, and her mother only cared about having a man around to pay the bills. She'd told Beth to keep her mouth shut when she told her about her husband.

They entered the diner, where the girls had spent the night a week ago, and grabbed a booth toward the back. A couple of early morning customers occupied several seats at the counter.

Janet greeted them, then looked twice at Beth. "I know you. How ya doin', kiddo?"

"Okay." Beth looked at Nick, then down at the table.

"So, what can I get ya?"

"Two hot chocolates and a couple pieces of apple pie." He looked at Beth who grinned. "A la mode," he added.

"Excellent choice," Janet said, winking at Beth.

When the waitress left, Nick said, "So, you're thinking you wanna go to California?"

Beth nodded.

"It's a long way. Don't know if that old car would even make it. It's a rusty piece of shit."

"We could hitch," Beth offered.

"Man, you really wanna get outta town, huh?"

Beth shrugged her shoulders. "I don't know what I want. I just know what I *don't* want."

"*Hmm*, well I guess that makes sense."

The waitress returned with pie a la mode and hot chocolate, piled high with whipped cream.

They kept conversation to a minimum as they concentrated on the melting ice cream.

"Thanks," Beth said, conquering the ice cream and then diving into the whipped cream on her hot chocolate.

Nick smiled. "You're welcome. Looked like you could use a little pick-me-up."

She smiled. "Food has always done it for me. As you can see," she added self-consciously.

"You look fine. Why is everyone so obsessed with weight? It should be okay, no matter how you look. And I really do mean it–you look fine."

"Thanks," she said again, feeling her cheeks flush.

"So, short term...what ya gonna do?"

Beth shrugged her shoulders.

"You can come back with me for a day or two until you decide...if ya want."

Beth thought of Tiny Tim *and Kath*. "I don't know."

"Well, finish your hot chocolate. You can decide later." He smiled, feeling alone and missing his girl, who was so far away in the City of Angels.

Chapter 68

Marco softly kissed her cheek. "Breakfast is served." He set a tray down on the coffee table next to where Tiara had fallen asleep on the sofa.

She opened a sleepy eye and smiled. A soft blanket covered her nakedness. He'd put on jeans and a black T-shirt. "Wow, I feel like a princess."

"You are my princess." He retrieved the other tray and sat next to her. "I hope you like it. Just something I threw together."

"Looks wonderful," she said, eying the feast of scrambled eggs, bacon, Italian bread with fresh strawberry preserves, sliced avocado arranged in a star design.

"I hope you like the coffee. It's my own special blend–I add cardamom and a few other spices." Marco took a sip and rolled his eyes heavenward.

Tiara picked it up, not much of a coffee drinker, but willing to acquire the taste. She took a sip. It definitely had a bite, but was drinkable. "*Mmm*, good."

Marco smiled, watching the beautiful girl eat like someone would steal her plate. He was falling for this strange girl and could tell, she felt the same way.

Tiara cleaned her plate in under five minutes, and leaned back on the sofa, the blanket falling below her breasts as she sipped the spicy coffee.

Marco cleared the breakfast dishes and refilled their coffee cups. "Shall we catch the morning sunshine out on the balcony?"

"Yeah, I'd like that. S'pose I should get dressed." She looked around the living room for her dress and panties, thinking that's where they had been removed the night before. She picked up the dark purple silk shirt Marco had been wearing last night and brought it to her face, inhaling his scent. She found him watching her. "I love the way you smell."

"How do I smell?" He smiled.

"Rich…and spicy."

He threw back his head and laughed from his gut, his eyes

watering. "Rich and spicy. I like that. Put it on."

She looked at him, slipped the shirt on, and buttoned a couple of buttons. It hung plenty big on her despite their height difference. He was very broad in the chest and shoulders. *A regular little powerhouse.* She grinned.

"Here." He handed her one of the coffees. "Follow me."

Opening the sliding door, they stepped into paradise. Small palm trees sat on each side of the balcony. The morning sun warmed the white stucco siding, despite the cool, crisp air. They sat at a small cast iron table twenty-some stories up.

"Beautiful." Tiara said, gazing out over the balcony.

"Yes, beautiful," Marco said, watching Tiara. "Drink your coffee while it's still warm."

She took a sip and looked at him over her cup.

"You like me, don't you Tiara?" His smiling lips quivered slightly as he watched her.

Tiara just looked at him, a sly smile playing on her full lips.

"Have you ever heard of Spanish Fly?"

She laughed. "Sure, it's an aphrodisiac."

"Very good. But did you know it's not really a fly at all. It is a beetle. An emerald green blister beetle."

"Really? How interesting, sounds nasty."

"It is in your coffee." Marco grinned.

"Yeah, right." She looked in her coffee and saw a greenish tinted residue on the inside of her cup. "You are fuckin' kiddin' me, right?"

Marco laughed. He liked her sassy attitude. "We'll see, won't we?"

"You better not of gave me no fuckin' Spanish Fly," she said, angry. "There *is* something in there." She swiped her finger around the inside of her cup and narrowed her eyes.

"Calm down." He laughed. "We don't need no stinkin' Spanish Fly. It's Cardamom, remember?" A smile still played on his full lips as he took her by the hand and led her back to the bedroom, where they made love for hours.

Chapter 69

Lizzy cleaned the apartment while Steve slept. She managed to find the cleaning supplies under the kitchen sink. She also found a loaded pistol, and another one on top of the refrigerator. *Must be backups–you never know when you're going to need to take someone out.*

Once the cleaning was accomplished, she started a large breakfast, first finding a pan and washing the dust off it. He actually had eggs and bacon. She made French toast, eggs, and bacon.

Steve awoke to the smell of bacon. Walking out into the kitchen he found the beautiful little blonde clad in one of his surf T-shirts and nothing else. "Lizzy, Lizzy." He wrapped his arms around her and buried his face in her hair, inhaling deeply.

"Are you hungry?" she asked, filling two plates with food.

"Yes." His hands roamed up and down her body.

"For food?" She giggled, giving him a quick kiss and scooting away.

They ate at the small kitchen table, comfortable with one another. It had become very easy to be together. They both felt it.

After breakfast, they cleaned up together, then took a shower together, then made love. It was after that, Steve asked Lizzy to move in with him.

She laughed. "I already have."

He looked at her in his T-shirt–bare legs, cup of coffee halfway to her lips–and grinned. "I'm in love with you, Lizzy. I love you."

Her smile faltered and she looked away, then returned his gaze evenly. "I love you, too." She felt her emotions churning inside, and used her behavioral training to keep them off her face.

"So, you'll stay here. We'll get you some new clothes. Do you drive? How old are you? Really? I know you told me seventeen. Is that the truth…you aren't fifteen years old are ya?" He grinned, suddenly feeling like a nervous schoolboy.

Lizzy laughed and thought, *Oh, if only you knew…I am only*

three years younger than you. "No, I'm not fifteen. Yes, I know how to drive. Why, are you going to buy me a new Corvette?"

"Is that what you want?"

She looked at him and frowned. He was serious. "No."

"Well, okay. You can drive mine if you want." He grinned.

"You have an SUV," she said.

"I have a couple more cars in storage, and a Harley," he added sheepishly.

"A motorcycle?"

"No, you're not riding the Harley."

She grinned and pushed him lightly. "You're no fun."

He picked her up as if she was a small child, then carried her into the bedroom and tossed her on the bed. "I am too, fun…let me show you just how much," he said. He traced her jaw line and trailed a finger down between her breasts, as he lowered his mouth onto hers.

Melting together like flames in a fire, they became lost in one another for the next two hours, all other thoughts and plans temporarily forgotten.

Chapter 70

The last three hours had been spent making love, taking passion to an entirely new level. Tiara felt euphoric and content at the same time. Shaky, but blissfully happy.

Marco looked at her as they lay spent, in the middle of his king size bed. "You...you are beautiful," he said gasping for breath, his black hair wet with perspiration.

Tiara opened her eyes and gazed at him. "So are you."

He laughed. "I am beautiful?"

"Yes." She laughed and rolled on top of him.

"Perhaps, you are too much for an old man."

Tiara laughed. "Old man? You?"

"What is so funny?" He smiled seductively, feeling himself harden again as she lay on top of him.

She reached down and rubbed him. "This...is not an old man."

"Well, I am more than twice your age."

"Who cares? I don't."

"Are you sure? What about our height difference? Does that bother you?" He held her head in both hands, gazing directly into her large brown eyes. "You have beautiful eyes...they are windows to your soul. Your soul is beautiful as well."

She shook her head. "I am crazy about you, okay? Nothing bothers me." She touched his full lips and kissed him. "Does any of it bother you? What about the fact that I'm a different color?"

"So am I." He smiled. "Perhaps we are *meant to be*."

She felt her heart beat faster. She loved the way he talked. So refined, with just a slight accent. "Yes, perhaps we are."

"I want you here all the time, Tiara." He laughed. "It may kill me. We seem to have *hmm*...how shall I say..." He looked up at the ceiling, thinking of the correct phrase. "Insatiable sexual appetites."

She smiled. Her dreams were really coming true...how lucky could she get? "I would love to be here with you. I could keep your place clean...help you out."

He propped himself up on one elbow. "Silly girl. You do not need to do that. That is what maids are for."

"You have a maid?" She raised her eyebrows.

"Yes, she comes in four times a week, does everything, even windows." He loved the innocence he saw in this girl. He was falling deeply in love with her. *So open, so willing to please.*

"Even windows, huh? Well, I bet she doesn't do this." She slowly slid down his taut muscular body, and took him into her mouth, feeling her heart race as he moaned in pleasure.

Chapter 71

Louie woke up around three in the afternoon. He'd had an unbelievable nightmare. He dreamt he was running Vinny through the band saw at his brother's butcher shop. *Crazy shit.*

He sat up, rubbing the sleep from his eyes...and remembered. "Holy fuck," he said, not quite believing it.

Catapulting out of bed, he hunted for his jeans on the bedroom floor, then dug into the pocket. He pulled out the hunk of plastic with the ear wrapped inside and dropped it on the floor, then covered his eyes. "Holy fuck," he said again.

Walking over to the bedroom window, he gazed outside in the afternoon sunshine. Looked like a beautiful day. January first. New beginning.

He shuffled to where the ear lay. It had come partially unwrapped and looked disgusting. Dried blood and cartilage. Hairy mole. He rewrapped it and placed it back into his jeans pocket. What had possessed him to save the fuckin' ear? *Proof.* For Marco, and he suddenly realized, for himself.

Louie recalled everything–whacking Vinny, the car that showed up out of nowhere just as he was finishing up. Then the butcher shop and the burial. *Whoa, what a fuckin' night.*

He picked up his cell and selected Marco's number from the contact list. It rang twice and went to his voicemail. He listened to the clipped accent telling him ever so politely to please leave a message.

"Yeah, hey, Marco. It's Louie. Was just hopin' we could touch base at some point today. I'll be around." He flipped shut the cell and tossed in on the bedside table.

He'd jump into the shower, then try Marco again. Maybe he'd go to the car wash, too. *Clean it real good–inside and out. Can't be too careful.* He headed for the bathroom.

Marco checked his messages while Tiara was in the bathroom. He had a message from his cousin in New Jersey. They had just given birth to a baby boy. *A New Year baby.*

Marco had *promised* he'd pay a visit when the day came. "Shit." He hated babies and animals–too messy. However, family was family and he did promise. *May as well get it over with.* He'd fly out in the jet, spend a couple hours, and fly back as soon as possible. Besides, he needed to speak with his cousin Frank concerning a business venture he'd offered to help fund. Jersey was fertile ground. Finally, he listened to the message from Louie. He'd stop and see him on his way to the airport.

Tiara came out of the bathroom naked, hair wet and clean smelling. She walked over to Marco and bent down, giving him a kiss.

He wrapped his arms around her. "*Hmm*...you smell delightful."

"Wanna do it again?"

Marco laughed. "I should take you home...for now," he added seeing the crestfallen look on her face. "I have a quick business trip to take. I will be back tomorrow evening at the latest. Believe me. You can get your things together back at Stephen's and I will pick you up tomorrow."

"Okay." She looked skeptical.

"Tiara, I promise. Don't you believe me?"

She shrugged her shoulders, feeling like she could cry. "Whatever." She would not bawl like a baby.

"I will pick you up tomorrow. Come on now, let's get you to Stephen's, so I can do what I must and return home. It is your home now, too." He looked at her, his dark eyes passionate for this strange beautiful girl.

As Marco drove her back to Stephen's apartment, Tiara stared out the window. *What the hell are you doing?*

She thought of Lizzy and what she would say. Before they left his penthouse, he had peeled off five one-hundred dollar bills from a wad of cash in his fat wallet. He then gave her enough H and weed to get through the next twenty-four hours–the syringe was ready to go with a rubber stopper on it and rubber tubing wrapped around it. She wondered if the filled syringe was from last night. He didn't do any, but told her he had. He lied. And all that money–five hundred bucks. She had never held that much money at one time. As exciting as it was, it cheapened their time together, making her feel like a paid whore.

"What are you thinking about, baby?"

Tiara took a shaky breath and looked at him. "Nothing."

He put his eyes back on the road. "Nothing? Tiara, there is only one thing I ask of you. You must be honest with me...at all times. Do you understand? I will tolerate nothing less." He looked over at her, waiting for a response.

She returned her gaze out the window. "I just hope you're not–" she stopped, realizing how ridiculous it sounded. She was a runaway, a prostitute, or that's what she had come to L.A. for anyway.

"You hope I am not what?" He looked at her, a slight frown creased his brow.

"Using me." There, she said it, as stupid as it sounded.

"*Hmm*...well, I could say the same about you."

Tiara laughed. "Yeah...guess you could. I'm not, though." Her smile faltered. "I...I love you."

Marco smiled. "That is the best thing I have heard in a long time. Tiara, I love you, too." He placed a hand on her knee.

She felt a rush of happiness at his touch and his words. This was all she wanted. She suddenly had everything she wanted in life. *It doesn't get any better than this. True happiness. We love each other.*

Marco brought Tiara back by mid-afternoon. Lizzy felt like a worried mother by the time they walked in the door. Marco pulled Steve aside and they spoke quietly before he left.

Tiara hugged Lizzy. "Lots to talk about, girlfriend," she said excitedly. "Let's go up to the loft...my former bedroom."

"Former?" Lizzy inquired, following her up the ladder. Steve remained in the kitchen.

Tiara hiked up the dress she still wore from the evening before, and sat cross-legged on the bed. She patted a spot next to her.

Lizzy sat down, not wanting to hear what she knew was inevitable.

"Oh my God, Lizzy. You would not believe the night I just had."

"You seem...excited."

"Woo-wee, girlfriend. Is that ever an understatement. It was...magical. Lizzy, I have never been with a man like this. He is...amazing. Knows exactly the right place to touch and kiss and fuck."

"Tiara, he is a lot older than you. You are being swept off your feet."

"He told me he loves me."

Lizzy laughed, and then registered the hurt look on her friend's face. "Oh, come on, T. He doesn't even know you. How could he love you?" She touched the girl's leg, concern in her eyes and a sick feeling in her heart.

"I love him," Tiara offered, defiantly.

Lizzy just shook her head.

"Well, look at you–miss high and mighty. Do you love Steve?"

Lizzy felt her face flush.

"Well well well, looks like I got my answer. See, that's the thing about white folk–they always give it away. Now with a black person, you can't notice it so much when they blush."

Lizzy shook her head and smiled. "Okay, I get your point. Sorry. Just...just be careful, T. I mean it," she said, noting the stubborn look on the girl's face, knowing she'd get nowhere. "Marco Santini is a different animal."

"Yeah, he certainly is," Tiara offered, a dreamy look in her eyes, vividly recalling the past twenty-four hours.

Chapter 72

Nick talked Beth into spending the night at the apartment, despite her dislike for Tiny Tim. They planned to make the trip to L.A. by end of the week.

"Well, looky here. Look what the kitty-cat dragged in. Beth, Beth, Beth," Tiny Tim said joyously when they entered. Now he'd have someone to help with the girls. They were almost more trouble than they were worth. Always crying and demanding and sulking. He was ready to boot them out in the cold.

"Hey, Tiny," Beth said. "How ya doin'?"

"Much better now." He smiled, ignoring Nick and placing his arm around Beth. "Still trouble at home?"

Beth backed away from him. "Yeah, you could say that."

Nick stepped up. "We're taking a road-trip."

"We are? I love road-trips. Where are we going?" Tiny Tim clapped his hands like a small child.

"Not you. Me...and Beth. Not sure where we're going yet." He looked at Beth, hoping she'd get the message. She did. She nodded imperceptivity. "Maybe Canada."

"Canada?" Tiny Tim laughed. "Why in fuck's sake would you want to go there, of all places?" He looked at them as if they were crazy.

Nick shrugged his shoulders. "I don't know, change of scenery." He glanced into the living room. Dani and Shawna huddled together, watching cartoons.

"We just wanna get away for a little while," Beth offered. "We probably won't even be gone that long."

"Yeah," Nick said. "Couple of weeks at the most."

"*Hmm*, sounds like you have it all figured out. Now, what would Tiara say?"

Beth blushed and Nick looked pissed. Tiny laughed, and sauntered back into the living room to watch cartoons with the girls.

Nick and Beth sat at the kitchen table. He gave her a thumbs up and she smiled. Tiny Tim was none the wiser about their trip to California.

Supper was late tonight. Maria tried to do fifty things at once, knowing they'd be taking a trip soon, for who knew how long. *Until it's over.*

Everyone seemed preoccupied. Maria watched Tony mindlessly swirl mashed potatoes around his plate, and Tess stared off into space. She looked at Joe. He caught her eye and smiled. He didn't want to go to L.A., had a bad feeling. She did, too.

Tomorrow was back to work for them and back to school for Tony. Tess remained off until January 18th. Perfect timing for their trip, because she'd be home to keep an eye on her younger brother.

"I want to run something by you guys," Maria announced, breaking into everyone's thoughts.

All eyes on her, she continued, glancing at Joe who nodded in encouragement. "Your dad and I will probably have to take a trip. Not sure exactly when, may be as soon as a few days, though."

"Where are you going?" Tony asked. "Can we go with?"

Maria smiled. "No, sweetie. It's business."

"Chasing bad guys?" He looked at her through narrowed eyes.

"Yes, something like that." Maria noted the kid's defiance.

"Figures." Tony went back to his mashed potato mess.

Tess looked from her mother to Joe and already knew where they were going. California.

"So, where are you guys going? How long will you be gone?" Tony fired questions at them, suddenly eager to know when he'd be free from their rules and regulations.

"We still aren't sure. We'll let you know when we do." Joe said, looking at the boy sternly. "Your sister will be in charge while we're gone."

Tess looked at her brother and grinned. "You will do as I say, little bro."

He rolled his eyes at her. "Yeah, don't I always?" He grinned. She'd be busy with her boyfriend, Mike. He'd have free rein to do what he wanted, when he wanted, ninety percent of the time.

"So, is everyone okay with this?" Maria asked, not sure about anything. She wanted to go, but at the same time didn't want to leave the kids. Then there was the ill fate she felt at the mere thought of everything that awaited them in Los Angeles.

"Sure, Mom. Don't worry. We'll be fine won't we, Tony?" Tess gave her a brother a look that said he'd better say, yes.

"Yeah, we'll be just fine," he offered, smiling convincingly.

Chapter 73

Marco called Louie's cell, a block from his apartment, loving the element of surprise. The man was waiting for him when he arrived.

"Thanks for dropping by. Come on in, Boss." Louie held open the door and smiled nervously. He looked down the hall in both directions to make sure no one waited in the wings, before closing the door.

"Hello, Louie." Marco smiled. "How are you? I cannot stay long. On my way to New Jersey. Short trip."

"Okay. Well, I just wanted to let you know the job, you know…that you gave me? It went well. Went fine." He looked down at the floor, then at Marco.

"Good. That is very good to hear, Louie. I know it was probably difficult. I told you I would make it worth your while, did I not?" Marco reached into his jacket pocket.

Louie wondered if he'd get a reward or a bullet between the eyes.

Marco pulled out an envelope stuffed with cash. "For your trouble and a little extra for emotional duress." He smiled openly.

Louie took the offered envelope and peeked inside, running his thumb through the stack. Hundred dollar bills. Lots of them. He looked at the Boss and grinned. "Thanks. Oh, I almost forgot." He reached into the front pocket of his jeans and pulled out the small package still wrapped in garbage-bag plastic. He handed it to the other man.

Marco looked at Louie, one eyebrow raised. "And what do we have here?" he questioned, tentatively taking the package.

Louie grinned. "Well…thought you might want proof. Open it."

Marco looked at Louie, wondering if the man was stable. He seemed a little…disturbed or something. "Okay."

Louie watched with excitement as the Boss opened the plastic. "It's his ear."

Marco smiled. Sure enough, there was the hairy mole that

had been on Vinny's right ear. He threw back his head and laughed. "Well done, my friend. Well done."

Louie laughed, too. "Thought you'd like that."

Marco handed it back. "You keep it. For now."

Louie looked confused. He'd figured Marco would want it. He shrugged his shoulders, wrapped the ear back up, and stuffed it into his pocket.

Marco patted the other man on the back. "Once again–good job, my friend. We will be in touch when I return. I see you going places, Louie. Big places." He smiled and left, anxious to get the impending trip over and return home to his beloved Tiara.

Tiara started having stomach cramps a couple of hours after she returned to Steve's apartment.

Lizzy thought perhaps she was hungry and made the girl something to eat, but she barely nibbled a piece of toast. Steve had left about half an hour ago, saying he had to go the office to look up some stuff for Marco concerning the trip to New Jersey. He said the Boss was supposed to call for the requested information in a couple of hours.

Tiara had been in the bathroom close to fifteen minutes. Lizzy waited on the couch, anxious to talk more to the girl about Santini. She needed to find out *everything* she could about this man. *Now.*

The girl came out looking sickly, perspiration beaded on her forehead. She moaned and collapsed on the couch next to Lizzy. "Oh, man…think I'm dyin'."

"What's wrong? Did you throw up?" Lizzy grabbed a blanket and tossed it over Tiara.

Tiara held her stomach. "No, but lemme tell ya, gives the term 'the shits' whole new meaning. I swear it is bloody with hunks of stuff…looks like my fuckin' guts."

"Tiara, are you serious? What happened last night? What did you do?" Lizzy held the girl with her stare.

Tiara knew a guilty look was plastered all over her face. She felt too crappy to hide it and lie. "Mainlined some H."

"You shot up? Why? I thought you were smart when it came to drugs!" Lizzy was pissed.

"I did it cuz I thought he was gonna, too. I think he may

have given me Spanish Fly, too. I think...unless he was kidding, but the coffee looked weird this morning and the sex afterward was unfuckinbelievable." Tiara moaned and pulled her knees closer to her chest, wracked with stomach cramps.

"Spanish Fly. That doesn't even work. It causes more damage than anything." Lizzy suddenly realized she sounded too knowledgeable but Tiara seemed too sick to notice. She'd have to be careful.

"Damage...how?" Tiara started to look worried.

"Just drink a lot of liquids." She jumped up from the couch and ran into the kitchen to fetch a bottle of water. "Here." Lizzy handed the water to the girl. "Drink that."

Tiara did as she was told.

"Did Marco shoot up, too?" Lizzy asked.

Tiara shrugged her shoulders. "Like I said, I don't know. I don't think so. I was too wasted to know for sure, but I don't think so." She thought of the syringe that waited for her, hidden under her pillow, along with five hundred dollars. "He's a rich man, Lizzy. I struck gold."

Lizzy shook her head, wanting to shake sense into the girl, but instead she smiled. "How rich?"

"He has a safe. Stacks of cash, drugs, other stuff. It's so cool, just like in the freakin' movies, hidden behind a picture in the living room. Oh..." She sat up. "Oh, fuck. I'll be right back." Tiara scrambled off the couch and stumbled toward the bathroom.

Lizzy thought that was interesting–a safe, loaded with cash, drugs, and who knows what other kind of incriminating evidence for the Family. *Thanks, T.*

Steve found the file Marco needed. From the brief information he'd been given, it was supposedly a lucrative real-estate deal in an affluent section of town, somewhere in New Jersey. Marco planned to lend his cousin some cash if everything seemed legit.

Pouring a drink, Steve put his feet up, looking out over the city of Los Angeles, and thought of Lizzy. She seemed to be on his mind all the time. He was in love. Head over heels. Life was good right now. It didn't get better than this.

His cell phone rang.

"Did you find it?" Marco asked impatiently.

"Yes. Have you landed yet?"

"No, the weather is terrible here. So, do you have the file in front of you?" Without waiting for an answer he said, "What I want you to do is look into the location. I think it is located on fucking swampland. A potential disaster. It could cost a lot of money draining, excavating, and filling it."

Steve powered up the computer and entered the information from the file into a program his older brother had created, before he was murdered. Within a span of a minute, he had an answer. "Well, I wouldn't say it's exactly swampland. It is lowland."

"Same fucking thing, isn't it?" Marco sounded upset.

"Swampland is worse, but yeah, this could be a problem, too."

"I am not investing in a no-win situation. I will pay my respects to the new bambino, then I shall return with all the money I came with."

Steve laughed. "Sounds like a good idea, Boss."

"Thank you, Stephen. How are the girls?"

Steve grinned into the phone. "Fine. Very fine."

Marco almost made a derogatory comment concerning Lizzy, but decided it was best approached in person. After all, perhaps he was mistaken. He hoped so for Stephen's sake. Love is a very powerful emotion. He could attest to that. Time would tell, but he would not go down. *Not at any cost.*

Chapter 74

Although Maria and Joe arrived early, Homicide was chaotic, and Chief LaSalle was in *a mood*.

"I'd like to see you both in my office." She glared at them. "When you have a minute. Please," she added with a sharky grin.

"Jeez, wonder what's going on," Joe said under his breath, as they hung up their coats.

"Who knows? She's been like this for the past week."

"We may as well get it over with. What do ya say, kiddo?"

Maria grinned. He'd always called her kiddo right from the start, when they were partners, before they became involved.

Joe led the way as they filed into the chief's office.

"Please shut the door," she said from behind her desk.

Maria closed the office door and they sat opposite the chief.

"Okay, guys, I'm going to be straight with you like never before." She looked from one to the other, total sincerity on her pinched face. "This trip to California is dangerous. I've said the same thing to Agent Slade. Our little rendezvous is not for the weak of heart or mind. I can almost guarantee someone won't come back alive."

Maria couldn't believe the woman would say something like that. Talk about jinxing them right from the beginning. She saw Joe shift uncomfortably in his chair.

"I'm going to give you a way out. Right now. If you don't want to go, speak now or forever hold your peace."

Neither Maria nor Joe said a word.

The chief grinned. "That's what I thought." She took a sip off her coffee and grimaced. "I'd start preparing to leave."

"We are," Joe said.

"Good. Do you have Powders down for the Spencer autopsy?" she asked Maria.

"Tentatively. I have to check my messages. I expect there's something from the M.E."

"Let's keep this trip as hush-hush as possible, okay? The fewer people who know about it, the better. Okey-dokey?"

Maria and Joe nodded, then stood to leave and get back to work, anxious to get out of there.

"Hey, Dynamic Duo?"

They turned around expectantly. Maria visibly cringed, and Joe looked ready for battle.

"I am proud of you–both of you. This really means something to me. Tina means something to me. Thank you."

Maria smiled and Joe mumbled a 'welcome'. They left, feeling strange at the sudden change of demeanor from the woman who had shown only cynicism in the past.

Chapter 75

Lizzy got up early. Everyone else was still asleep. Steve didn't get home from the office until very late. She had sat with Tiara and talked for much of the night, between bathroom runs. The girl had drunk enough water to float and had finally gone up to the loft to sleep.

Lizzy climbed the ladder when she first woke up, and found Tiara sound asleep.

She was on her second cup of coffee, perusing the morning paper left on the table. Steve must've picked it up on his way home. She wondered what time he had come in. She hadn't retired until after 2:00 a.m.

Hearing a strange noise from the loft, she set down her coffee and walked into the living room. She looked up the ladder and whispered loudly, "Is that you, T?"

No answer.

She headed back toward the kitchen when she heard a moan. She spun around and clambered up the ladder.

Tiara lay sprawled on the bed naked, the empty syringe next to her. She had one hundred dollar bills placed in strategic locations on her body.

Lizzy stood there, watching the wasted girl. "T, what are you doing?"

"Flying." She smiled.

"Where did you get the money?"

"Boyfriend. He's rich." She laughed, rubbing the cash on her naked body.

Lizzy turned, disgusted, and climbed slowly back down the ladder. She paced the length of the living room, thinking. She wondered how much time Tiara had. Considering what she just witnessed, if Marco didn't kill her, the drugs would.

She tiptoed into the bedroom and checked on Steve.

Sound asleep, a soft smile on his lips, so peaceful. She loved him, really loved him. A tear slid down her cheek.

Quietly closing the bedroom door, she walked into the living room. Partially climbing the ladder, she listened. Tiara hummed a nonsensical tune to herself. Lizzy returned to the floor and went into the kitchen.

Picking up the telephone, she punched in the calling card number, then the chief's number. Marco would return from his trip and pick up Tiara sometime this evening.

Within the next day, two at the most, it would be time to act. It was now or never.

Chapter 76

It sucked being back in school. Tony's mind focused on anything and everything, except his studies. *Who gives a flying fuck about school?* He looked at the clock on the wall, wishing for a smoke or *something* to clear the agitation he felt. One hour, ten minutes to go before freedom. He was meeting a buddy after school to score some X and possibly more weed. Smiling to himself, he liked to think about twisting the knife to the cops who ruled his roost. That's how he looked at Maria and Joe–cops, not parents.

Tony was counting the months until he was eighteen and could get the hell outta Dodge. He'd been thinking more and more–maybe he'd go back to his roots.

The latest autopsy was scheduled for mid-morning. Tom Powders wasn't happy about attending. He held Maria personally responsible and periodically shot her offending looks from his desk.

"I think you've made an enemy, darlin'" Joe whispered, leaning toward his wife, as they shuffled papers, attempting to find some semblance of order in the paper trail that surrounded this case. He nodded toward her ex-partner when he had her attention.

Maria snorted. "He'll get over it. Heaven forbid you ask him to do his fuckin' job."

Joe grinned. "What a bad-ass you are, Detective Sanchez."

"Who me?" Maria looked genuinely offended. "You know me better than that. We have a lot going on here and it appears things are coming to a head soon." She looked toward Powders. "Everyone needs to pull their weight around here."

Chief LaSalle's door suddenly flew open and she exited in a flurry, scanning the office. Her search came to rest on Maria and Joe.

Joe saw her coming. "Barracuda straight ahead. Coming right at us," he warned his wife.

She arrived at her destination and in much too loud of a tone, told them to pack their bags. "You're leaving for California day after tomorrow."

Maria and Joe looked around the office. Everyone seemed to be busy, not paying attention to them. Even Powders had his head stuck inside a file cabinet, hunting for something, instead of focused on them.

"Okay," Maria offered quietly.

"We'll be ready." Joe looked at the chief and smiled, which always set her back a step. She never knew how to take kindness from others, especially subordinates.

"Tina's in deep. I fear for her life." The chief's voice was now barely above a whisper. "I've already spoken with Slade. We'll pool our resources."

Maria and Joe both nodded their assent.

Chief LaSalle started to walk away, then turned back. "You know, you two owe me."

Maria looked at the other woman, eyebrows raised in surprise at the bold statement. "And why is that, Chief?"

"Agent Foley demanded to go along. I put the kibosh on it. Told him he'd only get in the way considering his feelings…"

"Well, thank you for that," Joe said.

"He didn't take it very well. In fact, I could probably have him written up." She looked at the two of them. "He actually called me a cold-hearted bitch." She smiled, then spun on her heel and headed back to her office.

"*Hmm*, imagine that." Maria looked at Joe and they both laughed.

Powders shut the file cabinet after extracting the file. He didn't even look at them. But he had heard everything. *Everything.*

Chapter 77

Tiara seemed to be back to her old self. Up in the loft, she and Lizzy packed her few things, awaiting Marco's arrival. The bloody diarrhea had worked its way out of her system for the most part. She still had periodic stomach cramps, but nothing like last night. The H seemed to help.

Lizzy felt she had to try one more time to talk sense to the young woman. "Ya know, T, and this is just an observation, so don't get mad, okay?"

"Oh oh, more motherly advice?" Tiara stood with hands on hips.

Lizzy ignored the sarcasm and continued. "Any man who would give you Spanish Fly does *not* love you. He could have killed you. He knew exactly what he was doing. You are lucky."

"Lucky? I had the bloody shits all night, girlfriend. You call that lucky?" Tiara threw her toothbrush and hair pick into her backpack.

"Yes, considering what the alternative could have been. And the heroin."

"Okay, okay. I know. I'll be careful. No more Turkish coffee and no more smack."

"After this morning, right?"

Tiara looked away, guilty as charged. "Hey, it was just sitting there, calling me, and I felt like complete crap. Figured I may as well do it. And what a glorious trip it was."

Lizzy shook her head. "You are smart, T. At least you used to be. Don't give it all away for anyone or anything...it's not worth it."

The door buzzed. They could hear Steve talking to someone on the main floor.

"He's here," Tiara said excitedly. Grabbing her backpack, she scooted down the ladder in record time.

Her heart caught in her throat upon seeing him. He was so handsome. She loved him so much.

"There's my girl," Marco said.

She ran to him and planted a kiss on his lips, almost bowling him over. "You're early!"

He laughed. "Did you miss me?"

"Yes, yes, yes."

"Are you ready? Do you have everything?" He looked at the backpack slung over one shoulder, his eyebrows raised.

She grinned. "Yeah, believe it or not, this here is all my worldly possessions." They were *so* different. He had everything, she had nothing.

"That will change," he offered, grinning. "Let's go."

Lizzy hugged Tiara and told her to keep in touch.

"I will, don't worry. We'll have to go shopping."

Lizzy glanced at Marco, sensing his scrutiny. "Yes, let's...in a couple of days. Let's."

They left. Lizzy felt as if she had somehow failed Tiara. *I will see her again.* They would go shopping in a couple of days.

Chapter 78

Maria telephoned her daughter, informing her they'd be leaving the Twin Cities day after tomorrow. She didn't mention where, but Tess already knew.

"You're going back to California, aren't you, Mom." It wasn't a question.

"Tess, let's talk about it when we get home, okay? Is Tony home from school?"

"Yeah, he got home a few minutes ago. He's in his room."

"Big surprise. Tess, honey?" Maria faltered. "I hope you can connect with your brother. I'm worried about him. Maybe it will be good, ya know, the two of you alone."

"Great minds think alike, Mom. That's exactly what I'm hoping."

Maria hung up, feeling mixed emotions about leaving. Tess was twenty years old, very responsible. Always had been. *Yet.*

Maria had called their next-door neighbor earlier. He was a retired firefighter, with a passion for woodworking. He promised to check on the kids several times a day.

They'll be fine.

The officer sat parked on the corner, car idling, watching the young couple make their way down the metal stairs. *Must be an apartment above the Chinese restaurant.* He remembered one of the detectives from the night shift, passing on information to keep an eye out for a brown-haired girl in a dirty pink jacket.

Watching the car pull out, he radioed in and was dispatched through to Homicide.

Maria happened to be walking by Tom's desk when he received the call.

"Girl in a pink jacket?" he questioned, a look of confusion on his face.

Maria stopped at his desk. "If you had read the morning report, you'd have a clue about what's going on." She placed the sheet of paper in front of him, handed out to all detectives every morning.

She snatched the phone from Powders, knowing she wouldn't score any points, but not giving a shit. "Sanchez here. You found the girl?"

"Well, she just took off with a kid in an old rust-bucket car. They came out of a dive above a fast-food Chinese restaurant on Seventh Street. We have two choices: I can follow the kids and pull 'em over, or hit the apartment they came out of."

Maria chewed a fingernail, thinking. The girl had been seen at the hospital asking questions about Kathy Spencer, but she wasn't really their target. Maria laid odds this was where Lizzy had made her initial connection to Santini. "Get the license plate so we can do a trace on the vehicle, then hit the apartment. See what's cookin' up there."

"Already got the plate number." He rattled it off to her. "Think I should call for backup?"

"Yes, there are a couple of squads in the vicinity...it shouldn't take long."

Within ten minutes, two officers clambered up the metal stairs, and knocked on Tiny Tim's apartment door.

No answer.

Five minutes later, they broke the lock, and entered through the kitchen.

Chapter 79

Marco looked over at Tiara. *My God, she is so beautiful.* She felt his gaze and smiled at him, then placed her hand on his leg and squeezed.

He smiled. "How are you?"

"Fine...now. I missed you terribly." She thought about what Lizzy told her. *Any man who would give you Spanish Fly does not love you. He could have killed you. And the heroin....* "Me, too. We can go home now. Are you hungry? We could stop somewhere and eat."

"No, let's just go to your place."

"*Our* place," he corrected her. "You seem very quiet. Is everything okay?"

She looked at him, remembering his demand for honesty from her. "Spanish Fly is poison. It can kill you."

He just looked at her, a slight smile on his lips.

"Marco, I was sicker than a damn dog. I mean sicker than I've ever been in my life. Bloody diarrhea with chunks..." She tried to gross him out.

"It must have been something you ate. Many people don't realize just how easy it is for bacteria to get into their food. Tiara, I did not give you Spanish Fly. I was joking when I said it put it in your coffee." He looked at her sincerely. "Joking, okay?"

He certainly appeared to be telling the truth. Very convincing, but still... Somehow, the facts remained undeniable.

Forget it. He loves me.

Lizzy needed to emotionally distance herself from Steve. Everything was going to turn upside-down soon. *How can I be in love with this man?* Her thoughts turned to Tiara, her friend and confidante. Too many feelings churning inside. One never got emotionally involved when going undercover...it was literally suicide.

Marco pulled into the underground garage and parked. They

rode the elevator up to the penthouse apartment.

"Oh my, I almost forgot." He pulled a long narrow box out of his pocket. "I saw this in a jewelry store window and thought of you." He handed the box to Tiara. Marco looked up into her large brown eyes, then his gaze traveled to her small, firm breasts, moving down her long slender legs, finally coming back to the crotch of her skintight blue jeans.

Tiara was surprised. No one had ever given her presents for no reason. She took the satin box. If the gift was simply the box it would be enough, it was so pretty. Eyes wide, she looked at Marco and smiled nervously, then carefully opened the box. A sapphire and diamond bracelet lay inside. She took a deep breath and held it.

Marco smiled. "Do you like?" He removed it from the box and clasped it around her narrow wrist. The jewels sparkled against her deep golden brown skin.

"Oh Marco, I more than like...I love," she said, bending down and planting a kiss on his lips just as the elevator door opened onto their floor.

A nerdy looking yuppie stepped inside, taking in the scene before him. The tall teenage black girl in the risqué clothing was in such contrast to the small Italian man in the expensive suit, one thought came to mind. *Hooker.*

Marco glanced at the young man and read his thoughts by the look plastered on his face. He didn't mind, in fact it amused him. *People will think what they think.*

Marco slid one arm around Tiara's waist. They stepped off and just before the door slid shut, he stated, "There's more where that came from, baby." He laughed at the expression on the young man's face.

Marco unlocked his apartment door and pushed it open. "Ladies first."

Tiara loved it here. It was so beautiful, open and airy. Rich.

"Would you care for some wine?" Marco set down his briefcase and overnight bag.

"Sure. Hey, how was your trip?"

He picked out a bottle from the small reserve he had in a wine cabinet. "My trip...*hmm*, let's see. I'd say uneventful, boring, a waste of my time."

He opened the bottle and pulled two crystal wineglasses edged in gold from the cupboard. Filling both, he handed one to Tiara. "Let's enjoy our wine in the living room, baby."

She sat on the leather sofa and he joined her, stopping to press a button on the stereo system. Soft music filtered into the room.

"To us," he said, touching her glass to his. "I missed you, Tiara."

"I missed you, too. Really a lot." She took a sip of her wine and set it on the coffee table.

Marco set his glass down as well. "May I kiss you?"

"You don't even need to ask, silly." She scooted onto his lap and lowered her mouth to his.

Their kisses became hot and passionate, no awkwardness at all, nothing but a searing hot desire that never seemed to be quenched.

Chapter 80

JJ thought Alex had been acting strange lately, but now it was way past strange. The guy talked about heading down into the Florida Keys. When JJ mentioned going back home–Christ, the guy practically blew a fuckin' gasket.

"What the fuck do you have...a fuckin' death wish?" Alex grew pale despite the deep tan acquired from drinking Corona beer and falling asleep on the beach every day. "Fuckin' fucker."

"Hey, take it fuckin' easy, man." JJ looked at him. "What the fuck's up your ass lately? What did I do?"

"Nothing...sorry. You didn't do anything." Alex was already shit-faced, and a couple of hours of daylight remained. "It was me."

"What do ya mean?"

Alex sat down on the couch, put his bare feet on the coffee table in front of him, and decided to spill it. "Remember, I told you Santini contacted us?"

JJ nodded, joining his friend on the couch, concerned about what he was going to hear.

"Well, the cops found something after we whacked the snitch."

"Found something? What the fuck did they find? What could they find? We were really fuckin' careful. Weren't we?" JJ stared at Alex, wondering what the fucker was holding back.

"They found a wooden bead." Alex appeared near tears. He rubbed his face with both hands, grabbed a handful of hair on each side of his head. "Fuckin A, man."

"A wooden bead?" *What the fuck is he talking about?* "Hey, man–you're drunk. Let's talk about it later," he said, watching tears slide down Alex's face. *Why is he bawling, for Christ's sake?*

"No, no. I don't wanna talk about it later. We gotta now. You can't go back to Minneapolis. You can't go back to Minnesota. Ever."

"Ever? That's an awful long fuckin' time. Why not?"

"The fuckin' wooden bead they found came outta my fuckin' pocket. I bought this necklace at that new hemp store." Alex looked at his friend, hoping for compassion, but finding none. "Well, the fucker broke about two days after I bought it. I stuck it in my jacket pocket, then tossed it in the garbage, but must've missed a couple of beads. I guess."

JJ put his head in his hands, letting it sink in. He looked up. "You guess? Shit."

"The fuckin' cops must've traced it back to me. They probably know we killed the snitch. We're fucked. One way or another, we're fucked, cuz if the cops don't get us, Santini will. I fucked up."

JJ looked at Alex. *You fucked up, man. Not me...I shouldn't have to go down for your stupidity, asshole.* He said nothing, just stared straight ahead while Alex cried like a fuckin' little girl.

Tiny Tim and the girls lay wasted on the couch, naked, when the door crashed open to the sound of heavy footsteps and shouts.

"What the bloody fuck!" Tiny sat up, saw cops, and totally freaked. He jumped up, reached behind the TV, and pulled out a small pistol. Waving it the air like a mad man, he shouted, "Fuckin' pigs–get away. Get away."

"Take it easy, man. Take it easy now," the first cop into the room calmly stated.

Tiny Tim shook so badly, the gun jerked back and forth wildly. "Fuck," he cried, tears streaming down his fevered cheeks. He dropped the gun and collapsed into a heap on the floor, bawling like a small child. Scared.

The two officers approached the hysterical naked man. The larger cop, Dan, had cuffs on him within seconds and the other cop instructed Dani and Shawna to get dressed.

Three-quarters of a block of heroin lay on the coffee table, along with a fix kit, a bag of weed and a pipe. Tiny Tim was *so* busted. Add to that the weapon and two naked underage minors. He was going down hard and long.

Beth slept most of the way through Minnesota. She hadn't gotten a good night's sleep in a long time. Her last evening at home was spent half-awake expecting her stepfather to steal into her room.

He hadn't disappointed.

It would never happen again. She was done. Finished. Her mother wasn't there for her. Only cared for herself.

She looked over at Nick. She liked him. A lot. However, she wasn't stupid. *Why would someone like Nick ever want anything to do with someone like me?* She always sold herself short, but past history had made her wary.

Nick had one thing on his mind–*Tiara*. He missed her terribly...couldn't live without her. He wondered how many guys she'd fucked by now. *Half a dozen, probably.* She was beautiful, smart, and too good to be a whore. *I love her.* He watched the pavement fly by as they sped down the highway, California bound.

Chapter 81

Lizzy figured this might be the last time she and Steve made love. Her heart ached. Why had she ever let her emotions play into this? How could she not have seen this coming? She was a very intelligent woman and street smart. That's how she'd survived this long in this crazy line of work.

She waited for him, naked and warm, ready to give herself to him fully, before crashing his world into oblivion. She needed to look at it as a game from here on out. She *would* come out on top. She had to.

"Hey, babe," Steve said. He removed his clothes and slid under the covers. He wrapped his arms around her small frame and drew her to him, kissing her deeply.

Tiara wore only her sapphire and diamond bracelet. Their rhythm matched one another perfectly. Marco met her every thrust with equal velocity.

"I love you, Tiara," Marco whispered in her ear.

They climaxed together, and it brought her to tears. Tiara had never felt this intense passion, desire, love, whatever it was, and she couldn't get enough. She would do *anything* for this man.

Marco's eyes were moist as well. "Are you okay?" he softly asked, wiping tears from her face. "Why are you crying?"

Tiara wiped her eyes. "I...I don't know. I guess it was earth moving." She grinned. "Was it good for you?"

He smiled and kissed her bare stomach. "Unlike no other," he said seriously. "You're like no woman I've ever been with, and I've been with many women. There is something different about you...and you're all mine."

Marco always knew the right thing to say. He made her feel beautiful, smart, unique. "Hey, how 'bout some weed and maybe a little H." She ran her fingers down the middle of his chest. "Please?"

He frowned slightly. "You should not do that shit. It is bad." He got up and walked to the picture with the safe hidden behind it.

Tiara watched his butt, and smiled. He was extremely fit. Muscular, yet wiry at the same time. He returned with the heroin and fix kit. She was amazed at his muscle tone–every muscle appeared contoured in his flat stomach. And he was always hard. *Always. No wonder he's such a wild man in the sex department.* She smiled.

He sat next to her. "What is so amusing?" He smiled, preparing her fix. He was somewhat worried she'd get hooked, but then, it would keep her right where he wanted her–here.

"Nothing really," she said. "Just admiring your amazing body."

"For an old man?" He smiled, but it did bother him slightly that he was so much older.

"I told ya, you're not old. What is that saying–you're as young as you feel." She watched every step he made preparing her fix, so she'd know how to do it right when alone.

"Okay, it's ready." He took her arm, tied a piece of tubing around it, then briskly rubbed up and down, tapping a large vein with two of his fingers. "I'll do you." He looked into her large expressive brown eyes, and felt he could see into her soul. She was beautiful inside and out.

"Ooh, yeah–do me." She smiled, holding his gaze, the luckiest girl on the face of the earth.

Marco kissed her deeply, then smiled. "Here we go." He inserted the needle, and watched it take effect on the woman he loved.

Tiara laid her head back, feeling euphoria creep into her brain, her body, her entire system.

Marco began at her feet, licking and sucking her toes, then slowly worked his way up her calf, her inner thigh, finally coming to the most important part. He raised his head and spoke to the wasted beauty. "I love you, Tiara."

She locked eyes with him and felt her soul shift. "I love you, too."

He went back to the task at hand, as she moaned in pleasure.

Chapter 82

Joe and Maria were waiting when the two officers brought in Tiny Tim and the two young runaways. They ran the make on the license plate of the old car that carried the girl in the pink jacket. The vehicle was registered to a Nick Dupree, who also lived there. He didn't have much of a record, and was only guilty by association.

Tiny Tim, whose real name was Tim Johnson, shook uncontrollably. His glazed, bloodshot eyes and paranoid gestures told them he was still stoned. The two girls were high as well.

"Tim...Tiny. Where did you get the H?" Maria asked.

Tiny Tim shook his head, looking at her, sweat pouring off him in rivers, despite his shivering.

"It will make it easier for everyone if you tell the truth. I want to help." Maria stared at the junky, could smell his fear. She would never understand why people did this to themselves. She wondered if he was having fun yet.

Joe questioned Dani and Shawna in a separate room. He eventually gave up and returned to where Maria interrogated Tiny Tim.

The girls were worthless. One had passed out and the other appeared on the edge of consciousness. They'd be checked into the hospital after their parents were notified. Questioning would continue when they became more coherent. They were no more than thirteen or fourteen. A camcorder had been confiscated and showed sex acts between them and Tiny Tim. Joe was getting pissed just looking at the greasy little fuck.

"Bloody hell," Tim said, wiping the sweat from his face with a trembling hand. "It's fuckin' sweltering in here."

"Would you like something to drink?" Maria looked at Joe, who quickly stepped out to grab a can of soda.

Joe returned, opened the can, and handed it to Tiny, wanting to hit him at least once.

Tiny Tim took a long drink. "Oh, man, thanks." He belched, then took another long drink, trying desperately to get his thoughts together and decide what to do. He was up shit creek any way he looked at it. *If he gave up the big boys, it would score points with the pigs, but at what cost in the end? Death?*

Joe stepped up and took the can of soda.

"Hey..." Tiny Tim looked crestfallen.

"Enough already. Spill it. Where did you get the heroin? Those girls, they are *way* under age. Babies. Had a look at your camcorder. Do you know what the other inmates do to sex offenders?" Joe glared at the frightened man. "And with your petite physique, you'll be an easy target." He grinned, returned to his chair, and set Tiny's can of pop on the floor just out of reach.

Tiny Tim tried to focus. He shook violently. "Okay, okay. You gotta make things go easier for me if I tell you anything."

"We'll do what we can," Maria promised. "If you tell us *everything*."

Joe shook his head. *No, we won't.*

"Steve. Stephen Freyhoff." Tiny reached for the can of pop, clutching his throat. The big male cop obliged, handing it to him.

He told them everything he knew, embellishing a bit. He had met the big boss, Marco somebody only once, but described him perfectly as a fancy man with quick wit and an even quicker temper.

Tiny Tim told about Tiara and Lizzy. He even mentioned the dead girls–Mel and Kathy. He came clean...totally clean. He felt light as air by the time he was done talking. He had no problem implicating his roommate, Nick Dupree. The fucker deserted him–deserved it.

Maria and Joe looked at each other and smiled, feeling things finally come together. Ammunition was what they needed. They had more than enough.

They needed to leave for California as soon as possible.

Tomorrow.

Chapter 83

JJ talked Alex into going for a walk on the private hotel beach. They wandered down to a deserted spot. It was just getting dark. A wind had picked up, making sand fly, and chasing all the rich tourists back to the comfort of the expensive hotel. Alex whined about sand getting in his eyes, but JJ insisted they get fresh air. It was what they needed to clear their heads, and think about what to do next.

The tide came in, loud and strong. A few dim stars sparkled in the darkening sky when JJ pulled out the gun.

Alex never knew what hit him. One minute he was watching the tide roll in and out, the next he was dead.

JJ took his time returning to the hotel, relishing the warm wind hitting his face with hard granules of sand. Made him feel alive.

Entering their room, he proceeded to pack his bags, combining Alex's items with his own, then made an important phone call.

Marco looked at the window of his cell phone. Tiara was in the bathroom. Once again, they had made the most beautiful incredible love, discovering a rare place where only they lived. He could not get enough of her. She was literally a dream come true. He answered the phone. "Marco."

JJ reported in, hoping for kudos and wanting to go home.

Marco shook his head, listening, then smiled. "Yes, go home. I'll have someone meet you at the airport. Get the first flight out and let me know your arrival time." He disconnected, then made a call to one of his best hit men.

Unfortunately, JJ would not have a very welcome homecoming.

Chapter 84

Chief LaSalle explained that she'd made special arrangements, pulling everything together last minute. She stressed her main concern–Lizzy. "Tina didn't sound like herself. More is going on than meets the eye. I'm worried."

As the chief handed them the itinerary, Tom Powders hovered near his desk, prepared to leave for the evening, but finding the conversation way too interesting.

Tom took his time, sent one last e-mail before powering down his PC, then straightened his desk. Everyone was too excited to even look his way, which suited him just fine. He hated the 'Dynamic Duo'–glad they would be leaving. And Lizzy. He had finally put two and two together. That was the little kid whom he had questioned Sanchez about earlier, but she wasn't a little kid. *She's undercover.*

Bitch. He glared at Maria

Maria and Joe finally made it home, exhausted, but with a busy night ahead of them. They would be leaving on an early flight, arriving in Los Angeles by mid-morning.

Calling a family meeting, they looked at their children. "We're leaving in the morning."

Tess took a deep breath, glancing from one to the other. "Okay," she offered with a resigned sigh.

Tony stared straight ahead, appearing to not care one way or another.

"Tony? You okay with this?" Maria asked, leaning forward, trying to make eye contact with her son.

He snapped out of his reverie. He looked at his so-called mother and father and shrugged his shoulders. "Sure, I'll be fine." He looked over at his sister. She was the only person he loved. "I got Tess."

Theresa grinned. "We'll be fine, guys. Don't worry. Just- just, *please* be careful."

Maria gave her daughter a look.

Tess met her gaze and glanced away. She knew all about it. Her mother had confided in her, wanting her to know, in case something should happen. It was Santini all over again. She had a bad feeling, but it wouldn't be the first time.

Joe and Maria went to pack, while Tess sat with Tony on the couch, watching HBO.

Tony was so quiet it scared her. Something was going on in the kid's head. Tess wanted to find out what was bothering him. Her studies in psychology might be helpful; she hoped. "Hey, little bro–what's wrong?"

Tony shrugged his shoulders and looked at his sister. "Dunno. Worried I guess. Not knowing where they're going, what they're doing, when they'll be back. No one tells me shit. Why is that?"

Tess put an arm around her little brother. "Tony, they're just trying to protect you. It's all part of their job."

"I know they tell *you* stuff. More stuff than me, by far."

"Well...I'm older." She thought about how honesty was so important in a family. Without it, things went crazy. Tony was a perfect example. He had spent his early years in a web of lies and deceit.

Tony wiped a tear from his eye. "I just wish people would let me *in* once in a while. Maybe I would do the same."

Theresa made a decision and hoped she didn't live to regret it. "They're going to California. They need to rescue an undercover agent and take down some Mafia bad guys."

Tony's eyes became huge. "Cool."

"Yeah, cool, but dangerous." A worried look crossed her face. She felt that familiar dread in the pit of her stomach when she thought of Mom and Dad battling the bad guys again. She'd never get used to it.

Tony sat for another ten minutes with his sister, then retired to the privacy of his bedroom and his computer. He knew just what he needed to do.

Chapter 85

The morning dawned brightly. Lizzy had been up for hours already. She'd finally found the opportunity to call the chief yesterday, as promised. Everything was coming to a head. They *had* Stephen Freyhoff and Marco Santini. There was so much evidence, they wouldn't see the light of day for quite some time. Even with their hired lawyers it would be a battle, but with them on the losing end. No way could they could squirm out of *all* the charges.

She would meet Maria and Joe, and possibly an FBI agent or two, at the corner market at 1:30. Stephen had already left for the office, and would be gone all day if history proved itself right. Their lovemaking had been incredible this morning. She took a drink of coffee, reliving it one last time in her head as she stared into space. She could not afford to think about it ever again. Would not allow herself that luxury.

Her main concern now was getting Tiara safely out from under Marco. They wanted to pull Tina out now and then rush in for the bust, but she made a promise to herself–Tiara would be safe before they made their move. Bullets were certain to fly.

She suddenly realized that for all essential purposes, she was no longer Lizzy. She was Tina again–tough as nails, no emotion. She could do this. She had to. Tiara's life depended on it.

Marco let Tiara sleep. He covered her nakedness, and kissed her smooth forehead. She didn't move. Her youthful body still needed a chance to recoup from the heroin and frantic lovemaking.

Closing the bedroom door, he headed for the office. Today would be busy. There was a sizzle of excitement in the air. He could feel it. He wanted to make an early start, and would bet Stephen was already there.

Marco thought of JJ and smiled to himself. The stupid fuck did not have a prayer. He had no doubt the hit would be handled efficiently and professionally. *Nice and neat, not too messy.* He paid top dollar and had used this particular source in the past with one-hundred percent success rate.

Not too messy. The thought brought to mind Louie *doing* Vinny. Despite his doubts, Marco had to give Quiet Louie credit, although the mess-factor *was* a bit much. Thinking of the ear and the tale of the band saw, he shook his head and chuckled. "Louie, Louie, Louie..." he said, locking the door behind him. He already looked forward to being with his beautiful Tiara upon returning home later this afternoon.

Steve fired up the computer, and started a fresh pot of coffee–using one of Marco's favorites, a Nicaraguan blend.

Lizzy remained constantly on his mind. He found himself grinning like a fool for no apparent reason. He was actually happy, for the first time in a long time. He couldn't imagine life without her.

The aroma of rich coffee filled the room. Steve filled a large mug and sat down in front of the computer. They hadn't heard from their source in Minneapolis for a while and he wondered when the next e-mail would come. He logged into Microsoft Outlook and did a send/receive, making a mental note to call Tiny Tim at some point today. He hadn't heard from the creepy little guy in a while.

He scanned the new e-mails, looking for the name. "Speak of the devil," he said aloud. He selected and opened it up, then read it with mounting concern.

"I knew you would already be here." Marco strode into the office, just as Stephen finished reading the e-mail. He stopped, focused on his partner, taking in the serious look. "What is wrong?"

Steve reread the e-mail, straining his brain to come up with the right scenario here.

Marco came up behind him. "You are in my e-mail account."

"I thought it was *our* e-mail account." Unlike his deceased brother, Nicholas, Steve hated computers. He knew how to get around on them–could send an e-mail, or surf the net–but that was as far as it went. He had a computer at home, but never turned it on.

Marco read the e-mail. "What the fuck is this? Did you read this, Stephen?"

"Yes," Steve said. He looked at Marco and glanced away. His heart sank to his stomach, then his bowels. He thought he would be ill. "We don't know if this is true."

Marco laughed. "Yes, we do. Our source has not been mistaken in the past. Ever."

Marco knew he should have trusted gut instinct. Lizzy, or whatever her name was, had seemed older despite her appearance. Something about her had alerted his internal radar right from the beginning. The little bitch was a cop. A soon to be dead cop.

He smelled a set-up. Marco would finally get a chance to personally meet the two detectives who had brought down his Uncle Roberto almost a decade ago. Perhaps he'd finally bring closure to the pattern of vengeance his uncle had started years ago. The e-mail did not say when they would arrive–only very soon.

"Stephen, please listen to me. I know how you must feel…betrayed…sad." Marco looked at his friend sympathetically. "But we must make plans. Don't you agree?" He looked at his watch and smiled. JJ would be landing soon in Minneapolis and his ride would be waiting to take him home.

Steve nodded, numb.

Chapter 86

JJ stepped off the airplane, and gazed out at the wintry landscape. He was tanned and healthy looking. He had walked no more than ten feet when a man approached him.
"JJ?"
He smiled. *This must be the contact Marco sent.* "Yeah. Already got my luggage." He held up two carry-on bags. Even with Alex's stuff, it didn't amount to much.

He followed the guy through the airport to his vehicle, parked in the farthest end of the visitor lot. "Christ, could ya have parked any further away?" JJ asked when they finally reached the car.

The man unlocked the passenger door, and placed a hand on JJ's shoulder. "Welcome home," he said, smiling, then placed the gun with the attached silencer, to the other man's temple and pulled the trigger.

Flight 408 landed in Los Angeles around ten-twenty in the morning. Peter Slade waited as Maria and Joe stepped off the plane.

Slade hugged Maria and shook Joe's hand. Like old times– but that wasn't necessarily good.

The local FBI was lying in wait, ready to take control if things went awry. Their goal was to get Tina wired, send her into the lion's den one last time, get Tiara Jackson out safely, then bust Santini and Freyhoff.

They drove in Peter's rental car to FBI headquarters in relative silence, each thinking their own thoughts, wondering where the end would take them, or if they even wanted to go there.

Tiara was getting extremely agitated. Marco had left for work without leaving her any heroin. "Now why the fuck would he do that?" she asked the empty room.

She walked to the picture with the safe hidden behind it. She had watched him open it many times. Tiara doubted if she could get it open, but it was worth a try.

Grabbing the edge of the frame, she pulled, exposing the safe. She placed her ear next to the tumbler, not sure exactly what she was listening for, but she'd seen in done in movies. "A click," she told herself. That's what she listened for. She heard it, and slowly turned the other way. Back and forth.

She tried several times, to no avail. Tiara felt ill and started sweating like a pig. "The little fucker," she hissed. How would she make it all day? She wondered when he'd come home. He had given her his cell phone number. What did she do with it?

Tiara went into the bedroom and dug through the pockets of the jeans she wore yesterday. She pulled out the tattered piece of paper, and debated if she should call him. She didn't want to appear needy, but she was...needy.

She picked up the telephone in the kitchen and dialed the number, got his voicemail. She left a brief message, simply stating she needed *something*, and he knew what it was.

She went back into the bedroom and climbed between the sheets, hoping sleep would take her away until Marco came home. She needed a fuckin' fix. Was desperate for a fix. Would die for a fix.

Chapter 87

BCA Agent Foley arrived in California around noon. Time was pressing and Foley knew he had to move fast to be part of the operation. He loved Etina. He had to be here. There was nowhere else he *could* be but here. Nobody understood. He tried to persuade the chief, but she wouldn't listen. She said his heart was too close to the situation. *What the fuck did she know?*

Picking up the keys to his rental car, he planned to head toward the local FBI office, hoping to catch Sanchez, Morgan, and Slade there.

He walked quickly, half-running through the airport, perusing the map as he went.

Maria, Joe, and Peter piled into the back of the van. It was customized, with high tech surveillance equipment hidden behind wooden cabinets on one side.

Two agents sat up front, ready to roll, when a maniac in a rental car slid into the parking lot.

"Jesus Christ," Maria called from the back, looking out the window at the cocky little bald-headed man emerging from the vehicle. "It's Foley," she sighed.

"Shit," Joe said, rolling his eyes. "What the fuck we gonna do now?"

Maria opened the sliding side door and walked toward the man. "Foley?" She stood before him, scowling. "What are you doing here? The chief told you—"

"I don't give a shit what the chief told me," he interrupted. "I'm going, Sanchez. There's absolutely nothing you or anyone can say or do that will deter me."

Maria blinked at him in the bright afternoon sunshine. She sighed, resigned. What could she do at this point? He was already here. "C'mon, then."

Foley smiled, for once in his life happily following the detective he loved to hate. One thing, and only one thing, was on his mind–Etina.

* * *

They arrived at the designated corner at 1:22.

Maria was anxious to see the beautiful blonde Russian. She watched the sidewalk from both directions.

"There she is." Foley spotted her crossing the street, walking toward them. His heart caught in his throat upon seeing her again. She appeared so confident, despite the eminent danger.

Tina spotted the van immediately and slowed her pace. She observed her surroundings before approaching. She stopped to check her backpack, pretending to look for something while checking the reflection in a store window, to ensure no one followed. She was relatively certain.

Situating her backpack, she strolled to the waiting van. The sliding door opened, revealing Detectives Sanchez and Morgan. Her eyebrows rose in surprise upon seeing the BCA agent, then she smiled.

Maria helped her as she stepped inside. "Tina. It's so good to see you."

Tina hugged Maria, then Joe and finally Foley.

The two FBI agents sitting in front looked at each other. The driver turned. "We need to get her wired and ready to go."

"Of course," Tina offered. "Sorry."

One agent stepped into the back of the van and proceeded to wire Tina. They discussed the plan, which relied on many factors coming into play, but the Russian would make it happen. She would find a way to get Tiara safely out, then they'd take care of the Family.

Chapter 88

Steve felt ill driving back to his apartment. *Lizzy.* She wasn't a runaway. *An undercover cop.* He still didn't believe it. *No way. No fuckin' way*, his brain kept telling him, as he thought of the two of them together. He loved her. She loved him–he knew it. He shook his head, and pulled into the parking lot of his apartment building.

Marco smiled to himself, wondering what condition he'd find Tiara in when he opened the door. Her voice sounded shaky in the message she'd left on his cell phone. She would be pleasantly surprised he was home early.

Stephen would bring Lizzy over for a visit with Tiara–all according to plan.

Unlocking the door, he was surprised to find the penthouse exactly as he left it. She had not even straightened up.

Silence pervaded the large main room. *Where is she?* He noticed the picture over the wall safe had been moved. She had tried to crack the code. He grinned, and walked through the large apartment.

He found her in the bedroom, lying in bed, staring at the wall.

She sat up upon seeing him. "You're home." Tiara wrapped her arms around him.

He pulled her away. "What is wrong? Why are you in bed in the middle of the day?" He looked concerned.

Her hand shook as she rubbed her tear-streaked face. "It's the fuckin' H. Why the fuck did you leave without giving me any? Huh?"

"Excuse me?" Marco did not like her tone.

"Well...Jesus fuckin' Christ, Marco. You know I need it...now." She looked at him beseechingly.

"Perhaps that is exactly why you should not have it. Tiara, you do not want a monkey on your back."

She looked at him, panicked. What kinda shit was he trying

to pull now? "I'm fine. I want the heroin. Please give me some. Don't make me beg, okay?"

"Maybe I like it when you beg." He smiled, but it did not reach his eyes.

"Fucker."

"Excuse me?" Marco said again, getting pissed. "Tiara, this is not the way to act when you want something from someone." He walked out of the bedroom.

Tiara scrambled off the bed, following him into the living room. "Marco, *please*. What do you want from me? Okay, I'll do *anything*. I'm begging, okay? Is that what you want? Give me the fuckin' drugs."

Marco ignored her. He carefully selected a bottle of wine from the cabinet, opened it, and set it on the counter to breathe. He then removed a couple of glasses from the cupboard.

"Marco? Can you hear me?"

Still no answer. He filled each glass half full, turning, just as Tiara approached him.

"Calm down, please," he stated evenly. "Here, have some wine. It's very expensive and–"

"I don't want no fuckin' wine." Pushing it away, she knocked it out of his hand. The glass shattered, spraying burgundy liquid across the floor.

"You will clean that up." Now he was pissed.

"Fuck if I will." She turned away.

Marco grabbed her by the back of the neck. "I said you will clean it up. Now."

She pushed him away. "Look at you. Always giving orders. You think you're pretty hot shit, don't you?"

"Hot shit?" He saw the girl he loved suddenly turn into a crazy bitch.

"Yeah, hot shit. With your fancy clothes and your fancy wine and your fancy place." She spread her arms out. "Just look at this place–the best of everything. That is all that matters to you. Material shit."

Marco's eyes narrowed as he let her rant, becoming angrier at each word she spit out.

"You know what, though?" Tiara continued, on a roll. Since he always demanded honesty, that's exactly what he'd get.

"You're still just a little man." She saw him bristle, but the smart-ass black girl in her didn't know when to shut up. "Little Mister Big Man. Ooh-wee, look at me, Little Mister Big Man."

He calmly placed his glass of wine on the counter, stepped over the broken glass on the floor, and backhanded her.

Tiara wasn't expecting the blow and fell to the floor.

Marco was on top of her, his hands around her throat in an instant. "I am a good man. What is wrong with you?" he demanded, seeing nothing but another ungrateful woman. His hands squeezed tighter.

"Mar-Marco..." Tiara couldn't breathe.

His eyes bore into hers as he sat on top of her, pinning her arms to the floor with his strong legs. *Bitch. One more ungrateful bitch.*

She tried to kick her legs, then tried to buck him off her body. His hands squeezed tighter. Her eyes begged him. *I love you. Please, God. Please, forgive me.*

No air left. She felt her eyeballs bulge as if they would pop, then a shroud of darkness, and nothing.

Marco stayed on top of her, squeezing even tighter, feeling some of his anger subside as her life slipped away. "How dare you," he said to the woman who, only this morning, he had loved more than anything in the world.

Chapter 89

Tina had been back for only twenty minutes when Steve arrived home. He was early and she felt lucky.

She felt her insides quiver when he came up to her, and wrapped his strong arms around her.

"Hey, babe. How's it goin?" He tried to sound casual when in fact he was torn up inside.

"Hey." She turned around and gave him a kiss. "How was your day?"

"Interesting," he offered. He opened the refrigerator and grabbed a beer.

"Oh, yeah?"

"Yeah." Steve leaned against the counter and looked at her. "Tiara left a message on Marco's cell today."

"Is she okay?"

"She misses you. Wants you to come and see her."

Okay, this is almost too easy. "I'd like that. When?"

"I told Marco we'd be over as soon as possible. So, I guess whenever you're ready."

"I'm ready."

"Great, let's go." He drank the rest of his beer and belched.

Placing one hand on the small of her back, he ushered her out the door, knowing she'd never be coming back.

They listened to the conversation between Tina and Freyhoff. Watching his SUV emerge from the parking lot, they followed at a distance. One of the agents radioed in to report their direction. Extra agents waited in strategic locations close to Santini's residence.

"Okay, to reiterate: the plan is Tina gets the girl out to go for a walk or shopping or some fuckin' thing. Then we go in," Maria said.

"Yeah, FBI first," the driver stated sternly.

"FBI first," Maria agreed. "*If* things go according to plan. If not, we play it by ear."

"Fair enough." The agent braked as the SUV signaled a turn.

They loitered in the lobby waiting to be buzzed up. After a couple of minutes, they were granted access.

"I thought you said he was expecting us."

"He is," Steve said, shrugging his broad shoulders.

Marco stood waiting for them when they arrived at his door, apologizing for the delay.

"I am so sorry you had to wait. I spilled a glass of wine and was cleaning up the mess. I just hate messes," he said, looking at Stephen and grinning. He ushered them inside.

"Can I offer you some wine? I've just opened the bottle," Marco said, always the gracious host. "I'm sorry Stephen–I am fresh out of beer." He smiled.

"No, thanks," Steve said, wanting to get this over with as quickly as possible. No more games. He wasn't in the mood for games.

Tina shook her head, declining anything that would dull her senses. Her adrenaline was pumping and she sensed danger. Maybe it was just her own paranoia. "So, where is T?"

"Tiara?" Marco looked at her, eyes narrowed. "She's in the bedroom...resting, I believe." He looked at Steve and shrugged his shoulders, then laughed.

Steve looked at the Boss, knowing something else had happened that he wasn't privy to. Another fuckin' surprise.

"Do you mind?" Tina started walking toward the bedroom.

"Be my guest." Marco took a sip of wine.

"What's up?" Steve asked, getting vibes he didn't like.

"You'll find out soon enough." Marco loved games, and this was the ultimate.

Tina came out of the bedroom, followed by Raoul, Marco's bodyguard. He towered over her a good foot, maybe more. "You bastard. You killed her."

Marco laughed. "She is sleeping."

"She's dead." Tina had found Tiara lying in the huge bed, covered with a beautiful quilt–her throat bruised, body already cold.

"Okay, we're going in," Maria said, as she opened the sliding door on the van. "Plans have changed. Tiara Jackson is dead." She looked around the van. "Joe, Foley, and I will go in first and try to get Tina out. You guys, Slade, your other men, be ready right behind us."

"Wait," The FBI agent behind the wheel commanded. "I don't like this."

Too late. Maria, Joe, and the BCA agent were already on their way in. And moving fast.

They lucked out upon entering the secure building, getting in with an older lady who struggled with a large bag of groceries. They did have other ways of entering secure buildings, but this worked best. The element of surprise usually got better results. Plus, Santini might have men scattered throughout, waiting for them.

Approaching Marco Santini's door, they heard a muffled pop from inside. Maria and Joe exchanged nervous glances, suddenly grateful for their bulletproof vests.

Joe motioned for them to stay put, but the BCA agent was not about to wait for anything.

Agent Bill Foley pushed past Joe and turned the knob, surprised to find it unlocked.

Joe grabbed the man's shirt, but the material slipped through his fingers. "Shit."

Etina looked at the man she loved, through a veil of tears. He refused to look at her. Stephen stood next to Marco, united. She was dying. Raoul did to her what was done to snitches. The pain–she tried to push it away, but it wouldn't go. She curled into a tight ball.

Foley saw Tina first, then lost all sense of why he was there.

Raoul shot the agent between the eyes before he could even raise his gun.

FBI agents ran down the hall as Maria and Joe entered the penthouse, guns drawn.

"Surprise, surprise," Marco said. "You're early." He fired at the woman who had killed his uncle, hitting her vest and doing little damage. Maria returned fire. Raoul took her down as he dived at her, but not without her bullet entering its intended target.

Marco screamed in surprise, grabbed his crotch, then looked down at the blood seeping between his fingers, and the bitch on the floor. Raoul sat on her back. "Kill her."

Raoul put the gun to her head.

Stephen knew it was all over, and focused on the man who had killed his brother.

Sensing movement, Joe trained his gun on Stephen, watching the man slowly advance toward him, when his attention was diverted to Maria.

FBI agents poured through the open door and everything that happened next, happened within chaotic seconds.

One of the agents shot Raoul, just as Joe shifted position to help his wife.

As Joe turned, Stephen rushed, took him down, then shoved a gun under his chin. "This is for my brother, Nicholas." He pulled the trigger, blowing a chunk off the back of the cop's head.

Maria watched her husband's skull disintegrate. FBI agents tried to help her up. She was in shock. Numb.

She heard her name and looked across the room.

Marco was still alive, his crotch soaked with blood. "I know a secret," he croaked between clenched teeth, knowing what he had to do before he became forced to live like this.

Maria stood on shaky legs and stepped closer to Marco. Agents swarmed the apartment. Two of them hovered next to Marco, not seeing the gun hidden underneath him.

"It's about your son...he really *is* one of us." Marco smiled, watching confusion cross her features. Two agents hauled him up, and he pulled out the gun he'd covered with his body.

He briefly thought of turning it on Maria Sanchez, but then he'd have to live like this. Placing the gun into his mouth, he pulled the trigger, spraying blood and brains into the face of the agent directly behind him.

Maria watched Marco Santini's brains fly out the back of his skull. *My son? Tony?*

She looked around the room–dead bodies and bustling agents surrounded her. Tina lay crumpled in a heap, the horseshoe necklace glittering around her throat. Agent Foley's body lay sprawled ten feet away, one arm outstretched toward the woman he loved. *Joe...where's Joe?* Already she had forgotten.

Then she saw him, lying in a pool of blood and remembered. *Dead.*

Everyone's dead.

Epilogue

It was hard returning home without Joe. Peter Slade stayed by her side to help with funeral arrangements, and to deal with the press.

Tess and Tony took it hard–especially Tony. He had confided everything to his sister. He had been feeding information to Marco Santini for months. It had been his way of seeking revenge for what he thought was his parents' fault–the death of his birth mother. It remained undetermined what his punishment would entail.

Tom Powders was innocent–only guilty of online dating and trying to e-mail potential future wives. One of which happened to be the chief, who used the same dating service.

Maria was done with the Minneapolis Police Department. She wanted nothing more than to crawl into a hole and die, but had to persevere for the sake of the children. Tony needed a lot of help and she would be there to provide it for him, once again.

Stephen Freyhoff would pay with a life prison term for killing a cop, among many other charges.

Raoul wasn't killed, but injuries and a future of incarceration, made him wish otherwise. The Minneapolis Police Department was working on obtaining names associated with the Family, rounding them up like cattle.

Within a couple of weeks, the department would indict seven more members of the organization.

Nick Dupree and Beth arrived in Los Angeles, California. They had made the trip in record time, but still too late.

He wondered where to begin looking for his beloved Tiara. It was a big city, lots of people. He didn't care. He would find her. They were *meant to be*.

The End

C. Hyytinen is a Wisconsin transplant and has been a Minnesotan for more than twenty years, embracing the land of 10,000 lakes as her home. Living in a male dominated household with her husband and two sons has proven to be a challenge at times, but has also given her insight into the finer qualities of life. With a demanding career in the fast-track computer world, she uses her writing as a form of escape. When she's not busy with her family or work, you'll find her hunched over her laptop, pounding out another crime thriller.

NORMANDALE COMMUNITY COLLEGE
LIBRARY
9700 FRANCE AVENUE SOUTH
BLOOMINGTON, MN 55431-4399